By Dean Murray

The Society

Dean Murray

The Society is a work of fiction. Names, characters, places and incidents are the products of the author's imagination or are used fictitiously. Any resemblance to actual events, locales, or persons, living or dead, is entirely coincidental.

Published by Fir'shan Publishing

ISBN 978-1-9393635-7-2

www.FirshanPublishing.com

First Edition

For Matthew

I wasn't there during the Desolation when the bombs started dropping—it happened nearly a century and a half before I was born—but despite that, I've never had any problems envisioning what they must have looked like. All I have to do is close my eyes for a moment and I can see silvery, flame-driven nails streaking out of the sky, barely visible in the split second before they impact.

The history books all say that the people of that time feared nuclear bombs—and they were right to do so—but it wasn't the shockwave or the heat that nearly destroyed the world as they knew it, it was the electromagnetic pulse.

Invisible, non-lethal, and perfectly suited to destroying the computers that were such an integral part of life even back then. The bombs did exactly what they were supposed to. They turned cutting-edge jet fighters into useless ornaments and immobilized tanks in a heartbeat, but that wasn't all they did.

Food production ceased, and pharmaceutical factories ground to a halt at the same time that radios and cellular phones stopped working with predictably catastrophic results. Relatively few people were killed in the initial attacks—the attacking nations all wanted to capture as much of their rivals' infrastructure intact as possible—but the societies of that day were ill-prepared for such rapid shocks to their ways of life.

They were selfish and petty. Rather than turning inwards to realize the highest possible version of themselves, they turned outwards. They wasted their time and resources pursuing profit and depriving their brothers and sisters of equal opportunities, and the results were catastrophic.

The bombs didn't destroy civilization, it was the people turning on each other who did that. It was surprising how fast it happened--within a few decades once-great cities were already starting to crumble. The survivors tried to leave the cities for a better life in the wilderness where food was more plentiful, but we didn't let that happen.

The precepts—the belief system that had seen us through the terrors of the Desolation—were clear that letting people rebuild before they'd come to accept our beliefs would just see the world consumed once again in another apocalypse—possibly one even worse than the Desolation.

We couldn't allow that to happen—even if it meant that some of our people would be forced to don uniforms and pick up rifles rather than pursue their highest self. At ruinous cost in lives and human potential, we embarked on a long vigil to ensure that the descendants of the men and women who'd come so close to breaking the world wouldn't have a chance to repeat their ancestors' mistakes.

We call ourselves The Society.

Chapter 1

The sight of the city lights rising up through the darkness to meet me at more than two hundred miles per hour was nearly enough to make a proper Society girl regret agreeing to jump out of a perfectly good airplane. The sense of vertigo was threatening my ability to function—just like on the last jump—but I gritted my teeth and tried to focus on the explosions blooming like destructive roses all across the city.

The full-face mask I was wearing kept the wind out of my normally impassive brown eyes, and allowed me to breathe at an altitude where the thin air otherwise would have killed me, but neither of my other two jumps had been from such a high jump point. I was starting to feel like the goggles were closing in on me, like my air supply was running out.

Hot orange tracers swept upwards from more than a dozen gun emplacements scattered across the city. The thought of one of those heavy-caliber rounds ripping through my body should have sent me over the edge, but somehow it had the opposite effect—it meant that things were going exactly to plan. Everything was unfolding just like the strategists from the Society's military had said it would.

Another round of bombs went off below me and then a loud tone in my ear warned of the imminent deployment of my gravity chute. The buildings were terrifyingly close now, and I angled my descent towards an alley, counting out loud to keep myself focused.

The chute deployed with a whine as capacitors fed energy into the cylindrical device mounted to my back. Nearly a dozen different straps connected the chute to me, wrapping around my legs, chest, shoulders, and stomach in an effort to spread the stress of my deceleration across my entire body. It still almost wasn't enough.

The Society's doctors had long ago established that twelve G's was the maximum safe deceleration for the average human body attached to a grav chute. My chute ratcheted up to nearly twice that over the course of less than a second as the onboard computer used a laser rangefinder to confirm the distance to the ground and plotted a safe landing for me.

The shock as the straps dug into my flesh knocked the wind out of me, and forced my vision to narrow into an ever-narrowing tunnel, but I stubbornly refused to lose consciousness. The brutal stresses being inflicted on me were not without reason. The grubbers—the residents of the city—didn't have any proof that this particular attack was being used as cover to infiltrate their home, but that wouldn't stop them from watching the sky in an effort to locate any jumpers. We'd never used an attack like this to infiltrate the city with a spy—I was the first of my kind—but we had used them in the past to cover larger assaults where hundreds of soldiers were inserted into cities like this one.

Black clothing, jumping under the cover of darkness, the self-destruct mechanism on my chute, it was all designed to make me as hard to spot as possible, to let me cross the danger zone as quickly as the limits of biology and technology would allow, but it still wouldn't be enough to save me if I collapsed into unconsciousness once I hit the ground.

Twenty G's was a crushing burden to put any human body through, but I had advantages that normal humans didn't.

The whine on the chute took on a softer edge as the sonic baffling went to full power, and then the ground reached up and slammed into my feet with the force of a twenty-foot drop. I reacted as I'd been trained, throwing myself forward to convert the fall into a roll at the same time that my left hand slapped the release button that let my chute collapse flat against my back.

The cobblestones under my shoulder were cold and gritty, and despite everything I still hit hard enough to add to the impressive set of bruises I'd already acquired from the chute's straps. I rolled through two complete rotations and then stood, slamming my palms into the building in front of me to bleed off the rest of my momentum.

It took exactly two seconds to shrug out of the harness connecting me to the chute and then arm the self-destruct mechanism on the face of the flattened cylinder. I waited for the readout to flash twice and then took off at a sprint—I had less than thirty seconds to clear the area before a bomb would be arriving in the alley.

I almost didn't make it.

The bomb landed two seconds before it was supposed to, and the blast from the shockwave slammed me into a nearby building as my outer layer of clothes started smoking.

I ripped off the black jumpsuit, revealing a set of much bulkier garments underneath—still black, but worn and holey so as to blend in with the grubbers. That last bomb—like most of what we were dropping that night—had been armed with an incendiary warhead, and I could feel the heat building behind me as the buildings that had survived the initial blast caught fire.

I double-checked the position of the moon to make sure that I was still heading north and picked up my pace to a three-minute mile as my straight brown hair fluttered in the wind from the speed of my passage. It shouldn't have been possible—almost wasn't possible even for me—but it was the minimum speed required to stay ahead of the waves of smart bombs even now headed down from the Society planes above me.

The first wave came down less than a hundred yards behind me, and bits of shrapnel shot past, nicking my arms and legs. Not fast enough. I was already breathing hard, but I forced my legs to push off from the ground with more force. I managed to pick up nearly five seconds before the next wave of explosions tore through the night behind me.

Glass windows shattered from the force of the concussion, and one of the ancient buildings listed to one side, slamming into its neighbors before twisting and crashing into the ground with enough force to knock my legs out from under me. This time even my unnaturally quick reflexes weren't enough to save me. I led with my face and felt the skin over my right cheek tear as it collided with a solitary island of asphalt in the middle of the cobblestones.

I pulled myself back up to my hands and knees, dazed. The bombing was supposed to stop now—the only other explosions would be secondary events, ancient gas lines or overloaded electrical panels, but I wasn't out of danger yet. I needed to get back to my feet and make my way further away from where I'd landed.

Bombing my entry point into the city into a hellish inferno was supposed to make sure that nobody would believe anyone could have survived, but it was still possible that someone had seen me moving impossibly fast through the city. I needed to clock another mile or two—at much slower speeds—before I could hole up for the night and assess my condition.

I made it only two more blocks before a horn sounded from deeper inside the city. The horn was quickly followed by a series of mechanical whistles from somewhere much closer. Within seconds people started emptying out of the buildings.

"There's a fire moving this way from Jenks' territory. I want every citizen of our fair province on the border with a bucket!"

The speaker was surrounded by half a dozen burly men armed with everything from clubs and swords to ancient-looking firearms. In the flickering light of the approaching fires, I could see that he was wearing a top hat like something out of the bootleg historical movies I'd watched during my citizenship tenure. It was obvious that he was mocking a speech given by some long-dead president of the Society, but he seemed no less serious for the levity—at least not based on the way that the unarmed people who'd been gathering in the street started moving toward the fire.

I was still too close to my insertion point; there was still too much risk that someone would think I was from the Society, but going against the flow of people would just make me stand out. I couldn't afford that, not if I wanted to survive.

I joined the stream of dirty, frightened people and it took no acting ability to appear just as worried as they all were. As we got to a rickety barricade in the street—a barricade that I had blown past by the simple expedient of running through one of the many holes at street level—some of the 'citizens' slowed as though thinking that they'd arrived at their destination, but a quartet of armed men rolled a section of the barricade back and waved everyone else through.

"Jenks is going to need our help to secure this block. As faithful citizens and honest neighbors, we will do exactly that."

"By secure you mean steal, don't you, Piter?"

The comment came from somewhere off to my left, but whoever had made the wisecrack was smart enough to have kept their head down. That didn't stop the guy in the top hat from frowning.

"Sedition is a serious crime, one that weakens us all against enemies inside the city and the ants who just finished bombing us. Anyone who can provide my men with information about who just said that will receive double rations for a week and an upgrade in their living accommodations."

Nobody volunteered any information, and within seconds the warlord's men were back to hurrying people past the barricade. Apparently securing additional territory was more important than punishing someone for daring to speak the truth.

I took my place in a long line of people who were passing buckets of water from a large pump to a series of low wooden structures that seemed to have been constructed of scrap wood and garbage. The first few buckets emptied onto the shanties drew curses from the inhabitants, but the profanity rarely lasted beyond the time required for the people inside to come out and see the approaching fire.

A few of the occupants tried to dive back inside for some prized possession or another, but Piter's men were already moving inside the building and throwing people back through makeshift doors and windows, ordering them to form additional bucket brigades.

My mind was whirling. My briefing had mentioned that the grubbers would organize to put out the fires started in the bombing, but the sterile descriptions I'd read in the classified files hadn't prepared me for anything like this.

They had formed more than a dozen lines that I could see in the flickering light—some from one well, some from another—as teams of six or seven people manned the manual pumps that were emptying water into large basins. Each line emptied a gallon or two of water onto a nearby building each second, but that was next to nothing against the blaze that I could feel moving in our direction.

Any group of free people would have stampeded away—that was what my fellows from the Society would have done if faced with this kind of danger, but Piter's citizens held their places. They shifted around nervously, but they kept the flow of buckets moving, and a few seconds later a new trembling started working its way up my legs.

It felt like a herd of monstrous beasts were stampeding in our direction, but the people in my line actually seemed less nervous now than they'd been just moments before. It finally made sense when the first few drops of water started cascading down out of the sky.

The grubbers weren't just going to fight the fires with low-tech bucket brigades, they had roof-mounted systems for spraying water over everything in the fire's path. Now that I knew what to look for, I could see clouds of steam coming off of the fire further away from them. They wouldn't have been visible—even in the flickering light of the flames—for normal, unaided humans, but that was just one of the advantages that I'd carried into the city with me.

"Don't stand there and lollygag. The water cannons aren't going to be enough to save your sorry hides all by themselves. Douse these buildings or you'll all go up in flames with them when the fire arrives."

The guy who'd talked to me was a big bruiser in his late thirties with an eye patch and a club. I looked away from him to take one last look at the rooftop water dispersal systems, and was nearly knocked off of my feet by a blow to my side.

My elbow clamped down against my fractured ribs and I dropped down halfway to the crouch that had been drilled into me during my two months of unarmed combat training. The guard tapped his hand against his club and gave me a sadistic smile.

"I said get back to work."

I ducked my head, hiding subserviently behind a thin veil of long, dark hair, as I stepped back into line and accepted the next bucket full of water. The bruiser watched me for several seconds, making sure that I was really as cowed as I'd let on, before walking down the line.

"Bash is a monster. You going to be okay?"

The question came from a guy about my age who was two places behind me in the line.

"Yeah. I think he broke some of my ribs, but I can still keep up."

The woman immediately behind me shook her head. "Not for long—not if they're really broken. Donner, you hear that?"

The slender man in front of me grunted and then took a half step back towards me at the same time that the woman moved forward. She patted me on the shoulder as she handed off the next bucket of water.

"Your new admirer is named Jack and I'm Sally. Try to pace yourself. Don't fall out of line or Bash will beat you to within an inch of your life."

Jack moved up, splitting the distance between Sally and the person behind him. All three of my benefactors were already sweating and obviously tired, but none of them seemed ready to throw me to the wolves. It was the last thing I had expected out of three strangers. All of the briefings had agreed that grubbers were suspicious and cutthroat.

Some of the leading minds inside of the Society thought that grubbers were that way as a result of the endless gang warfare inside of their enclaves. Others thought that it was a result of some fundamental difference in their physiology and psychology, but everyone had seemed unanimous on the fact that I would need to be on my guard at all times.

I fell back into a rhythm swinging heavy buckets from Sally to Donner with my right hand and then accepting empty buckets with the left as they came back. The ribs were definitely fractured. The lance of pain each time I breathed told me that, but I knew I wasn't in any danger of complications—not with my new-and-improved body.

"You're from Jenks' territory, aren't you? You came through the barricade with us, but I've never seen you before. That means you used the confusion of the attack to slip over to our side."

I nodded, unsure where Sally was headed with her questions.

"You're going to want to keep your head down. Your best bet is to try to slip in with some of your own people and pretend that you were just swept up in the confusion when Piter came over and took control of this block. Piter doesn't like deserters—he says if someone will desert one of his rivals, they'll desert him further down the road."

We'd all been talking quietly—little more than whispers—but as Bash worked his way back up the line, all of my neighbors fell silent and focused on moving the buckets even more quickly.

I continued to take in my surroundings as I worked, keeping my head down to avoid drawing Bash's wrath again. The water falling on our heads from the buildings around us had grown from little more than a mist to a heavy torrent that seemed like it should be more than enough to stop the fire that was less than half a block away, but based on the way that all of the bucket brigades were speeding up, that was less of a foregone conclusion than I would have liked to believe.

A couple of seconds later a heavy jet of water shot out from the top of the building, seeking the edge of the fire, and the burst of steam that shot back at the people on the ground was hot enough to redden exposed skin. It probably would have scalded my entire brigade if not for the cooling mist of water still coming down from the building just behind us.

It was hard to tell for sure, but it looked like the other areas I could see were having better luck stopping the fire.

"Is there a wind driving it this direction? Why is it getting so close?"

Sally double-checked to make sure that Bash was too far away to overhear, and then shook her head. "Piter's men were slow getting the water flowing on this block. The fire-fighting equipment is all supposed to be standardized, but it never is. Part of that is because everything is jury-rigged, but it's also because none of the warlords are too keen to make it any easier than they have to for someone to come in and take over their territory."

I finally understood. "So Piter marched us all over here knowing that he might lose some of us, but he doesn't care because at the very least he's created a firebreak that should save his territory."

"Exactly. Anyone he really values is still back at his headquarters making sure that water keeps flowing up to the suppression systems on the top of our buildings. Why, was it different here? If so I wouldn't have expected you to try to run away."

My instructors had all warned me of the danger of getting too close to the grubbers—especially at the start of my mission—but I'd still stumbled into exactly the kind of casual conversation that was most dangerous to me.

"No—it's all the same here in Jenks' territory. I'd heard stories though that it was different on the other side of the wall. It's silly, really. I guess everyone always says things are better somewhere else, but it's all just a bunch of lies designed to make us believe that we could escape and be free if the breaks all went our way."

Donner laughed. It was a very unpleasant sound—more raspy than it should have been—but that wasn't as concerning as the way that Sally looked at me.

"Freedom. Listen to you, child. You sound like one of those bloody ants all lazing around like mindless drones inside the comfort of the city they build on our blood and bodies. There isn't any such thing as freedom. At least here in the city we know how the world works. That batch out there is too stupid to come in out of the rain."

The heat coming off of the fire had continued to increase while we'd been talking, and I suddenly wondered how often the pumps in the building malfunctioned. When it came to the crumbling technology so common to the grubber cities, it wasn't a question of *if* something would break down, but rather *when*.

If it happened while we were dumping our buckets of water into the inferno raging mere yards away from us, we would all be killed instantly. The icy water coming out of the sky was the only thing keeping the fire at bay, and even that wouldn't have been enough to save us if not for the fact that a recently arrived breeze was blowing most of the steam away from the bucket lines.

I picked up the pace even further, ignoring the pain in my chest, and I wasn't the only one. We turned the makeshift wooden buildings before us into a water-soaked barrier between us and the flame, a barrier that smoked as the water evaporated away.

It seemed as though we were standing there in that line for hours. Bash and the other enforcers came through at regular intervals and cycled the people in the front of each line to the very back, but it wasn't out of mercy. As the heat continued to grow, it got to the point that the people in the front of the lines couldn't withstand more than five or ten minutes before becoming so dehydrated that they started collapsing.

I was covered in soot, exhausted, and singed in more than one spot, but still I moved water down the lines, lines that were shortening as the heat drove us back. The shorter lines were a blessing because it freed up more people to form additional lines and increased the amount of water being thrown at the fire, but they also meant that the fire was that much closer to consuming the tall metal building at our back.

Everything hung on the edge of a knife for several minutes, and then the rest of the inferno was beaten down to the point where the closest buildings added the water from their big cannons to the single stream that had been battling our little corner of the blaze.

Between one heartbeat and the next, the fury seemed to go out of the flames. They were still going, still dangerous, but they lacked the intensity that had come within a hair of destroying all of us.

Piter climbed up to the top of the pump in the middle of the square behind us. "Once again, you've all shown why our little community is the premier group in the entire city. I thank you all for your service tonight, my good citizens. You're all released to go back to your homes. Those of you who work directly for me can take an extra hour to report to your posts tomorrow morning."

I had lost track of the passage of time, but between the disruption of having bombs dropped on the city and the time spent fighting the resulting fires, I was sure that Sally and the others had all lost more than an hour's worth of sleep. Piter was just as contemptible as my briefings had said he would be. For the briefest of moments I considered assassinating the pompous windbag before moving on to my actual target, but I shook off the thought.

THE SOCIETY

There was little doubt as to my ability to get to Piter if I put my mind to it, but my purpose inside the city was too important to risk on an ill-conceived assassination. If I succeeded, then Piter would be dead, but it wouldn't make any kind of lasting difference in the lives of Sally and the others.

My three bucket-brigade companions had turned out to be much kinder than any of my briefings had led me to expect, but Piter's death would just mean that one of his men would step into his shoes, and institute a reign of terror for weeks or even months until he felt like he had enough control over the territory to risk relaxing his grip.

As much as I wanted to do something to repay the kindness I'd been shown, that wasn't the answer. I needed to carry out my mission so that the Society's military wouldn't be forced to raze the entire city to the ground.

I joined the throng of individuals heading back through the barricade, grateful that each step moved me that much closer to my ultimate destination, and didn't realize my error until after I was already through the barricade. I stuck out just as much back in Jenks' territory as I did in Piter's, but at least back on the other side of the barricade I was one new face among many.

Bash grabbed me by the arm and pulled me out of the stream of humanity within seconds of my crossing through the barrier. My instructors had taught me half a dozen ways to break free of that kind of hold, but the pain from my broken ribs took me by such surprise that I didn't even consider executing any of the techniques that had been drilled into me.

By the time that I pushed the pain back into a corner of my mind and locked it away, Bash had pulled me into one of the tiny pathways that wound around the wooden shanties that took up the space between the buildings on either side of the alley.

"You're not from our territory."

Bash's voice carried over even the bedlam from so many people heading back to their homes, but it didn't stop me from hearing someone approaching from behind. I turned my head far enough to confirm the presence of another enforcer—a slender guy with a long scar that ran from his temple down to his chin.

"I—I'm from Jenks' territory."

"I'd like to believe that, but you have to know that Piter doesn't like deserters. I think you're only admitting to being a deserter because you're trying to hide something worse."

I shook my head. I was shaking and I didn't have to fake the fear in my voice.

"I was terrified. The bombs were dropping in the heart of our territory and I could see the explosions getting closer and closer with each wave. It's true, I ran away. I figured that Jenks had done something to piss off the...ants. I knew that I had to get out of there or I was going to end up dead."

Bash smiled, but it wasn't a pleasant expression. "Take off your shirt."

"I don't care what you think you have on me, I'm not going to take my clothes off. I—"

"You'll do what I say or your new home is going to be a pauper's grave. The perimeter territories keep a good watch on all of the approaches to the city, but Piter thinks that the ants are sending people in from the sky using some kind of fancy parachute. If you're really an ant, then you'll have the bruises to show for it—marks from the straps that stopped you from slamming into the ground."

I started to hesitantly lift the bottom of my shirt, and despite the poor lighting, there was no mistaking the flash of excitement in Bash's eyes. Regardless of whether he was right or wrong about me being part of the Society, he was still going to win.

My shirt was nearly high enough to expose the slender pack around my middle when I struck, slamming my right foot into his knee. He never even had a chance—my blow destroyed his joint before his brain had time to realize I'd started moving.

I didn't allow him a chance to react to my attack. Instead, I moved in and slammed my elbow into his throat, crushing his trachea and knocking him to the ground. He would suffocate over the next several seconds unless medical help arrived, but I'd already spun around to deal with the second guy.

The second enforcer had a knife out and stabbed at me, but despite his adrenaline and obvious experience in violent confrontations, he was still moving too slowly to have any chance of scoring on me. I stepped to the side and slammed my palm into his elbow, shattering the joint a split second before I reversed the course of his hand and slammed his own knife home into his chest.

Despite my superhuman reaction time, it had all still happened too fast for me to register what I was doing. I'd been reacting out of instinct, responding with counters that had been drilled into me by some of the most brutal instructors inside the Society.

I was supposed to be leaving the scene of the fight already, making my way to a safer location before anyone stumbled upon my handiwork, but I just stood there staring at the two men lying there on the ground.

The skinny guy was already dying. Society med techs probably could have stabilized him if they'd been onsite already, but nothing the grubbers had was going to be able to save him at this point. Bash was a different matter—even the low-tech grubber doctors could probably perform a tracheotomy if they arrived soon enough. All my training said that I should take care of him, should ensure that he couldn't come after me at some later date.

I looked back and forth between Bash and the knife in the other enforcer's chest, and then forced myself to walk deeper into the narrow alleyway. A single instruction to the computer riding inside of my chest was all it took for my face to start shifting. Five steps later Sally and the others wouldn't have been able to pick me out of a lineup. I was still me, but my features had been shrouded by localized swelling.

By the top of the hour, everything from my bone structure to my eye color would be different.

Chapter 2

The Presidential Administration Building
The Society Enclave
Six months earlier

The man sitting across from me always made me feel vaguely unclean. There was never anything I could quite pin down, and I'd told myself dozens of times that I wasn't being very enlightened by thinking such thoughts, but I hadn't been able to shake the feeling.

He didn't look at me with the kind of open sexual desire that I'd encountered so often from other citizens. I was well past the legal age of consent—an adult in nearly every way that mattered—so if that had been the cause of my discomfort I could have easily dismissed it as being insignificant.

At one point I'd thought maybe it was the way he carried himself. I'd been on half rations for the last two years, with no explanation given other than that it was for the good of the Society.

Food was one of the intermediate rights, granted free to anyone and everyone who wanted it, regardless of their contributions to the Society. Technically the administration couldn't enforce their decree that I take in only slightly more than fifteen hundred calories per day—it was unconstitutional.

I could have gone to any food dispenser in the entire city and requisitioned additional nutrition, and received thousands of extra calories if that was what I wanted. If I'd been concerned about the administration finding out about my 'excess' then it would have been a simple matter to have one of my acquaintances procure the food for me.

I wasn't particularly close to anyone, but there were easily half a dozen people I could have manipulated into giving me whatever I wanted. Most of them wouldn't have even realized what I was doing. The rest of them wouldn't have cared—most of them had tried to slip something to me at some point in the past because they thought it was unnatural for me to pass up the latest dessert crazes.

By any sane measuring stick I should have abandoned my starvation diet months ago and ballooned up by thirty or forty pounds, but whatever the Society wanted, the Society got. It was one of the rules I'd had drilled into me a decade and a half ago by one of the nannies assigned to my crèche.

What I wanted didn't matter. Following orders would eventually result in rewards beyond anything I could imagine. None of the kids in my housing unit seemed to have received the same lectures, but it didn't matter what other people did—or didn't—do. I was special. More was expected out of me than was expected out of them.

The longer I went before asking for a reward, the bigger my eventual reward would be.

My compliance with the restricted, bland diet had started out as nothing more than habit, but as time had gone on, I'd grown to appreciate the results. Unlike most of the kids my age, I was slender and fast. My instructors had pushed me for hundreds of hours in countless different exercises, and as a result I could perform athletic feats that were the equal of many of the top citizen-athletes in half a dozen different events—once my results were adjusted to reflect the fact that I'd not yet earned my franchise.

The level of speed and strength I'd obtained so far was heady and I could only imagine what I might accomplish once I was franchised. That—and complying with the needs of the Society—was more important than any concerns among my peers that I had some kind of eating disorder.

The administrator sitting behind the oversized desk was plumper than any of my friends, but he wasn't off of baseline for someone his age. I passed dozens of people in very similar physical condition every day and none of them ever made me uneasy.

No, it had to be something else. I just hadn't managed to figure it out yet.

"Your instructors are satisfied with your progress, Skye. I've read all of their reports and you are performing within specification. You are nearing the completion of several of your current courses of instruction. Would you like to make any requests regarding your next round of training?"

Additional physical education. Maybe a class in unarmed combat, or one in weapons mastery. That was what I wanted, but once again I suppressed any sign of my true desires. With sacrifice would come reward.

"No, Citizen-Administrator. I am happy to continue whatever units of instruction the administration judges to be most useful to the Society."

"Surely you must know how unusual your course of study is? The other young people your age have all completed as much schooling as they are ever going to complete. The most advanced stopped studying last year and the rest have been finished for three years. When they aren't campaigning for their elders to reduce the franchise requirements, they are all working hard—as much as two or even three hours a day—to make sure that they contribute to the

Society in a significant enough way to earn their franchise. Some of the ones who finished studying three years ago—the most dedicated social servants—are within a month or two of completing their long-held goal and finally entering into our Society as full, franchised citizens."

I wondered for a moment if he'd forgotten who he was talking to. It was doubtful given just how unique my circumstances seemed to be, but it was the only logical explanation. I routinely spent six hours a day undergoing extreme physical conditioning and then studied other courses of information for another four hours.

I was lucky to get two hours a day to spend on the leisure pursuits that most of the franchised citizens dedicated themselves to. My current schedule was nearly as demanding as that of the Society's small, but very elite group of military men and women.

It was hard to rationalize what I was hearing out of the Citizen-Administrator. In one breath he talked about the unusual nature of my decisions so far. Then in the next, he described two or three hours a day of work as being an exemplary level of dedication out of someone who would doubtlessly cut back to a few hours a week—if that—once they earned their franchise and received their injections.

"I'm aware that my current course of study is outside of the normal selections made by people my age, Citizen-Administrator. I'm aware that I'm lagging far behind most of my fellows with regards to earning my franchise, but that is a sacrifice I'm willing to make if our Society demands it from me."

"Don't you want to vote?"

"Yes, Citizen-Administrator. I would very much like to be part of our great democracy, I'm willing to wait for that day for as long as you and the rest of my instructors deem it necessary."

He studied me for several seconds before looking back down at his terminal.

"Since you left the juvenile housing and were allowed to pick your leisure activities, there have been no instances where you've visited any locations other than those designated with a green-one classification. Why is that? Surely you're curious."

I forced my face to remain relaxed. He was wrong. There had been one time when I'd ventured out into the wider world. The tracker buried in my arm should have alerted whoever was tasked with monitoring my activities of that fact.

I'd been young, curious about the world, and tired of being confined to the same thirty-thousand-square-foot facility that had been the limits of my world up until that point, but that hadn't been why I'd left the approved areas.

Thinking about what had nearly happened still gave me nightmares, but even that wasn't as disturbing as the fact that nobody seemed to know what had happened that day. Putting myself in a position where I could be forcibly taken from the approved areas of the enclave was a mistake that I'd never repeated, but the man sitting across from me had never given any indication that he was the kind to make excuses for anyone's actions but his own.

This felt like a test—something designed to establish whether I was willing to admit to my errors—but I forced myself not to follow my instincts. *She'd* told me five years ago that I must never admit to leaving, no matter what situation I found myself in.

"The social desirability index has been established for a reason, Citizen-Administrator. I may not fully understand the reasons behind why a given section of our nation has been categorized as being more or less socially desirable than another, but my understanding a given rule is not a prerequisite for obedience."

He smiled, and I finally realized what it was that bothered me about him. He did want me—just not sexually. There was something behind his eyes that seemed to indicate that I wasn't entirely real to him. It was unnerving.

I'd run into plenty of franchised citizens who'd retreated into virtual worlds once they no longer had to spend hours every day trying to earn their franchise. The Society's simulated reality equipment had been perfected more than seventy years earlier. For those citizens, the outside world often seemed to become less real to them than their simulated playgrounds. I'd had several of them treat me as though I was beneath their notice—unfranchised and locked out of their virtual worlds as I was—but this was different. He didn't just think of me as something that existed to entertain him, he viewed me as something that could be owned.

"...understand that many franchised citizens don't view the desirability index as anything other than an archaic holdover from days gone by—days when the Society was under attack from all sides. Given that, don't you feel a little silly detouring more than a mile out of your way just to avoid crossing into a blue-two zone?"

I slowly shook my head. The number of things that didn't add up were starting to bother me. The Citizen-Administrators worked directly for the Citizen-President. More than any other group, the administration was responsible for preserving our way of life.

"If the desirability index is really pointless, then the Citizen-President will abolish the color designations. Until then, I will continue to restrict myself to the most benign areas. Maybe there is some validity to the argument that the activities in the other zones are harmless. I've heard people say that the stresses put on our society as a result of those activities are so minor as to be insignificant, but if my training has taught me nothing else, it's taught me that under times of emergency even very small stresses can mean the difference between success and failure. I will not be a cause of a failure for our Society."

He cocked his head to the side. "Our Society is not under stress. The grubber cities are no threat in the face of our technology and military. There is no need to forgo pleasures and diversions when there is no emergency."

"With all due respect, Citizen-Administrator, emergencies by their very nature cannot be predicted with perfect accuracy. I stand by my words."

He looked down at his terminal and then nodded once as though acknowledging an order. A second later he'd levered his bulk up out of his chair and I was scrambling to my feet so as to show the proper respect to a Citizen-Administrator.

It was unprecedented. I'd never seen him standing. Every other time we'd met I'd been ushered into his office while he was seated, and then dismissed without him ever seeing me to the door.

I thought for sure that I'd offended him. I hurried to the door, hoping to get out of the office before he worked himself up to yelling at me, but he barked for me to hold my position. A second later the door opened and a slim, muscular man walked into the room.

"That will be all, Beck. Leave us—I'll let you know when you can have your office back."

I started to drop to my knees, but the new arrival grabbed my arm, easily supporting my weight.

"There's no need for any of that. The last thing you should be doing is kneeling before me."

"Mr. Citizen-President, I don't understand. Whatever I did wrong, please let me assure you that I will correct the failing immediately. I never meant to let down our people."

"Skye, you've got everything backwards. I'm not here because you've committed some kind of capital offense. I'm here because you are a very unique individual. Out of the two thousand young people born in your year, only two of you have demonstrated such a high level of loyalty to our Society."

"I've only done what was asked of me, sir. Surely there are dozens—hundreds even—of others who have done just as well as I have..."

"No, I'm afraid there aren't. I'm not just talking about the starvation-level rations or the extensive physical conditioning. I've got dozens of people in the military doing that specifically because they want access to the benefits given only to our brave armed forces personnel. I'm not even talking about your steadfast refusal to ask when you'll get a chance to earn your franchise, Skye.

"Out of everyone else born at the same time as you, there are only two of you who've done all of that and also refused to go into the zones that have been deemed less than socially desirable. A dozen trips into the blue zones would have been hardly remarkable given the predilections of your peers. Even those slated to join the military are allowed unrestricted access to zones that are much more habit-forming than that, but your competition has ventured out of the green cordon only once, and you've never strayed even a single time."

"I still don't understand, sir. The Citizen-Administrator was just telling me that the social desirability index was a relic."

"It was a test, Skye. Everything that's happened to you since you were born has been a test. You knew you were being tested back before you were released from the juvenile housing, but there was no way for you to know for sure that your tests went on for another five years after that. This was a test to see just how loyal to our people you are, and you succeeded magnificently. I've looked back through the archives from before my election and the last time someone passed the tests with such perfection was nearly three decades ago."

For a brief moment I almost asked what my reward was going to be. Surely after everything I'd done so far—after passing all of his tests—the Citizen-President was going to reward me with something magnificent. The temptation was nearly overpowering, but at the last second I heard the words in my head again—just like I'd heard them so often in my memories.

Never ask for a reward. Just continue serving—sacrifice will lead to the reward you seek.

"How can I serve, Citizen-President?"

"No thought for yourself? No request that I fast-track you to receiving your franchise?"

"Only if it is what's best for our Society, sir. I'm loyal to the ideals we were founded on."

He smiled, and I knew that I'd just passed another test.

"You're a strong young woman, Skye—stronger than almost anyone else I've ever met. Let's go infuse the same inner strength into the rest of your body."

Chapter 3

The Presidential Administration Building
The Society Enclave
Six months earlier

The next hour was a blur of preparations. The Citizen-President escorted me out of the Citizen-Administrator's office and deeper into the administration building than I'd ever been before.

It was common knowledge that the most important parts of the administration building were buried underground, but I'd had no clue just how far underground they were. A quartet of military guardsmen followed us from the office we'd just left to an elevator hidden behind a locked metal door that was more than a foot thick.

The elevator was just big enough for the six of us, and it required two different keys and the Citizen-President's thumbprint before it would move. When it did start moving, it did so with a

THE SOCIETY

shocking speed that left my stomach back at the ground floor. The panel in front of me only showed twelve floors, but that was misleading because we were moving for almost a minute before the first of the buttons lit up to signal that we'd arrived.

We'd just dropped down a shaft that was hundreds of feet deep, and there were still more floors even further down.

"We can't be too careful, Skye. The truth is that most of our population isn't ready to know just how hard we have to work to keep everyone safe. The core of our belief system is that the inhabitants of the cities out there beyond the energy barrier need to be given a chance to correct their ways. They need to be given time to develop and accept the sublime perfection of our system of living—the system that their ancestors rejected so long ago."

I nodded. That was something every child born into the Society learned at the same time they learned colors and how to count to five. None of us were capable of understanding at that age, but memorization of the precepts meant that they became a part of us—understanding always followed with time.

"All men and women have an inalienable right to pursue the highest version of themselves they can imagine." I said. "Society's obligation is to support each member in that pursuit. The gift of the best of each of us back to society will result in plenty for all. That gift must always be

35

outstretched to those who have not yet started to believe."

The Citizen-President nodded like a proud father at my recitation of the first precept. "Very good, Skye. I've dedicated my life to that ideal, to becoming the best version of myself I can be—just like every president since the Destroyer betrayed the Founder and snatched the promise of immortality away from us. The truth, though, is that the cities beyond the barrier are much more dangerous than most of our people realize."

I shook my head—in astonishment rather than denial. "I thought that their technology was still centuries behind ours. We should tell everyone, sir. Knowledge of the full scope of what we are up against would inspire tens of thousands of people to reach higher, to find the better version of themselves that has been just out of their grasp."

"I wish that were the case, Skye. I would be lying if I said that I hadn't considered doing exactly that. The unfortunate reality though is that far too many of our people pay only lip service to the ideals found within the precepts. Even if that weren't the case, the addition of stress has been proven to reduce people's ability to realize the best version of themselves. I have a depressingly large section of the storage on my computer terminal filled with the results of research studies that prove that particular fact over and over again."

He paused as though inviting comment, but I was already feeling like I'd overstepped my bounds.

"As for your other concern, Skye, it's true that the general technology base of the cities beyond the barrier is tragically primitive, but it never pays to underestimate the ability of humankind to turn even relatively simple inventions to terrible ends. The little technological progress that has been realized over the last few decades has been disproportionately focused on developing new ways for people to kill each other."

"I understand, sir. The cities are still a threat, but one which we are honor-bound not to wipe off of the face of the planet. How can I help?"

That earned me another proud, almost paternal, smile. "We have a number of different methods for gathering information about the activities of the various petty warlords in each of the major cities—everything from electronic and radio surveillance to semi-autonomous mobile listening devices that we've maneuvered into place over the course of years. Up until now, that has always allowed my predecessors to head off any developing technology that could cause us problems."

"That's not the case anymore?"

"No, Skye, I'm afraid not. We're getting reports of a new warlord rising to power in the city inside of Sector One. He's begun the construction of a device—one that has the potential to destroy everything our ancestors spent such unimaginable effort building."

"What kind of device are we talking about, sir?"

"It's a power source—one that will serve as a foundational technology for a whole host of weapons that will be more than capable of penetrating the barrier and killing us from hundreds of miles away. My first instinct was to call in airstrikes and make sure that we destroyed the prototype Brennan is constructing, but unfortunately our best efforts have not been equal to locating the precise position of the generator."

"Meaning that we can't blow it up—not without destroying the entire city."

"Correct, and given that this new warlord has constructed a jammer capable of interfering with the signals from our normal micro drones, I can't use our normal methods of tracking it down. What I'm about to ask you is unprecedented, Skye.

"In the entire history of our people this has never been done before, but our Society needs you to go undercover inside of that city and locate the device that Brennan is building. We need you to be our eyes and ears inside his headquarters—we'll send you in with a special transmitter capable of piercing the jamming—so that we can make sure the device is never used against us. It's a mission more dangerous than even the ones undertaken by our brave military men and women, but you won't go in unprepared. We have enough time to train you before you'll need to leave—all indications are that Brennan's device is still months away from completion."

An overwhelming fear of the unknown surged through me for two full seconds—seconds that felt like an eternity—and then the fear retreated back inside me, chased away by the mantra I'd heard since childhood.

"Will I have to kill him, sir?"

The Citizen-President pursed his lips for several seconds before shaking his head. "I don't believe so. The construction of the device requires very rare, very specialized components that he'll never find again. The destruction of the prototype should be sufficient to make sure that the integrity of the barrier is never threatened.

"If I'm wrong though, you'll be doing the world a service—these warlords are all the same. You won't feel bad about killing a man like that. Please know that I wouldn't ask you to undertake such a dangerous venture if it weren't vitally important."

"Yes, Citizen-President. I understand the dangers, but I'm willing to serve. I stand ready to commence preparations whenever you want me to."

"There is no time like the present, Skye. You still haven't asked about your franchise, but I'm happy to tell you that you'll be preemptively earning the nanite injections right now. I—"

He looked at the guardsmen who'd accompanied us down in the elevator, and pointed back at the door.

"Please wait for us at the elevator. I'm perfectly safe with Skye."

We watched the guards retrace our path and then once the door was closed behind them, the Citizen-President led me through another set of doors.

"As I was saying, undertaking this mission earns you your franchise as a full citizen inside our Society, but you actually won't receive the standard set of injections."

"Of course, sir. I'm aware that our military personnel receive a different set of injections to increase their strength and speed. It only makes sense that you'd want to give me every possible advantage before sending me out to infiltrate Brennan's organization."

"You're right that I want to send you off with every advantage, but there is a reason that I sent my guards away, Skye. The nanite injections our military receives has always been the best available to anyone in the Society—until now."

My mind was reeling. "We've done it? Our scientists have finally managed to crack the secret to immortality after all of these decades?"

"No, I'm afraid that is still outside of our grasp, stolen by the Destroyer when he sabotaged the research he was pursuing with the Founder, but we have made advances. They are still limited—much more so than I would like—but real advances nonetheless."

He opened a glass refrigeration cabinet and pulled out a handful of syringes—three were full of clear liquid in various shades of light green, the others full of a gray metallic fluid.

"These nanites are incredibly expensive to produce—several orders of magnitude more costly than even the military nanite pack—but they will drastically increase your odds of survival. These will slow the aging process by an additional ten percent over the military nanites—twenty percent over what the general franchised citizen receives. You'll gain more than double your current strength levels, with corresponding increases to your speed and reaction times."

He stared at the syringes with the metallic liquid in them for several seconds before continuing. "This is the next step in the evolution of mankind, Skye, but it's imperative that you never mention this to anyone. If all goes well, I'm told that we might be able to ramp up production over the next two generations to the point where all of our military forces can be equipped with the same variant you're going to receive, but you must understand that word of this can't get out."

"Of course not, sir. There would be riots in the street. Even the most self-actualized person is going to want a shot at an improved nanite pack with those kinds of benefits. Even once you explain that they are too expensive for use by the general populace, there are people who will start demanding military injections."

"I know, but the simple fact is that injecting even half of our citizens with the military nanites would bankrupt our economy. We would have to pass across-the-board increases to the franchise requirements. Provisional citizens would have to work for thousands, possibly tens of thousands of additional hours to provide the additional resources for that kind of upgrade program. Our entire society would be thrown into disarray as people stopped seeking self-improvement, abandoning the precepts in favor of unsustainable increases to their life expectancies."

"I will never speak of this to anyone, Citizen-President."

I was having a hard time containing my excitement, but he seemed to understand that it wasn't simple greed that was driving me. It was vindication. My mantra—*her* mantra—had finally proven to be true. I'd made sacrifices—greater sacrifices than anyone not in the military track—and now I was receiving a reward commensurate with that sacrifice.

"Let's go ahead and get started then, Skye. If you'll lie down on the table over there, I'll administer the first injection."

I complied with his instructions, but couldn't stop another question from slipping out.

"You're going to administer it yourself, sir? Aren't there usually doctors present for these kinds of procedures?"

"Generally, yes, but as you're aware, this is a special circumstance. The general medical staff isn't cleared to know about this nanite variant, and the scientists behind the development of the upgraded nanites aren't any more qualified to be administering injections than I am. Don't worry, the procedure is very low-risk and I've been studying for weeks in preparation for this moment."

"Yes, sir."

He placed both sets of syringes on a nearby counter as he picked up an iodine solution. "You'll need to lift up your shirt to expose your ribs, Skye. Even the regular injections are location-specific, but the upgraded version has additional injections that also have to be administered to precise parts of the body.

"The first injections are designed to prepare the body to host the nanites. At the time of the Desolation, the creation of nanites was understood, but their uses were limited to short-term injections that eventually washed out of the recipient's system."

He finished swabbing a spot about halfway up and just to the right of my sternum, and then picked up a syringe.

"The invention of this solution changed all of that. In what was one of the most impressive scientific advances in the history of mankind, the Founder discovered a way to merge nature and machine. The Destroyer was the one who hit upon a method for powering mechanical and electronic constructs from the reserves of the host body, but it was the Founder who made it so that the host body wouldn't attack the mechanical components once they were installed.

"This injection will prepare the site for the nanite factory that will be responsible for creating replacement nanites to insure that your nanite load never drops below specific levels. You're going to need to hold absolutely still, my dear."

He stabbed the needle into my flesh without further warning, and I wanted to scream. The only thing that stopped me was the fact that I knew just how close he was to my heart. I held my breath and hoped that his hands were steady enough to avoid damaging my heart.

"I'm sorry, I know that stung a little, but there is an anesthesia included in the formula so the next injection to that site won't hurt as badly."

He reached for the top of my shirt and slipped it down off my left shoulder. Once again, he swabbed my skin down with disinfectant—without jostling my shirt enough to expose me or have it slip back down and contaminate the area he'd already disinfected.

"We need to give the first injection a little time to take effect before injecting the nanites, but there's no reason not to proceed with the preparation for the second injection site. This one will be injected up above the heart next to the spine."

He waited for a second while I took a couple of preparatory breaths, and then once I'd exhaled halfway he plunged the second needle into my chest. The pain was just as bad as the first time, but I managed to hold still again, and a couple of seconds later he finished pushing the plunger home and withdrew the needle.

"Very good, Skye. You're doing great. That second site is where the nanites will tap into your nervous system. They'll run a biomechanical interface directly into the center of the spine and up into the base of your brain so that the computer at that location can interface between the nanites and your conscious mind."

"Computer, sir?"

"Yes, Skye. These nanites are going to do more than just make you stronger and faster, they are going to accept a primitive set of instructions—something that has never been possible before now. We're going to have to make a number of additional injections at secondary sites—creating a kind of network of biomechanical computers at key locations inside of your circulatory system—but once that is done you won't just be faster and stronger than the best of our military personnel, you'll be able to instruct the nanites to change the actual structure of your face."

Chapter 4

The Society Military Training Complex
The Society Enclave
Six months earlier

The Citizen-President was as good as his word. Despite the discomfort inherent in the injections, they went off without a hitch. He prepared each of the main and secondary sites over the course of ten minutes, and then he proceeded to inject the specialized nanites into each of those sites, talking me through what was happening at each stage.

As he made the first injection, he talked about the marvel of technology that the nanites had just started constructing in the space between my lungs, the factory that was capable of creating nanites to replace those that inadvertently got expelled from my body. Apparently this strain of nanites was even better at staying out of the digestive tract, respiratory system, and per-spiration ducts than any previous breed, but there was still going to be some loss no matter how good the technology was.

When the plunger went home for the nanite injection into the second site he talked about how the nanites would soon be constructing a flexible metal ring around my aorta. Apparently it would serve as a transmitter so the computer could interface with the nanites as they used my circulatory system to move around my body.

"The interface between your central nervous system and the computer is unfortunately not capable of transmitting complex commands, so you won't be able to do much more than command the nanites to change your face between two or three different structures, but the computer still provides other benefits that aren't possible with the other two nanite strains."

"How so, sir?"

"It will register the presence of adrenaline in your system and instruct some of the nanites to take up position along key neurons inside of your body. Electricity normally travels at about one-tenth the speed of light. You're probably not aware of this, but nerve impulses in the human body are much slower than that. At their best, they only manage about fourteen percent of the speed that electricity would travel down a metal wire.

"Fortunately a chain of nanites stretched alongside the body of a given nerve can register the presence of signals coming from the brain and then send that signal down the chain of nanites running down the spine. It means that the signal can cross a significant percentage of the distance it needs to travel at more than six times its normal speed.

"It's going to take some getting used to, but once you've finished your training I'm assured that you'll gain additional speed over and above even what your increased strength would otherwise suggest."

Each of the secondary injections created another processing node that wrapped itself around another vein or artery to ensure that the nanites would react as quickly as possible to any changes in my body.

Once all of the secondary injections were completed, the Citizen-President went to the back of the room to retrieve two big syringes that looked like they were filled with graphite, and injected them into the site where the factory was being built. Apparently that was another benefit to this strain of nanites. For franchised citizens and soldiers both, it was important for them to eat special dietary supplements to make sure that they consumed enough heavy metals to provide the factories with the requisite raw materials for nanite construction.

My nanites—my factory—were capable of safely storing extensive amounts of heavy metals so that I would be able to go for long periods of time without worrying about my nanite load dropping below peak operating levels. Given that I was going to a grubber city, it was less of a concern than it otherwise would have been—the water in the cities tended to have more heavy metals in it than the purified water consumed inside the barrier—but it was still nice to know that I had plenty of reserves and wouldn't find myself deprived of a key edge at a critical time.

The Citizen-President monitored my vitals for half an hour, and then pronounced me to be in perfect health. Twenty minutes later I was being escorted back to the juvenile dorms to gather up my few possessions and carry them over to my new home in a special, classified section of the administration building.

I was on cloud nine for the first week. There was some residual soreness and exhaustion for the first twenty-four hours as the nanites finished constructing the factory and the computer systems inside of my body, but after that I felt like an entirely different person.

I needed slightly less sleep than before becoming franchised, was stronger, faster, and my bones were the next best thing to un-breakable—a fact I learned fairly quickly once my revised training program started up.

My new instructors all thought that I was running the standard military nanite pack, but they still managed to stress my body nearly to its limit simply because nobody had bothered to tell them that I was doing PT sessions twice a day rather than just once as was standard for military candidates. Obstacle courses, weapons training, hand-to-hand, it all added up to a ruinous toll that would have killed me if not for the superior regenerative properties of my new body.

I woke up wearing my old face—the one that I'd worn my entire life—and then once my morning training was over I switched to the new face—the one that looked older with higher cheekbones and a different eye color. I had my doubts at first, but the Citizen-President was right—none of my instructors realized that Skye from the morning training sessions was the same person as the Stacy their colleagues were so busy trying to kill in the afternoon sessions.

I thought the gig was up the first time I missed a block while learning how to use a baton and had my ribs broken by my six-six, two-hundred-and-eighty-pound instructor. I just knew that I was going to favor that side in the afternoon session and not be able to explain how Stacy ended up with broken ribs, but they healed up over lunch to the point where I didn't have to favor them, and by the time the next morning arrived they were completely healed. I spent the next couple of days acting as though they were still a little sore in my role as Skye, and that was that.

The injury did provide a secondary benefit though. After watching Skye favor her ribs like that, anyone who might have been suspicious of the similarities in weight and height between Skye and Stacy *knew* that Skye couldn't possibly have survived the beating Stacy received in hand-to-hand—not with a set of broken ribs.

I'd always been dedicated to my classes, but my fervor had reached new heights by the time that I made it to the end of my first week. The nanites—even the experimental version inside of me—didn't replace a person's normal strength, they just acted as a multiplier.

The stronger I was underneath the new advantages I'd received, the more of a benefit they could provide. I suddenly had an incredible incentive to strain for every possible ounce of muscle I could pack on my body.

The fact that I was sleeping less and training harder than anyone else meant that it took less time than I'd been expecting to get the hang of the speed assist that the nanites sometimes provided to my nervous system, and once that happened, my skill level soared. I was well on my way towards feeling invulnerable when I was ordered—as Skye—to take a morning weapons class over on the other side of the compound from where I normally trained.

My mood instantly soured when I saw what was waiting for me. I'd been expecting to be added into a normal class of newly-franchised military recruits. Instead, I was sent to a class that before my arrival had included a grand total of one student.

The Citizen-President had told me just days before that there were only two people in my age-group who'd done everything that had been asked of them rather than dropping out of school and training to go off and start working towards their franchise. I was one of the two, and I knew without asking that Megan was the other.

We'd never been friends, but even as a child I'd known that there was something unnatural about Megan. I'd had to be coached into obeying the rules—chided with the mantra that my nurses had repeated to me at every turn. Megan had never seemed to need any prompting. She followed the rules even to the point of alienating the other kids.

I'd learned early on that if I wanted to both obey the rules and not make enemies I was going to have to be careful to make myself scarce when my companions started thinking about testing the boundaries. It wasn't pleasant because it meant that, as time went on, I spent more and more time by myself, but I knew it was the only way I was going to earn the reward that was waiting out there for me.

Megan, on the other hand, never tried for that kind of subtlety. She went wherever she pleased—inside the strictures of the rules we'd been given—and she reported every sin or misdemeanor with a smirk that told everyone around her that she'd known all along that they wouldn't measure up to her standards.

THE SOCIETY

My isolation was self-imposed. Megan's isolation was because she'd made an enemy out of every single person she'd had even the slightest contact with. By all outward evidence, she'd spent every waking moment honing herself into whatever our Society needed her to be. I, however, knew the truth, a truth that I'd never even suspected before the Citizen-President had walked into that office and changed my life forever.

He'd said that I'd never left the zones with the highest social desirability index, but I knew that wasn't true. I'd left—only once, but I'd left. That meant that the system wasn't perfect, that it didn't track us as completely as I'd always suspected it did.

He'd said that Megan had left once, but the fact that some trips didn't register meant that she'd actually left more times than that. Megan was a hypocrite. Her holier-than-thou attitude had been hard enough to stomach when we'd all believed that she really meant the things that she was saying. Now that I knew it was all an act, that she was off doing something that wasn't strictly in keeping with the precepts, she turned my stomach.

She smirked at me as I stepped onto the textured, no-slip training floor, and I wanted so badly to wipe that expression off of her face. I knew I could take her—she'd always had a slight edge in hand-to-hand during the few instances when we'd crossed paths in training sessions, but even if she was franchised now, there wasn't any way that she could hope to take me down now, not with my newfound advantages.

All that work, that hypocritical, catty mask she'd worn for years, and she'd ended up coming in second place to me. Only this time the gulf between first and second was even bigger than normal. There'd only been one dose of the prototype nanites and I'd gotten it.

"Okay, you two. I want to see what you're capable of—no killing blows and nothing that will take more than twenty-four hours to heal. I'm under orders to make sure that you don't interfere with the training schedule that's been laid out for you. Don't make me break the two of you up."

The instructor slapped his stun baton against his leg, emphasizing his point. The baton was plenty deadly enough—for a blunt weapon—on its own, but the handle carried a battery capable of emitting a charge that would drop a buffalo.

We nodded at each other and then I stepped forward and sent out an exploratory jab. What I found made me grit my teeth. Her reaction time was better than I'd been expecting. Despite my best efforts I hadn't been training hard enough. Apparently she'd always been a hypocrite, but she'd pushed herself harder than I'd ever done. Given a few more weeks our baseline capabilities would level out as I caught up with her, and then the greater multiple from my nanites would make a fight like this child's play.

Unfortunately this wasn't taking place in the future, it was taking place now, and our capabilities were too close for comfort. She dodged my jab and stepped into me with a punch to my short ribs. As quickly as that, the fight was full on and the two of us blurred into a flurry of blows that no normal human could have hoped to follow.

I checked her punch with my left elbow and launched my knee up towards her midsection. She blocked that with her shin, using enough force to nearly knock me off balance, and then moved forward with a palm strike to the base of my throat.

I slipped to the side, just far enough that her hand shot through the empty space next to my ear, and then I slammed a punch home to her ribs, smiling as I heard a pair of cracks that signified she was going home that night with at least two broken bones.

I expected her to back down—broken ribs weren't the kind of injury you could fight around without feeling every muscle contraction. Instead, I saw something change behind her eyes. I'd always suspected that none of the rest of us were really real to her, now I had confirmation. She wasn't just fighting to hurt me now, she was going to try to kill me—she just needed to find a way to make it look like an accident.

She hooked her heel around the back of my leg and pulled as she threw her weight forward and slightly to one side. I'd put too much into my punch to her ribs; my balance was too far off.

I was going down—there was no stopping it—but I wasn't going to make things easy for her. I grabbed hold of her mid-fall and tightened every muscle along the front of my body to generate the maximum possible force as I drove my knee into her gut.

She screamed out in pain—something I'd been convinced I would never hear—as the shockwave from my blow sent fragments of rib up into her lung. I expected to feel the lash of the instructor's stun baton at any second, but until it actually landed I had no choice but to keep going at her with everything I had.

A split second later I hit the ground with her on top of me, and her elbow slammed into my chest with enough force to break several of my ribs. Even nanites could only go so far when it came to overriding involuntary muscle contractions—she'd knocked the air out of me.

Before I could knock her off of me she repositioned, throwing me into an arm-bar as she flipped me over on my stomach. She'd won—there wasn't anything I could do to get out of the hold—but I knew that wasn't going to satisfy her. She needed a pretext for killing me; she was going to let my arm slip out of her hands.

I felt her pull back and knew she was about to make her move. From a kneeling position with only my back exposed to her and no weapon there were only so many options open to her. She was going to try to snap my neck.

My timing had to be perfect. I heard the faintest whisper of breath and chose that moment to move. I tore my arm free of her hands at the same time that I brought my right leg around and slammed it into her knee, destroying the joint.

She was falling, but I knew I couldn't just back off—not against Megan. I had to prove I was the more lethal fighter. I wrapped both of my legs around her upper body and used my hip as a fulcrum to snap her arm.

A second later I felt the paralyzing jolt of the instructor's stun-baton. Darkness tried to claim me. I couldn't move, but I still refused to let myself fall unconscious until after I saw the baton slam into Megan as well.

I'd underestimated Megan, secure in the supposed superiority of my nanites, but I wasn't going to repeat that mistake. Shattered ribs, blown knee, broken arm, none of that mattered as long as Megan was conscious. As long as she could still move she was dangerous.

Chapter 5

Present time

Traveling at night was dangerous, but I needed to get out of Piter's territory before sunrise or I risked being trapped on the wrong side of his barricades. I'd gotten extra sleep before my drop into the city, but hadn't wanted to get too far off of a normal sleeping schedule—it was one more difference from those around me that I hadn't been sure would have been justified.

It meant that I was exhausted by the time I reached the barricade on the far side of Piter's territory. Luckily I seemed to have arrived before word of Bash and the other enforcer made it to the border. That meant that security along the barricade wasn't as bad as it could have been, but it was still significant. I saw the expected collection of clubs, knives and swords hanging from the belts of the enforcers on Piter's side of the barricade, but there were also several blocky, two-hundred-year-old firearms in evidence.

That was concerning—I was fast, but nobody could outrun a bullet. The Society's intelligence on this section of the city was better than what we had on the territories of most of the other warlords, but it still left a lot to be desired. I knew there had to be ways through the barricade, routes used by smugglers and others who profited on moving goods and people to other territories, but I didn't have any contacts on the ground, and despite my hopes from before I'd jumped out of the plane, I wasn't going to have time to perform any kind of detailed analysis of the perimeter.

If Piter was anything like most of the warlords, he couldn't care less about murders that happened inside of his territory—unless they happened to his enforcers. Crimes against his men were one of the few things that he couldn't afford to turn a blind eye to. Piter would have someone publicly executed before the sun set again.

Justice inside of grubber cities was swift and less concerned with accuracy than it was with creating deterrents. I knew better than to let my guard down though. Executing some poor individual who was in the wrong place at the wrong time wouldn't stop Piter from continuing to look for the actual murderer. He couldn't afford to let me get away any more than he could afford to let his 'citizens' think that I'd gotten away.

My only way to make sure that I was beyond Piter's grasp was to find a way across the barricade and into the territory to the north of his, the territory where my target lived.

I spent nearly twenty minutes scouting Piter's northern border without any luck. I found a couple of likely holes in the wall of metal and wood that ran from building to building, but each and every one of them was guarded by at least two guys. It spoke volumes that Piter was so concerned about keeping everyone in his territory from leaving, but I suspected that it was much the same in any of the territories controlled by the various warlords who ran the city.

I could feel the clock ticking down with each passing minute. With all of the disruption from the bombing, and the late start that Piter had awarded all of his people, there was a chance that the two bodies I'd left behind me wouldn't be discovered until dawn, but it would be foolish to rely on that. There was no choice but to go inside one of the buildings on the border.

It was risky—once I was inside there were fewer options when it came to running away from any pursuit. Even more concerning was the likelihood I would quickly be recognized as a stranger by the building's normal occupants, but the buildings were the last possible vulnerability.

My clothes were already worn and singed in several spots. Even without the damage from the bombing and the fire I'd wanted to make sure that I would blend in with the rest of the grubbers, so I'd made sure to tear both the shirt and pants before I'd left home. I picked a couple of likely rips and strategically lengthened them to show some upper thigh and a healthy chunk of shoulder.

Then I took a deep breath and walked into the nearest building with the confident stride of someone who belonged there. I should have known that the doorway would have a guard on it, but my ruse worked. The guard flinched at the bruising and swelling easily visible all over my face, but he didn't ask me who I was going up to see. I walked past him with a gait that was part shame and part strut, and then once I was out of sight I hurried up the closest stairwell.

At some point this had been an office building. That meant a plethora of windows, but I knew that Piter wouldn't have left the first two floors unsecured—not as paranoid as he seemed to be about security, not for a building that bordered the territory of one of his rivals.

I ducked out of the stairs on the third floor and bit back a curse as soon as I got to where I could see the closest window. Metal plating had been welded across the space that had once contained a window. As I headed back towards the stairs, arm pressed against my ribs, I heard yelling. The odds of anyone having tracked me to this building already were astronomical, but I had to assume that was what had happened.

Maybe Piter's men had access to radios and someone had seen Bash pull me off into the alley. If so, the guard downstairs had probably alerted his fellows to my presence in his building just based on my height, build and gender. I hurried up to the fourth floor, but the first window I checked was blocked off by a steel mesh that would take equipment I didn't have to cut through.

I debated going up one more floor. There was a limit to how much metal even a psychopath like Piter would be willing to dedicate towards sealing off egress from this particular building, but the paracord I'd brought with me hadn't been measured with a hundred-foot drop in mind. I had to find an exit from this floor or I wasn't going to survive the drop.

At least the fact that they'd used steel mesh rather than welded sheet metal was a good sign. I could hear a group of people running up the stairs as I crashed through the plywood separating the next-door office.

This room wasn't abandoned, but I subdued the two occupants—a guy and girl roughly my own age—with a pair of carefully targeted blows that left them unconscious. I turned to look at the window and felt a surge of relief. There was nothing more than plywood sealing the room off from the elements.

The relief lasted only as long as it took to rip the plywood down and see the bars that had been welded across the opening. It was a patchwork mess, but there weren't any spaces big enough even for someone as small as me to slip through...unless...I checked a suspicious-looking bar and confirmed that the weld to the rest of the framework was corroded.

I gritted my teeth and then lashed out with a kick that sent a jolt of pain shooting through my foot. I'd just fractured the reinforced bones in my foot, but the blow had succeeded in breaking the top of the bar loose. I grabbed the free end and started working it back and forth in the hopes that I could fatigue the bottom weld. It wouldn't have worked if not for the kick that had broken the top free, but between my first blow and the corrosion, the bottom weld gave just a few seconds later.

I pulled the paracord out of the pack wrapped around my waist and tied one end to the most secure part of the remaining framework. The other end went around the metal bar I'd just finished tearing free, and then it was time.

More screams rang out from the third floor as Piter's enforcers went room to room looking for me. I wriggled through the opening I'd created in the framework, and then stood on the windowsill with one hand on the framework and the other wrapped around the bar that connected me to the paracord.

I told myself that it wasn't going to hurt as bad as I thought it would, and then I stepped off into thin air.

My length of rope was just over forty feet long—long enough to be useful, but not so long that it would be impossible to believe I could have scavenged it from somewhere inside of the city. By the time I'd used several inches tying into the bars crisscrossing the window and several more inches securing the knot around the bar in my hand, there was a tad less than forty feet of slack racing past me as I fell.

I grabbed hold of the metal bar like a water-skier from back home, and locked the muscles in my hands and arms. Nobody—even an operative from the Society—was strong enough to absorb the forces involved in a one-hundred and twenty-five pound weight falling forty feet, but I came close.

It felt for a second like my arms were going to be ripped out of their sockets, and then the jolt of pain from my cracked ribs was competing with the agony shooting through my shoulders and up my arms. The bar tore itself free of my grasp, and then I was falling again—even faster this time because I was still carrying a significant amount of momentum from the first stage of my fall.

I had a split second to wonder exactly how hard I was going to hit, and then I crashed into a wooden shanty that had been built right up against the side of the building. It was sheer dumb luck that I'd found that window to jump out of, but the plywood roof was the only thing that allowed me to survive the fall as well as I did.

I hit with the unmistakable crack of breaking wood, and then screamed out as my feet made contact with the concrete and I felt the bones in my lower right leg break. It was a fracture rather than a complete break, so I knew I could still move. It hurt, but I needed to get to my feet if I wanted to avoid having Piter's goons shooting at me from above.

I made it half a dozen steps away from the building before a guard in all black appeared out of the darkness.

"Freeze!"

I knew that it was useless to try to explain. Every warlord in the city probably had the same industrial-strength paranoia when it came to people willing to desert one section of the city for another. I raised my hands above my head, grimacing from the pain, and waited for the guard to close.

He was much better equipped than anyone I'd seen on Piter's side of the barricade. Rather than just a collection of worn-out fabric, he had an actual uniform, including a utility vest and a rifle that looked like it was brand new.

Even more incredibly, he seemed to be by himself—something that would have been almost unimaginable for one of Piter's enforcers, all of whom probably had so many people gunning for them that they wouldn't dare walk around by themselves. He moved well too—almost as well as the Society weapons instructors who'd trained me.

Too bad he was no more than human.

I waited until he was within five feet of me and then threw myself to the right as I swept my hand across his barrel, knocking it to the side. He got a single burst of shots off—all of which slammed into the building I'd just left—and then my palm-strike took him in the base of the throat and he was gasping for breath.

Unlike the strike that I'd used against Bash, the base of the throat wasn't a killing blow, but I couldn't just leave him conscious and potentially able to follow me into the darkness once he recovered from the shock to his system. I slammed my forearm into the side of his neck, compressing the carotid artery and causing his body to react by decreasing blood flow to his brain.

My instructors would have killed him to make sure that he wouldn't be able to identify them later, but I wasn't one of them. There'd already been enough killing tonight.

I disappeared into the shadows, quietly working my way deeper into my target's territory. My face was already shifting back to the one I'd worn into the city. Within five minutes the swelling would start to go back down. My ribs and the bones in my leg were going to take longer than that, but I'd just successfully completed the first phase of my mission.

Chapter 6

I knew from my briefing that the warlord who controlled this stretch of the city was a guy named Brennan. Interestingly enough, the streets were much less dirty and cluttered in Brennan's territory than they'd been inside of Piter's. It was still nothing like the city back home, but it was obvious that an effort was being made to clean up the refuse left behind from decades of bombing and neglect.

Under other circumstances I would have been overjoyed. I was invulnerable to nearly every virus, parasite and bacteria known to mankind, but that didn't mean that I liked the idea of living in what amounted to a garbage dump. Despite that, as I walked through the flickering lighting of the city I found myself wishing that Brennan didn't run quite as tight a ship. The lack of shanties meant that there were fewer places to hide.

Luckily things got a little less orderly within a few blocks of the border I'd just left. I found the remains of a plywood shanty that looked abandoned and pulled a couple of the sheets of wood over me. It was too cold to sleep very deeply, but it got me out of sight and gave me time off of my feet so my bones would have a chance to heal.

The sun rising was one of the more welcome sights I could remember seeing. I pulled myself to my feet and started working my way deeper into Brennan's territory.

One of the first rules anyone living under the equivalent to martial law learned was to keep your head down once the shooting started, but there was still a chance that someone had gotten a look at me when I'd taken out the guard after jumping out of Piter's building. It was a loose end that I didn't like—something that I couldn't control—but all the reports I'd read indicated that the technology base inside of the city was fragmented.

There were no televisions and only a few aging radios for receiving centralized announcements. With no telephones or other forms of wired communication, most of the information flow was carried the old-fashioned way—by foot.

That meant the further I could get away from the incident, the less likely it was that it was going to come back to haunt me. Besides, I didn't know exactly where Brennan had set up his headquarters, but it was going to be roughly in the center of his territory.

The street signs had all been scavenged and used for other purposes decades ago, but it wasn't like I was trying to follow a set of directions or anything. I counted blocks, figuring that once I knew exactly how far Brennan's territory ran from south to north, I could measure the distance the other direction and then work out where his headquarters was likely to be located.

I was shocked to see how much the streets changed over the course of just three more blocks. They went from looking like the site of an industrial chemical spill, to clean and rubble-free. Even more astonishing was the gleaming wall that ran through the middle of the road a few blocks deeper in from that.

None of that had been in my briefings. Either this was a new development or my trainers had been keeping it from me. Neither possibility was particularly comforting.

I meant to keep moving once I saw the wall, to act as though it wasn't a surprise, but my feet ground to a stop despite my best intentions. I knew that it made me stand out, that it made me a potential target for Brennan's enforcers, but I just couldn't help it. This was too much like civilization—the last thing I'd been told to expect in one of the grubber cities.

"You must be a new arrival."

I spun around in the direction of the voice, hands up as though expecting an attack, but the woman who'd spoken looked anything but threatening. Her curly white hair was a shocking contrast to dark skin that didn't look anywhere near as wrinkled as her eyes seemed to suggest it should.

"Don't worry, Brennan doesn't worry about deserters like the rest of them do. He doesn't have to—not given the way that he's sealed off his inner compound from the rest of his territory."

I shook my head in amazement. "How did he do this?"

"He took down the building next to the one where he set up his headquarters. He had the other gang leaders frothing at the mouth. They figured that he wouldn't be able to hold his territory for very long, and they were worried he was destroying perfectly good housing."

"But he wasn't?"

The woman shrugged. "I don't know. It provided him with the metal he needed to build a wall and ever since then he's done nothing but bring more people into his compound—faster even than he's expanded the size of his inner sanctum. It kind of seems like he's finding somewhere to put all of those people, but nobody on the outside knows for sure. For all I know, he's a cannibal."

"Wait, you mean he recruits people, brings new bodies into his compound?"

She nodded, and gestured off to the right with her chin. "There's a recruiting center two blocks that way. Don't say that I didn't warn you though. Nobody but his guardsmen come out of there once they go in—at least not alive."

"What are you trying to say? You don't really believe that he's eating people, do you?"

"Doesn't matter if he's eating them or not, there are always at least two or three new bodies on our side of the gate every morning. Some of them are incredibly disfigured, missing limbs or fingers. You go in there, and as far as the rest of the world is concerned, you're dead."

The woman gestured around at the buildings to either side of us. "You don't have to go in there, you know. Whatever else anyone says about Brennan, he runs a tight ship. Even here, outside of his compound, things are better than they are anywhere else in the city—unless you're some warlord's favorite.

"We have food, all grown on the upper floors of the buildings, way more than the last place I lived. Brennan doesn't even make us carry the water up the stairs—he uses the pumps on the fire-suppression system. Murderers are hunted down, rape is punishable by death, and he doesn't turn a blind eye to thievery. There's no reason to go inside the compound when we're already living nearly as good as ants out here."

For the first time since I'd agreed to my mission, I was tempted to turn back. I was more than a match for any single enforcer. In a pinch, I was even capable of taking down two at the same time, but that was an entirely different proposition from walking into a fortress full of well-armed, well-trained men. I'd been in danger before now, but once I was inside, a single slip would blow my cover and get me killed.

"Don't you wonder whether or not the people inside of the compound are living even better than you are out here?"

"Sure, I wonder, but it doesn't matter if they are. I'm an old woman, old enough to know this isn't the first time something like this has happened. Brennan might have bigger ambitions than most, but there's one immutable law to our existence. If you try to climb above your station you get punished. For you and me the punishment comes from some enforcer or gang leader. For someone like Brennan, the punishment will come from the ants. You walk inside of there and sooner or later the bombs will be dropping right on your head."

"Maybe you're right, but I don't have anywhere else to go."

"Yeah, that's what your type always thinks. If you change your mind, I'm in this building here on the second floor. You just ask for Gladys and I'll put you to work in my garden."

I nodded my thanks to her and then headed towards the gate. A few minutes later I was standing on the outskirts of a crowd of more than forty people, all of whom were milling around as though unsure how close they dared get to the gates.

It wasn't until I got closer that I realized they weren't just scared—they were also keeping a respectful distance from the trio of corpses resting less than a dozen feet from the gate.

All three of the bodies were covered up. Part of me wanted to go check them for a cause of death, but that would just draw attention to me. Attention that would probably result in me joining them under a similar shroud before I ever got a chance to finish my mission.

"I'm looking to fill five positions this morning. Which of you are looking for a job?"

While I'd been staring at the three shrouds, the gates had swung open with a soundlessness that would have been enviable even back home. The man who stepped out of the compound to address us looked like he was in his late forties. He had dark hair and the slight build of someone who survived based on his wit rather than his fists.

This was my chance, but I knew that I couldn't just volunteer without asking about the deaths. Even the most desperate of volunteers would be concerned about the mortality rate inside the compound.

"What would I be doing?"

The man—the foreman—shrugged. "It depends on your abilities. Everyone starts at the bottom of the food chain unless they enter with some kind of specialized skill. You'll probably start out doing manual labor."

"Dangerous manual labor?"

The question came from someone deeper in the crowd which was good because it meant that the foreman's attention shifted away from me.

The foreman shook his head in response. "Everything about our lives is dangerous. Do you see that building looming behind you? It's more than two hundred years old and it hasn't seen any kind of significant maintenance for at least the last century. The superstructure has been exposed to the elements for decades now. Honestly, I'm surprised it hasn't already collapsed—probably killing hundreds or even thousands in the process."

More than one person in the crowd looked up at the buildings around us in fear—as though they'd never considered the possibility that our very surroundings might turn against us. The foreman wasn't done though.

"That's just the start of the risks we all face. Even if you didn't have to worry about being mugged or murdered in some senseless turf war, your life expectancy isn't much past forty-five. The water supply is contaminated. Not with bacteria—we could deal with that. It's got a thousand different chemicals in it that would have caused riots in the street back before the breakdown. Back then drinking water this filthy would have killed millions, but there aren't millions of us left to kill anymore. The Desolation saw to that, and those of us who are left have developed tolerances to the toxicity of our environment.

"There are a thousand different ways that you could die, most of which you've never even stopped to consider. Starvation, exposure, disease, they are all just warmup shows for the main event. Even if you do everything right, you're still going to be killed by the ants."

A low rumble of anger greeted his words, and I joined the nodding I saw all around me. That drew a smile out of the foreman.

"That's right. It doesn't matter how smart you are, how hard you work, in the end they hold all the cards. They fly in with their fancy planes and they drop bombs that we can't even see coming. These cities are kill zones, but there is no leaving them. We can scavenge within a mile or two of the city, but if you stay out past dark their drones will get you. They'll sniff you out in the darkness, see the heat coming from your body, and execute you from a mile away. We're here in this hellhole because the ants—the Society—don't give us any other choice."

"What are you saying? Do you think you can stand against them? It's been tried before and it never works!"

"You're right. It has been tried before, but this time we have something that those others didn't. We have a secret weapon—one that will buy us time to bootstrap ourselves up to a point where we can beat them."

He needed a better speech. There was no telling how often he'd practiced it out here in front of his shining gates with a score of heavily armed men at his back, but no amount of polishing was going to make this particular pitch workable. He'd lost all of his listeners right then and there.

Even the most angry, revenge-driven grubber knew better than to provoke the Society. For decades we'd laid siege to their cities, containing the infestation that they represented. They couldn't beat us, and their plan to stand against us was exactly the reason that I'd been sent to this city.

I'd been nervous about going into the compound. I couldn't go back to the Society—not without succeeding in my mission—but even being forced to live like a grubber wasn't as bad as being unmasked as an agent of the Society. They wouldn't just kill me, they would torture me to death.

That nervousness disappeared as I heard him admit that they had a weapon they were going to use against the Society, against my home. He'd used the wrong recruitment speech for a grubber, but he'd used exactly the right one to get an operative from the Society to sign onto his little endeavor.

I stepped to the front of the crowd.

"Where do I sign up?"

Chapter 7

The foreman was thrilled. My offer to join was the first crack in the dam that had been holding the rest of the grubbers back from signing up. It took a few more minutes, but by the end, he had the pick of the crowd. He turned away anyone obviously sick or otherwise unable to work, and still had more than enough volunteers to fill out the five positions he was recruiting for.

We were escorted inside of the compound and a few seconds later the gates were locked again and there was no hope of escape. I wasn't sure what to expect after that. Back home, there would have been psych studies and aptitude tests to determine our strengths and qualifications. No matter his delusions of grandeur, Brennan didn't have access to that kind of technology and resources.

Instead of undergoing testing to determine where we would be most useful, we were taken to the dormitories and assigned a bunk and a footlocker for our belongings. I spent the entire trip trying to stop my nervousness from showing.

This was a particularly critical time in the insertion phase. The few remaining items in my waist pouch were all fairly innocuous—other than the special transmitter that was my only way to radio my handler back home.

The device had been engineered to look like nothing more than a piece of scrap metal, but that wasn't a guarantee that it wouldn't result in my death if someone saw it. Back among Piter's men there had been a chance that whoever saw it wouldn't realize what they were looking at, but this was most definitely not Piter's territory, and for all of his foolishness when it came to announcing Brennan's intention to fight the Society, the foreman wasn't un-educated.

I kept my eyes peeled on the trip from the gate to the dormitory hoping I would see a place to stash the transmitter, but didn't have any such luck. I wouldn't have been able to secret it while being accompanied by the foreman, three guards, and my four fellow conscripts, but it still would have been nice to know that I had a plan.

The dormitory was likewise no good. The foreman gave us a couple of minutes to stow any belongings in our lockers, but I wasn't stupid enough to think that anything left there would be safe. The lockers might be proof against the rest of the dormitory's residents, but they wouldn't stop Brennan's security people, and that was the first place I would look if I was one of the people he probably had tasked to find spies among his new recruits.

A few minutes after our arrival at the dorms, we headed back outside. It wasn't until we were leaving that I finally realized that the building housing the dorms was new construction. That was unexpected—to the rest of the people who'd joined with me just as much as to me.

Here in the city, nobody had the skills or knowledge required to build anything more complicated than a wooden lean-to. Back home that hadn't been the case, but we built with such quality and forethought that it was rare that we actually had to put up new buildings. Our population had been stable for more than a century and there was more than enough in the way of housing and other facilities to take care of any conceivable need.

"You've never seen anything like this before, have you?"

The foreman put the question out there casually—as though not addressing anyone in particular—but I got the feeling he was talking to me. Luckily I was able to answer honestly this time.

"No, I haven't. The fence was one thing, but this is something else. You weren't kidding when you said that Brennan was trying to do something different."

He nodded. "The other warlords don't realize just how far Brennan wants to take us. The building is only two stories tall, and it's screened behind the other buildings inside the compound so that everyone outside of our group won't realize what we're really up to, but it's been laid out so that it can grow—someday it will be forty stories tall."

I pointed towards the sky, overcome by some urge that would have made my instructors throw their hands up in disgust.

"You can screen your activities from the other warlords, but there isn't anything you can do to hide a brand-new building from the ants—not when they control the sky."

That earned me a secretive smile. "You know you didn't fool me back there, right?" My breath caught, but he continued on after only the slightest of pauses. "I know that you didn't join up because you want to defeat the ants. It's okay though. We're in the middle of trying to rebuild civilization. We have centuries of knowledge that needs to be re-discovered, everything from running a foundry to building computer processors. It's a dangerous, brutal undertaking, but it's required if we're ever to claw the ants' boots off of our neck. We'll take you for whatever reason you want to join us."

He held out his hand. "I'm Foreman Tyrell."

"Skye."

"A magical name. I hope that someday we're able to put you back up in the heavens—that's where someone with a name like yours belongs."

We'd all stopped to take in the building housing the dormitory, but now he waved everyone back into motion as he pointed off to the east.

"Sergeant, please take those two to textiles. Lexis will slot them into whatever holes she's got right now. I'll take these three down to the foundry. The rest of your men can return to their posts."

Tyrell led the three of us who were left over to a ramp that led downwards into the ground. The scale of what we were looking at was nothing less than amazing, but I should have anticipated that just based off of the fact that Brennan had decided to build an entirely new building rather than converting one of the existing office buildings.

None of the other warlords would have ever considered digging down into the earth beneath us, but if they had, the entrance to their mine would have been barely wide enough for two people to walk abreast. Brennan had created a ramp that was large enough for two vehicles to move down it. He was building for the future in ways that stirred something inside of me that I hadn't anticipated.

We walked for five more minutes along the main shaft before coming to a heavy iron door. Tyrell pointed at it.

"If you'll do the honors, please, Skye? I'm afraid that these old arms aren't as capable as they once were."

I nodded, somewhat taken off guard by the admission of weakness from someone who seemed to wield the power of life and death over significant sections of Brennan's domain, and grabbed the large wheel that served as a locking mechanism.

I'd expected it to be nothing more than a little sticky—probably as a result of not having been lubricated in years. After all, he'd asked a seventeen-year-old girl who looked like she'd spent significant chunks of her life not getting enough to eat.

I'd been wrong. The locking wheel was poorly machined and I could feel metal grinding against metal as I tried to turn it. One of my companions, the burly twenty-year-old guy, laughed and said something dismissive.

Under other circumstances I probably would have backed off and asked for help, but this was still a grubber domain. No matter how progressive Brennan might seem, there was still one truth that reigned supreme. You couldn't appear weak.

I clenched my jaw and slowly increased the force I was using until the wheel finally broke loose, spinning enough to release the locks on the door.

Tyrell patted me on the shoulder as he walked past, leading us into the foundry. "You're surprisingly strong, Skye. I think I chose well bringing you down here. You'll need to be strong to survive underground."

Chapter 8

Saying that I was going to work in the foundry wasn't quite true. I was actually working above the foundry—a fact that kept me up more nights than I wanted to think about.

The city was powered by a mix of generation sources. Wood, wind, solar, gravity-fed turbines from water captured on the roofs of buildings more than a hundred stories tall, it was all in the mix, but none of it was very plentiful.

I knew from my pre-mission briefings that the solar and wind generators were all the better part of a hundred and fifty years old, and with every passing year the city's generation abilities dropped. Old age claimed many of the panels and windmills, but the biggest cause of the loss was bombing runs like the one that had been used to cover my arrival.

The Society was in a tough position. We wanted the grubbers to become self-sufficient enough to realize that the teachings of the precepts were a better way to live, but we also couldn't allow them to become a threat to our way of life.

If they directed their efforts towards redeveloping solar technology then we wouldn't be forced to continually bomb them. Instead they continued to focus on building better ways to kill us.

Good old-fashioned wood-burning power generation was very much within the capabilities of all of the grubber cities, but that posed a different set of problems. It was obvious to even the least informed individual back home that the grubbers couldn't be allowed to roam freely over the face of the earth.

The Desolation had taken place precisely because the various countries had been allowed to attack each other with a host of weapons capable of raining down destruction from half a world away. The precepts were clear that no group could be allowed to threaten the survival of our world in that manner again.

Even if that hadn't been the case, their cities were toxic dumps—letting them range more than a day or two beyond the edges of the urbanized areas would just allow the contamination to spread.

That meant that our drones and snipers picked them off whenever one of them stayed outside of the city after dark, which in turn meant that there wasn't a lot of wood coming into the city for fuel purposes.

What fuel did make it into the city was fought over for use as building materials and to provide warmth in the winter, and only if there was any surplus did it then make it into the rudimentary generators that powered critical machinery like the fire suppression systems.

It was no wonder that the warlords on the edge of the city were the most powerful. They were the ones who controlled most of the food production and all of the lumber trade. It was ironic. From what I'd been told, just two hundred years ago agriculture had taken a definite back seat with regards to the creation of wealth, a trend that had been progressing for centuries before that.

Now everything had reversed. All of the warlords were fabulously wealthy compared to the average grubber, but the value of the human lives controlled in the inner territories was completely eclipsed by the wealth generated by the farms and lumber operations on the edge of the cities.

Brennan's compound was different. There was an array of priceless solar panels stationed on the top of his headquarters building, but they had primarily been used to bootstrap him up to the compound's current method of power generation, a large, two-stage geothermal facility.

The first stage drew heat up from several miles below the surface of the earth and converted it into electricity, which was then used to power a small foundry buried several hundred feet underground. The second stage involved harvesting the waste heat off of the foundry and using it to generate additional electricity. That was where I was stationed, along with two of the other workers who'd joined up on the same day as me.

Back home a facility like this would have been fully automated so as to ensure that no human life would be lost in the event of a disaster, but I hadn't seen a working computer since I'd landed inside the city. Instead, Brennan and his foremen were using barely trained men and women to keep the geothermal plant running.

Each stage of the process was fraught with danger. Brennan had managed to drill down far enough that the temperatures in each of the main shafts was more than hot enough to boil water. The individuals in the first stage were responsible for regulating the flow of cold water to keep the generator operating at peak temperatures. That regulation was done by way of old-fashioned valves mounted on more than a dozen different pipes, and a round-the-clock watch had to be maintained to make sure that the temperatures didn't rise to dangerous levels.

The foundry was dangerous simply because they were working with metal that had been heated to a temperature measured in the thousands of degrees. Unlike normal foundries, this one was underground, which meant that there wasn't any easy escape for all of that heat.

Instead, the heat emitted by the molten metal was absorbed into the rock walls around the foundry and then shunted away with cold water piped in from above. The hot water rising back to the top of the loop then ended up in the second stage of the geothermal power generation facility.

Those of us in the second stage weren't in quite as much danger as the people in the foundry, but we had just as much or more responsibility. If we didn't correctly regulate the flow of water into the coolant headed down into the foundry, then everyone down there would die. If we dumped too much cold water down the pipes, then the secondary power generator stopped working and power that the rest of the compound was depending on disappeared.

That would have been plenty bad enough all by itself, but the added complexity driven by the hot water coming up from the stage one power generating facility meant that we were often juggling multiple variables with nothing more sophisticated than a few old-fashioned mercury thermometers and an ancient telegraph.

The crew I was working with was a mixed bag. Our team lead was a serious, silver-haired woman named Beth who'd been running the night shift inside of phase two for more than three months. Her right-hand man was a guy named Billy.

Billy rarely said more than two words at a time, but the two of them had a near-perfect ability to anticipate what the other needed at any given moment in order to keep the various pipes from getting too hot.

Those two were the good part of my new team. The two who'd joined up with me were decidedly less competent. Jerome was roughly the size of a house—an amazing feat for someone who'd grown up in the food-poor interior of the city. I suspected that he'd served as an enforcer for one or more of the other warlords before moving into Brennan's territory. He was only marginally smarter than a rock, which made me question the wisdom of putting him in such a critical location, but there was no denying the fact that his strength came in handy when it was time to open or close some of the more corroded valves.

My best guess was that Tyrell had assumed that Beth and Billy would be able to keep Jerome out of trouble. Nothing had gone catastrophically wrong so far, but I'd only been on the job for two days, and there was still plenty of time for Jerome to screw something up.

His girlfriend, Del, was an even bigger question as far as I was concerned. She didn't have Jerome's strength, which meant that she usually ended up monitoring the telegraph and master thermometer. That would have been okay if she'd been intelligent, or at least realized that she needed to check in with Beth on a regular basis, but she was dead set on appearing competent regardless of the reality of the situation.

I'd spotted a likely hiding spot for the transmitter I'd brought with me at the end of my first shift, and dropped it off on the way into work the next morning—a fortunate thing since everyone had started making pointed comments about my need for a shower. The transmitter wasn't waterproof—even assuming it wouldn't have drawn attention to shower in communal facilities with my clothes on—and I wasn't willing to leave it back in my locker.

I arrived to work the third morning freshly showered and only slightly embarrassed at being forced to shower around a dozen other women. I was beginning to understand why most of Brennan's workers were so happy to be working for him. Being clean again—even after less than forty-eight hours in the city—felt like the ultimate luxury.

The people who'd been working there for a while made it clear that the showers weren't always hot, but they often were, and being able to shower more often than just when there was a rainstorm was considered an amazing perk to working in the compound.

Beth looked up as I walked in. "Good, you're early—that means I'll be able to brief you."

"Something new going on?"

"Yeah, the foundry is shifting over to steel again, which is a first for you. Up until now they've been just turning out new rolls of copper wire."

"So we'll have more waste heat being dumped into the wall."

"Smart girl. Yes, more waste heat, which means more pipes turned on in order to keep the pressure from getting too high. This is the first time we've dealt with a steel pour in more than two months, which has me worried. Before this, Brennan and Tyrell always came down here to make sure that everything ran smoothly when the foundry kicked over to the more dangerous jobs. Between the two of them and Brennan's guards, we always had plenty of hands—smart ones—to make sure that nothing got out of control."

"So we're on our own this time? Any idea why?"

Beth shook her head, silver locks whipping back and forth. "They've moved on to some other project. It's the way of things around here. Brennan is always thinking several steps ahead, always working on the next step to getting us so that we'll be able to stand up to the ants. The foundry and stage one have both been working just fine for more than four months—since even before I got here. Adding the second generator up here only happened about three months ago."

"So the bosses figure that all of the bugs have been worked out of the system and with our arrival you've got the extra hands you need to keep up with all of the flow regulation that needs to happen."

"Yeah, that's the idea, but the truth is that it's never been done before with so few people. There are only five of us, and two more thermometers have gone out since then—with no replacements in sight—which means that we'll have to go in and take manual measurements."

I pursed my lips, debating. "You're worried about Del?"

"About all of you, but her most of all. Jerome needs to be inside turning valves—Billy and me too—which just leaves the two of you. If I had my druthers, I'd have you out watching the telegraph, but Del is worse than useless inside the pipe chamber. She doesn't have your strength, and she's as likely to shoot her mouth off as she is to obey an order."

"Can you get her replaced?"

That got me a shrug. "Maybe. I already asked, but the day manager says that decent people are hard to come by. He wants me to give things a go with her first. We should be okay. We'll keep an eye on things—keep the temperature on the low side of the operating range so that we have an extra safety margin to work with—and then you, me and Billy will all stop by the telegraph every chance we get to check that she's passing on the messages. You'll be working the area closest to the doors though, so it will mostly fall to you to keep an eye on her."

The thought of being in the pipe room if a pipe burst was enough to make my skin crawl. The bottom end of the generator's operating temperature was more than a hundred and fifty degrees. The pipes were supposed to be rated for three hundred and fifty degrees, which meant that a pipe that got too hot and burst from the resulting pressure was going to be unleashing scalding water on anyone in the vicinity.

If I'd been the team leader I would have given the day manager a piece of my mind, but Beth knew a lot more about the way the system worked than I did.

"Okay, if you're sure it's safe. I'll do my best to keep an eye on her."

"You're a smart girl, Skye. You and I both know that there isn't anything safe about any part of this process. Brennan is the smartest man in the city—maybe the smartest man on the whole continent—but he's figuring this out as he goes. We have accidents all of the time. For every thing he anticipates there's at least two more that he doesn't see coming—mostly interactions between complex systems.

"Sometimes grunts like you and me see the issues developing and can head them off, sometimes we can't. There's a reason that Tyrell drops off a body or two every morning and comes back in with an equal number of new recruits. None of this is safe."

"I thought it was mostly people who weren't paying attention who were getting killed."

"Tyrell say that?"

"I'm not sure—maybe."

"There's some of that happening, but that's not the only reason that people are dying."

"If this is all so dangerous how come you're still here?"

Beth grinned. "Same reason you are. Here's no more dangerous than out there. At least here we don't have to worry about being murdered or raped. Besides, maybe the two of them are right and we can finally put the hurt on those ants. Bombing runs killed both of my children when they weren't any older than you are right now. I'd give a lot to be a part of something that evens the score between us and them."

I tried to fake an enthusiastic smile, but it was harder than I'd expected. Being told it was going to be hard to keep my emotional distance from a bunch of grubbers wasn't quite the same as actually living among them and sharing life-threatening risks. Maybe I was more like Megan than I'd realized. On some level, I hadn't really thought of the grubbers as people. I'd expected them to all be like Piter and Bash, but so far a lot more of them had ended up like Beth and the three people—Sally, Jack and

Donner—who'd covered for me back in the bucket brigade.

I knew that Brennan had to be stopped—the lives of all of the people inside this city weren't any more important than the citizens, franchised or otherwise, back behind the barrier—but I was starting to realize just how much death and destruction ultimately needed to be laid at Brennan's feet. There were more reasons than I'd originally realized to make sure that I was successful with this mission.

Billy arrived a couple of minutes after Beth and I finished our conversation, but Del and Jerome were a full twenty minutes late, which meant that two of the workers from the night shift had to stay late. I could see Beth getting hotter and hotter under the collar with every minute that passed after the official start time, and I was pretty sure that she was going to have another conversation with the day manager once our shift was finished. Luckily the foundry wasn't scheduled to start heating up the steel until more than an hour after our shift started.

My new bed had included a set of utilitarian clothes made out of fabric that came in a loose, scratchy weave. There were several layers to the garments, which I hadn't understood at the time, but as I stepped away from the telegraph and prepared to go into the pipe room, I blessed the individual who'd decided on multiple layers as a way of staying warm rather than opting for a single set of thicker garments.

I'd already shed my outer layer of clothing when I'd arrived at work, but now I pulled off the long-sleeved shirt I'd been wearing and set it to the side as well. A few seconds later I was dressed in nothing more than a set of crude shorts and a halter top. I started shivering almost immediately, but I knew I was going to be grateful for the extra exposed skin once I was working around all of those hot pipes.

I strapped on a set of heavy pads for my knees and hips, and then pulled on thick gloves that ran all of the way up to my elbows. Once I was 'in uniform,' I opened the door to the pipe room and winced at the heat.

Everything about my current assignment was one long series of sub-optimal compromises. Back home this kind of job would have been handled by computers—even assuming that we'd used any technology so antiquated. If human intervention had been required, then the workers would have been dressed in special suits that would have both protected them from contact with the hot pipes and maintained a cooler temperature so that they could work in comfort.

In Brennan's territory, we were faced with the choice of bundling up enough to make burns unlikely—and passing out from heat exhaustion less than an hour into our shift—or shedding enough clothes to keep us from overheating and risking nasty burns from accidental contact with the pipes. Everyone in the pipe room would rotate out for water at least every half hour and take salt tablets to replace the electrolytes we were losing, but working in the pipe room was still a punishing assignment.

The generator was located just below us, which meant that Brennan had been able to install a primitive cooling system by running pipes circulating cold water through the walls and ceiling, but even when the foundry was just pouring copper, it still got hot inside of the pipe room. I could only imagine how hot it was going to get during a steel pour. Either Brennan had more confidence in the resilience of the unaugmented human body than I did, or he'd misplaced a decimal when doing the calculations about how much water he'd need to circulate through the pipes cooling the pipe room. That or maybe he'd just run short on building materials when constructing the second stage of the geothermal project and this was another of the compromises that were such a part of life here.

Within seconds I was coated in sweat and wishing that I could lose the gloves, but I knew better than to remove them—not when I could feel the heat coming off of my set of pipes even through the thick leather.

For nearly an hour I was able to lose myself in the work—mindless though it was. It was obvious that the piping system had all been built with scavenged materials. Brennan and his people had put the geothermal installation together back before they'd had the ability to melt down metal and then pour it out in new shapes.

That meant that they'd been working with a non-standard set of diameters and lengths. Throw in the fact that they'd had to accept bends in less than optimal locations, and it was amazing that they'd managed to run the pipes at all. Even more astonishingly, the tangled mass of pipes had still ended up with a high degree of order to their placement and grouping.

When I'd first stepped into the pipe room two days before all I'd seen was a jumbled mess with no apparent order, but now when I looked at the pipes I saw the work of a frighteningly capable mind. The pipes all came together into clusters that had thermometers mounted more or less at eye-level on smaller, bypass pipes, and for the most part they'd all been installed so that it was possible to see every pipe by walking no more than three-fourths of the way around the cluster—a good thing since not all of the pipes made it up above head-level for someone Jerome's size before bending and running horizontally toward the closest wall.

For one of the first times in my life I was glad that I was a tad under average height. Even knowing that all of the pipes in my area were tall enough that I couldn't walk into them by accident didn't stop me from worrying that I was going to slam into one at some point and collect a burn scar similar to the one prominently displayed across Billy's forehead.

It turned out to be a good thing that the foundry waited until an hour after our shift started to begin working with the higher temperatures—it meant that I'd had a chance to get into a routine. I started on the end closest to the door out into the control room and checked on all of the pipes in my first cluster, opening up valves where the thermometers were showing temperatures that were getting up into the two-hundred-degree range, and slowing the flow through any pipes where the temperature was dropping below one-fifty.

Then it was on to the second cluster, where I checked on the first pipe with a failed thermometer by the simple expedient of looking at the portable thermometer that I'd placed into a temporary bracket mounted to the pipe. It took only a second or two to make whatever adjustment was required on the first problem pipe, and then I moved the portable thermometer over to the second problem pipe so that it would have a chance to adjust to the temperature on the surface there while I checked the rest of the cluster.

By the time everything but the second problem pipe had been checked, the portable thermometer was showing a fairly accurate read of the second pipe, which meant that I could adjust the corresponding valve and then move the thermometer back to the first problem pipe on my way back out to check on Del.

"You don't need to be out here every fifteen minutes looking over my shoulder."

I shrugged. "I don't *need* to look over your shoulder, but I do need to make sure that I'm staying hydrated. I also need to check on the temperature of the water inside the generation chamber, and as long as I'm out here I might as well take a quick look at the ticker tape. There's no telling when Beth might want me out here monitoring the telegraph—I still need practice reading the codes."

"Don't kid yourself. Beth isn't going to put you out here. There's a reason that she chose me for this job. Neither of us can read and you're obviously not capable of memorizing seventy different codes."

The more time I spent around Del the more she reminded me of Megan. Under other circumstances I would have showed her up, but I just gritted my teeth and gave her an obviously insincere smile. I'd spent so many years doing whatever I'd been told and never asking questions that responding to those kinds of slights with the aggressiveness they deserved was far from second nature. When you threw in the fact that telling anyone I could read was almost certainly going to blow my cover, I really didn't have any choice at all.

As I turned to go, the telegraph started punching holes in the ticker tape. This message was coming from the headquarters building. I counted the longs and shorts. Three longs, six shorts and then three more shorts, all split up into nice even groups.

My memory was good enough that I was almost certain that it was an order to increase power generation, but I looked up to the steel plates mounted above the telegraphs and confirmed my recollection against the notes stamped onto the list of signals.

"Get back in there and let Beth and the rest know that Brennan needs more power."

I forced a smile onto my face despite Del's tone, and then slipped back inside the pipe room. A quick visual inspection of the closest of my pipes confirmed that they were still down in the same temperature range as when I'd checked them last.

I hurried past my section—taking care to avoid any of the pipes that bent horizontally soon after exiting the floor—and found Beth.

"We just got a telegraph from upstairs. Brennan needs more power for something and wants us to push up the temperatures inside the generator."

That earned me a frown. "Then he should have sent Tyrell down to keep an eye on things—that or come down himself."

"Yeah, except then he couldn't have kept working on whatever project it is that has him pushing for more power."

"I know, that's my point exactly. He's rushing along too quickly."

"Are you countermanding the order?"

She shook her head. "No, there are risks, but while you've been keeping an eye on Del, I've been keeping an eye on you. You're doing a good job keeping things under control. You're making small adjustments and giving it time to settle into a new range before making another one. Billy would have said something by now if Jerome was having problems, so there's nothing to do but continue on."

Beth dropped down to check one more thermometer and then pulled herself back upright with a groan. "You can go back to your station, I'll tell the other two."

"It's okay. I've got the smallest batch of pipes, so I'll go tell them. You should save your knees, we've still got almost an entire shift ahead of us."

"Thanks, Skye, that's kind of you. Just remember to emphasize to Jerome that we want to make very small reductions to the water flow. It doesn't take much of a drop across all of these pipes to start pushing the inflow temperature up and really get the generator spinning."

I nodded and set off looking for Billy, who had the area furthest away from the control room. He listened to the orders I was relaying and then waved me on wordlessly as he reached for his first valve and turned it a fraction of an inch to the right.

Jerome started scowling as soon as he saw me approaching. "What do you want?"

"Wow, somebody woke up on the wrong side of the bed."

His forehead wrinkled as he tried to decide whether or not to take offense. "Hurry up and tell me what it is you came to say. Del doesn't like it when I talk to other girls, and I don't want to be in the doghouse again."

"Isn't it kind of hard to go all day without talking to Beth seeing as how she's our boss?"

"Beth doesn't count—she's old."

At least half a dozen responses were jostling each other on the tip of my tongue, but I just shook my head at him rather than pointing out how stupid that statement was.

"We've got orders to get the generator up to speed, so we'll have to reduce the water flow, but Beth said to tell you that it doesn't take much to have a big impact on the temperatures hitting the generator, so make smaller adjustments than you think you need—if Brennan has to wait to get his extra electricity then he has to wait. It's not worth risking our lives to ramp the turbine up instantly."

"I'm not scared. This is just a little hot water—I've been in much more dangerous situations."

I wanted to tell him he was being an idiot, that scalding water would kill him as quickly as a knife in the dark, but I was pretty sure that would just make him bristle and then do something stupid to prove himself.

"I'm just passing along orders. If you have an issue with that, take it up with Beth. I need to get back to my pipes and make my next round of adjustments."

He mumbled something under his breath as I walked away, but my nanites didn't magically grant me better hearing, and I couldn't make it out over the low hum of the pipes vibrating as water circulated inside of them. It was probably for the best—I didn't particularly care what he thought of me as long as he did his job and stayed out of the way.

Back at my pipes, I checked each of the thermometers in turn and closed each valve slightly to make sure that my pipes were taking their share of the burden when it came to pushing up the temperature inside the generation chamber. The temperature had already started to go up slightly in several of the pipes even before I'd made any changes, but Beth had warned all of us about that back before we'd even been allowed to step into the pipe room.

Everything was one big interconnected system. When everyone else had reduced the speed of the water flow through their pipes, the waste heat hadn't just started building up in their pipes, some of it had started bleeding over into my pipes too.

I took manual readings off of the two pipes with broken thermometers, and then headed back out to grab another drink of water.

"Don't bother coming over here and trying to look over my shoulder again. I've got things under control."

Del hadn't even waited for me to fully exit the pipe room before mouthing off, but I reminded myself that my mission relied on not drawing attention to myself, and headed over to the water line rather than walking over and slamming my elbow into her face like I half wanted to. I swallowed a few sips of water and then headed back towards the door, detouring slightly so that I could at least get a feel for the temperature inside of the generation chamber.

It had spiked a lot further than I'd been expecting it to, but it was still inside the tolerances that Brennan and Tyrell had set out when they'd designed the system. If things continued to get hotter we would be in trouble in short order, but as long as everyone was watching their section we'd be okay—even just increasing the flow of water through a few of the pipes would be enough to bring the pressure down and stabilize the operating temperature.

I went back inside the pipe room, and nearly tripped over a spot where the metal plating wasn't as flush as it would have been back home. The Society built with perfect seams and everything was fastened down. Brennan had finished off the pipe room with a false floor that consisted of nothing more than plates of metal laid on a framework of steel girders. As long as all of the plates were in position it functioned like a giant interlocking set of puzzle pieces, but I was pretty sure that once you started lifting up sections of flooring you had to worry about other sections shifting—it made me glad that we weren't responsible for maintenance.

My thermometers were showing readings that were approaching the danger zone. The tiny, primitive part of my brain that was a holdover from the time before humans had figured out how to use tools was jumping up and down demanding that I open the valves back up, but I ignored that urge and opened up the valves in sequence, moving the wheels less than a third of the way back to where they'd been.

It was exactly what Beth had told us to do, but when I went back to my first cluster of pipes the temperatures looked like they were still climbing. That wasn't necessarily proof that anything was wrong—Beth had told us several times that there was a gigantic lag built into the system. It took time for the water to complete its circuit back to us so that it could be measured, and then even more time for the instruments to register any changes in temperature, but I couldn't get past the feeling that something wasn't right.

I ran over to the control room.

Del glared at me. "I told you not to—"

My eyes found the thermometer reading the temperature inside of the turbine and I cut her off with a look.

"You're not doing your job! That's all of the way up to the top of the acceptable operating range. You should have been inside the pipe chamber yelling for us to open things back up."

"There's a lag built into the system. You guys just opened things up, it's going to take time for it all to cool down."

I pushed past her and grabbed the ticker tape. The one from the command center was blank, but the one from the foundry was repeating the same code over and over again. Three shorts, six longs, three more shorts.

I rounded on Del and she stepped back as though realizing that it wasn't safe for her to be within arm's reach of me right then.

"Don't freak out—it's just the foundry acknowledging the fact that Brennan asked for more power."

"You've got the longs and shorts reversed. Even without that you should have known that something was up—there's no reason for the foundry to acknowledge an order from headquarters to us, let alone do so a dozen times. That code is signaling that they've had a failure down there—a feedback loop in one or more of the burners!"

I was already moving back towards the pipe room, but I paused for just long enough to yell back over my shoulder. "Get a pair of gloves and then get inside the pipe room and open up every valve you can see!"

Even if I hadn't just seen the ticker tape I still would have known that something was wrong. The pipes were all groaning and the temperature inside the pipe room had climbed at least twenty degrees in the last few minutes. It was like walking into a blast furnace—we didn't have much time. It might already be too late.

I wanted to stop and open up all of the valves in my area, but that would have to wait until Beth and the others had been warned—hopefully Del would manage to open up at least some of my pipes.

By the time I made it to Beth, she was already opening up her pipes an inch at a time. Her instincts were good, but she was operating without all of the information she needed.

"Open them up all the way—they've got a feedback loop on the burners in the foundry!"

"How did she miss—no, there isn't time. Tell Jerome. I'll tell Billy!"

I'd already started running towards Billy's section. Now I veered to the right, recklessly leaping over pipes that I normally would have detoured around. My foot caught on another lip where two of the plates in the floor weren't quite the same thickness, and I started falling, headed right for a pipe that was so hot that it was shaking like it was going to come apart.

I wasn't going to get second-degree burns, not from something that hot, I was headed towards third-degree burns. I was off balance and moving far too quickly for such a dangerous environment, but I managed to get my right hand up and slam it into the pipe, knocking myself away. It wasn't enough to stop me from falling, but I managed to hit a clear piece of ground and stopped my roll by slamming a boot into another pipe before I could burn the entire left side of my body.

Even the floor was hot enough to burn the bare skin of my back and shoulders, but I didn't stop to assess damages—if we didn't get the temperatures under control we were going to all end up dead.

I pulled myself back up to my feet and stumbled around another big cluster of pipes to find Jerome struggling with a frozen valve. The temperature gauges on his pipes were all reading temperatures beyond anything the pipes were supposed to withstand.

"Leave that one—we've got to get as many open as fast as we can—hopefully the other pipes can suck some of the heat out of that one if we work fast enough."

I grabbed the nearest valve and heaved against it, increasing the flow of water by a good quarter turn, and then threw myself towards the next pipe. My gloves weren't keeping the heat away from my palms now—it hurt to grab hold of the metal—but I forced the next valve open and moved on to another.

The thought of what was going on back in my section was making me desperate, but Jerome's gauges were even hotter than mine had been. All I could do was hope that getting his pipes cooled down would draw some of the heat out of my pipes before everything exploded.

Valve after valve turned until it hit the stops, and then it was down to the last couple, which I left for Jerome to take care of as I raced back to my section. I arrived to see temperatures every bit as high as what Jerome and I had been dealing with just seconds before.

Del was there, struggling to get valves open, but she lacked both Jerome's size and my nanite-infused muscles. Her gloves were smoking, but she was gamely hanging onto the superheated metal in an effort to get the flow of water moving more quickly.

I joined her at the valve she was working on, throwing everything I had into it, but it refused to budge. I grabbed her by the shoulders. "The heat made the valve expand—we're not going to get it to move without more help. Open up the rest of the valves—hopefully that will be enough to cool it down too."

I got two more valves opened up before a terrible, unearthly groan brought me around. The pipe we'd been working on was starting to deform under the pressure of all that hot water. I traced the path the water was going to take when the bulge finally gave way, and realized that Del was standing directly in the space the stream was going to hit.

She'd never done anything nice to me, never even acknowledged me as being worth talking to other than to tell me off. Even more than that, everything that was happening was her fault, but I still couldn't just let her die. I raced over to her, heedless of the fact that I could feel my bare skin getting tight from how close I was getting to the other pipes, just as the bulge started to give way.

It was too late to get her out of the way—too late to save either of us. Instead I bent down and grabbed the edge of one of the metal plates from the floor, lifting it up as I yelled her name.

The stream of superheated water hissed as it left the pipe headed towards us like a living organism. The sheet of metal shook from the impact of all that pressurized water, but I managed to keep it from coming back over on top of us. My efforts had been enough to stop the water—and bits of shrapnel—from hitting us directly, but not enough to stop all of the ricochets that were hitting nearby pipes.

I'd grabbed Del with one hand once I had the floor plate levered up to provide some protection, but she was further back, which meant that she was further outside the pocket of protection I'd created. She screamed in agony and collapsed against me as a shard of metal took her in the right side of her chest, but already things were cooling down.

The cool water being flushed through the rest of the pipes had come too late to stop my section from overheating, but it had been enough to make sure that only the first couple of moments of the breach had been potentially lethal.

A split second later Jerome picked Del up off of the ground and carried her towards the control room. I dropped the metal plate back into place in the floor and followed him—I could already see that the temperatures in my section were starting to drop.

Beth and Billy met us at the door. "We need to get the bleeding stopped. Jerome, you get her on the table. Skye, grab the first-aid kit."

I grabbed the first-aid kit and turned back around just in time to see Billy disappear back into the pipe room. Beth saw my questioning glance. "He'll make sure that all of the valves in your section are all of the way open—we can't afford to just leave them be and hope that the rest of the system can soak up the extra heat."

Beth snatched the medical supplies out of my hands and set to work taping up Del's wound with a surprising amount of skill. It wasn't going to be enough to keep Del alive—not unless we got her somewhere they could stitch her up soon—but it was more than I'd been expecting out of a grubber. More importantly, she'd bought us time to transport Del through several hundred yards of tunnels in the hopes of finding real medical assistance once we got to the surface.

"You two grab the stretcher and bring it over here."

Jerome and I were moving to comply when a group of men barged into the control room. "What's going on?"

The guy asking the questions looked too young to be in charge of anything, but based on the way that Beth all but saluted, he was important. Maybe he was one of Brennan's favorites. Jerome and I carefully shifted Del onto the stretcher while Beth responded.

"We had a pipe burst on us, sir. We got the order to ramp up power production and started slowing down the flow of water, only to have the foundry report a malfunction in one of the voltage drivers for the heating process on the steel they were melting down."

The guy in charge waved to two of the men who'd arrived with him—big, well-armed men—to pick up the stretcher. "Get her up to the hospital and make sure that she gets treated."

He pointed the other two guards toward the pipe room. "You two get some gloves on and make sure that everything is under control in there. The last thing we can afford right now is to have one of the pipes in the walls burst—that would set us back months."

It was odd. By that point I'd had time to get a better look at the younger guy—the supervisor—and he was every bit as young as I'd originally thought. He might be eighteen, but given how quickly living inside the city aged someone, that was a long shot. More astonishingly, he was surprisingly attractive with short, dark hair and a build that wasn't starved like most of the grubbers I'd met so far. Unlike the shapeless bulk so common to enforcers like Bash and Jerome, this guy looked like he had well-defined muscles underneath the clothes he was wearing—clothes that were light years better quality than what I'd been given upon arriving in the compound.

His eyes were remarkably clear for someone in a position of authority. Piter and his men had all looked like they spent half of their time drugged out of their mind. This guy looked like he'd never touched anything at all mind-altering. His eyes weren't dull, bloodshot holes in his face; they were hard, brown orbs that right then looked like they could stare holes in sheet metal.

He didn't look like a spoiled dandy, and all four of the bigger, older men with him hopped into motion like their lives depended on obeying instantly. It was an interesting response. I'd seen very few people move with that kind of speed since I'd moved into the city. Whoever this guy was, he'd either earned his team's respect or he had carte blanche from Brennan and wasn't afraid of dishing out punishments at the drop of a hat.

Jerome and I stepped back as the guards picked up the stretcher and hurried towards the tunnels. Jerome made as though to follow them, but before he could take more than a couple of steps the supervisor resumed talking.

"Damn it, Beth, how did this even happen? Were you guys asleep down here?"

For the first time since I'd arrived down at the geothermal installation I saw Beth actually get mad.

"This is your fault! You can't leave Billy and me here with no other help than a trio of untrained workers who are so new they don't even know how to operate a shower. Not and still expect us to make everything function the same way it did when you and Tyrell were down here with half a dozen men. I told Simms that it was a mistake to pour steel with a crew this green, but he insisted."

"Beth—"

"Don't you 'Beth' me. I did everything by the book. The damn girl didn't fall asleep at the switch, but she was too stupid to tell the difference between a command for more power and a warning from the foundry that they had a runaway voltage regulator. This is squarely on your shoulders, Brennan. You were a damn fool to think that you could get away with pouring steel at the same time that you demanded more power out of us."

The revelation that the 'supervisor' was actually *Brennan*, the guy with the power of life and death over everyone living inside the compound, rocked me back on my heels. Maybe that was why I didn't anticipate what happened next.

Jerome had nearly made it to the tunnel by the time Beth finished up with her rant. Unfortunately he was still well within hearing range, and he moved with a suddenness that proved he'd worked as an enforcer at some point in the past.

He turned and shot towards Brennan like a bullet out of a gun, and one look at his eyes told me that he wasn't going to be satisfied with anything less than death.

"This is your fault! You're the one who stuck us down here hoping we would die."

I reacted without thinking, but my reaction time wasn't what it should have been. Jerome brushed past Beth with enough force to send her windmilling toward a wall, and then grabbed Brennan's throat with both hands.

This was the reason that the warlords—large or small—all had enforcers and bodyguards. Unfortunately, all of Brennan's guards were out of position, too far away to protect their charge.

I stepped into Jerome and slammed a punch into the side of his neck in the hopes that it would shock him into letting go. He did—at least with one hand—but only so that he could try to backhand me into last week.

I ducked, but he was a lot faster than I'd been expecting. I turned the blow into a glancing one rather than the monstrous attack that would have snapped my neck, but it still hit with enough force to almost make my knees buckle.

Brennan was grabbing at his throat, clawing at Jerome's left hand, but he didn't have any leverage—even assuming that he knew the first thing about fighting with his hands. Beth was probably smart enough to grab some kind of club before she joined in the fight, but she'd hit the wall with enough force that I'd heard something snap.

The guards inside of the pipe room couldn't have possibly heard what was going on, and the ones from the tunnel were still several seconds away even if they'd realized that their leader was under attack. It was all up to me.

Jerome's arm was headed back my way, but now I had enough adrenaline coursing through my system for my nanites to be enhancing my reaction time. I stepped forward and slammed a punch into his left arm, targeting a nerve cluster that I hoped would render it useless, and then spun and checked the blow from his right arm with my elbow.

I couldn't stop him—not a blow with that much windup, not when he was so much bigger and heavier than me—but somehow I managed to keep my feet under me, and then it was my turn to really go on the offensive. I bent my knees, lowering my center of gravity a split second before exploding upwards with an uppercut that started from down at my calf and involved every muscle in my body from my legs up through my shoulders and arms.

My fist hit his crotch with enough force to pick him up off of the ground. Even my nanite-reinforced bones weren't up to transmitting that much force into something as hard as his pelvis. I felt my hand break in three or four places, but I did even more damage than I took, and I had the pleasure of seeing him hit the ground and not get back up.

It was only then that I realized what I'd done. I'd just saved Brennan, the single most dangerous man in the entire city, the very person I'd been sent in to stop.

Chapter 9

My instructors back at the capital would have reacted without thinking. Elbow strike to the neck to finish off Brennan, break Beth's neck, and then grab one of the big wrenches off of the workbench and use it to kill Jerome.

It wasn't guaranteed—no plan ever was—but it had a near perfect chance of killing Brennan at the same time that I eliminated all of the witnesses. Unlike my instructors, I hesitated. I looked Brennan in the eyes and the hard, flinty orbs had been replaced by something else, something more vulnerable.

He'd been shocked by what happened, but he wasn't responding with the bluster of a tin god. He looked like a real person, one who'd had their mask stripped away, and what I saw didn't justify murder. My orders had been to find the location of the new power source and report back in. It was still possible that I would have to assassinate Brennan before everything was said and done, but those weren't my orders—at least not yet. The fact that another operative might have taken him out right then didn't mean that I had to do the same.

I hesitated, gave myself a chance to connect with him on a human level, and suddenly my chance was gone. His guards came running back down the tunnel, guns drawn, and it was too late to do anything other than just help him to his feet—hoping the entire time that he hadn't seen death in my eyes when he'd looked at me.

One of the guards made as if to club me away with the butt of his rifle, but Brennan stopped him. "I'm fine—she's the last person you need to worry about protecting me from. Without her you would have arrived to find that guy over there standing on my corpse."

The bigger guard slammed his rifle into Jerome—knocking him unconscious—while the closer guard lowered his weapon without taking his eyes off of me.

"Are you sure that you're okay, sir? We should probably get you up to the hospital. You've got a nasty set of bruises around your neck already and we need to get you checked out."

Brennan shook his head. "You and I know that there's very little the hospital could do if I've got a broken hyoid. I'm still talking and breathing, which means that there's no point in trekking all the way up to the surface. Especially not given that I'll just be coming back down here to check out the damages. Get that lady up to the hospital while there is still time—that's an order."

The guards shot each other dissatisfied looks and Brennan sighed. "Leave me your sidearm. If the big bruiser over there wakes up before help gets here, I'll shoot him."

It was obvious to me that I was the unknown quantity who had the two of them so worried. Beth was an old woman, and she'd been around Brennan any number of times before now without attacking him. I, on the other hand, had just taken down a guy more than twice my size. I didn't blame them for being worried.

I took a couple of slow steps backwards and then turned towards the pipe room. "I'll go tell the guards in with Billy that you need them back out here. Given that the pipes are all wide open by now, there's no reason for both of them to be in the pipe room. Billy and I can handle monitoring stuff in there until you can send down more help."

I heard grumbling from behind me, but by the time I picked up my gloves from the floor where I'd dropped them while grabbing the first-aid kit, there was a presence at my back. I tucked the gloves under my right arm and reached for the door with my left, but Brennan was already pulling it open. He had a sleek black pistol stuffed down his waistband, and a pair of heavy gloves in his free hand.

"Let me get that for you. I saw that punch and you shouldn't be using your hand until after we get it looked at. It's probably broken."

I shook my head—the last thing I could afford was to have a doctor poking and prodding me. "It's just sprained. I'll avoid using it for the next day or two and it will be fine."

"You've broken enough bones to know the difference? That's a hard life."

"Yeah, that's the way of things here in the city. We all have tough lives—everyone gets broken in some way."

I was shocked at how easily the words came out. I hadn't been expecting to fall into my role so easily. I'd lied a dozen times just in the short time I'd been inside the city, but this was different somehow—it felt more significant.

"Where did you learn how to fight like that?"

I shrugged. "If you see enough people get beaten down by enforcers you eventually learn a few things."

I stepped through the door, hoping that he would let my evasions stand. All I needed was to make it through the next hour or so without saying anything to make him suspicious. As soon as he'd taken stock of the damage to the pipe room, he'd go back to his headquarters and I'd never see him again.

He was obviously smart and used to getting his way, so I expected him to keep pressing as we got inside the pipe room, but as soon as he stepped through the door he was suddenly all business.

One of the guards met us before we'd even made it out of my section of pipes, but Brennan just waved him off. I started checking the thermometers in my section of the room, hoping that Brennan would move on and leave me behind, but he simply picked the other cluster of pipes in my section and started double-checking that all of the valves were open.

"Get them all open, then we'll go through and inspect all of them to make sure that none of the rest of them are damaged."

I nodded, and went back to work, stopping from time to time to watch Brennan tap on a pipe with a wrench that he'd picked up somewhere along the way.

"It's not a perfect test, but it's possible if we've got a problem on some of these that I'll be able to hear a change in the pitch. Someday maybe we'll have x-ray machines that we can bring down to test welds and look for structural flaws. For now we do things the old-fashioned way—eyeballing everything and then stress testing different parts of the system under the most controlled circumstances we can manage."

I nodded and then paused. "What about the people in the foundry? If it got this hot here, it must have been terribly hot down there. I was so caught up with trying to keep the pipes from rupturing that I didn't even think about the fact that people might be dying down in the foundry."

Brennan nodded. "That's actually how we ended up down here. When the control room down there couldn't get any kind of response out of the girl Beth had on the telegraph, they contacted us. Tyrell headed down there to try to hold things together while I came directly here."

"How bad do you think it got down there?"

He stepped over to the ancient, corroded pipe that had partially burst and tapped on it. "Given just how hot this had to have gotten to deform like that, I'm guessing it got hot enough down there to have killed anyone who didn't get out in time. Hopefully they all got clear. We probably lost some of the machinery down there. Who knows how much work it's going to take to get us back into production again."

"You don't sound that worried about the machinery."

Brennan shrugged. "I am, but there's no use fretting about it until I get a report from Tyrell. We've got commitments we've made to the other leaders in the city, and every hour we lose puts us one more hour behind a schedule that we weren't sure we could hit in the first place. The only thing I can do right now is focus on getting the secondary power generation machinery back up and running again. I can't make more guns without a way to reclaim structural steel—which means I need the foundry—but until I get this location working again, I can't afford to power up the foundry anyway."

"Why not? The power from the stage one generator is what provides the electrical current to power the foundry in the first place."

That earned me a smile, which affected me in ways I wasn't expecting. I got the feeling that Brennan wasn't someone who smiled very often.

"It's true, but if I took away the power and the hot water both from everyone upstairs at the same time, I'd probably have a mutiny on my hands."

"That doesn't sound very much like the person running the last area I was in."

Even as I said it I knew it was the wrong thing to be saying, but Brennan just cocked his head to the side. "You might be surprised what the leaders of the rest of the territories worry about—most of them are holding on by a much slimmer margin than their people realize. Not that it matters though. The difference between them and me is that I'm looking for more than just dumb animals. We aren't growing a few handfuls of wheat or chopping down trees.

"I need the people inside the compound for their minds. We can't do any of this without a lot of hands helping, and most of them need to have a decent brain attached to them. You can make a man—or woman—work, but you can't force them to use their mind. I need skilled people. It's looking like Tyrell and I are going to have to start out almost entirely with people who don't have any skills. If this is going to work, we'll have to train them up into what we need them to be."

"Do you realize how egotistical that sounds? You make it sound like we're all just playthings. You haven't even asked me what my name is."

We'd moved on to Beth's section of the room. My comment earned me a scowl from Brennan's guard, but Brennan just paused to meet my gaze.

"You're surprisingly articulate—probably better educated than most of my people, even the ones like Beth who've been here with me almost from the start. You're also capable of taking orders, but you're not afraid to speak your mind. Just that would make you quite the find, but you're also a good enough fighter to take down someone more than twice your size, someone who obviously had experience as an enforcer at some point."

He looked away from me for several seconds before looking back, and once again his eyes were less guarded than they'd been when he first arrived. It made no sense whatsoever, but he seemed to care what I thought.

"You're not a pawn to me—none of the people inside of my compound are. I've been learning about you since the second I arrived down here. I guess I was so caught up peeling back all of the more important layers that I forgot to ask you for your name."

"So a name isn't important?"

The words could have come out mocking or insubordinate, but they didn't feel that way, and Brennan didn't seem to think that I'd crossed any lines.

"I've spent months now trying to turn people who've never had a day of formal education into a working middle class who are capable of creating everything from food and clothes to gunpowder and firearms. That's the kind of investment in human capital that nobody inside this city has ever made before now.

"To be honest, I'm not sure anyone on this entire continent, other than the ants, even bothers to invest in people anymore, but that's beside the point. If there's one thing I've learned since I started this project, it's that people can tell me anything they want about themselves. A name tells me absolutely nothing about someone. Changing your name is easy. Changing who you are—what you know and how you go about things—is hard. Not many people ever really manage it."

"Skye. My name is Skye—just in case you decide it matters at some point down the road."

I had exactly three days of experience as a spy, but even I knew I was playing a risky game. I needed to avoid notice so that I could figure out how to find and destroy Brennan's prototype energy generator. The last thing I should be doing was having extended, probing conversations with the man I'd been sent to stop.

Despite all of that, I couldn't make myself look away from those deep, brown eyes. There was plenty to Brennan, things that were obvious at first blush to anyone, but I was starting to realize just how much more there might be underneath the surface.

He held my gaze for several seconds before smiling again. "Well then, Skye, I'd like to offer you a job. We're going to need to get things cleaned up here, but once that is done I think that you'd make an excellent bodyguard. Tyrell has been pressuring me to add to my guards. Would you like to follow me around and make sure that nobody twists my head off in a fit of rage?"

Chapter 10

I didn't know what to say.

I knew what I was supposed to do. Being Brennan's bodyguard was the perfect opportunity to get access to wherever he was keeping his prototype generator. It was the kind of master-stroke that only happened once in a hundred missions. It even redeemed my earlier hesitation when I'd had a chance to kill Brennan but failed to take it.

It was the perfect in, the perfect way to advance my mission, but it took conscious effort to get a response out. Brennan was the enemy. He was the man who was developing a weapon capable of breaching the energy barrier pro-tecting the Society from external threats. He was a grubber who was getting dozens of people killed every week in a crazy drive to rebuild this city into something more than a primitive, hunter-gatherer society.

His efforts would have been admirable if he'd been guided by the precepts, but he wasn't and they weren't. He represented everything that I'd been taught to despise, but something inside of me was yelling that I would be making a mistake if I said yes.

The odds were that I was going to be able to finish my mission regardless of which choice I made. The only question was how quickly I was going to be able to do it. The difference was that if I said yes to the job he was offering me, then I was going to have to betray his trust at some point down the road.

Actually, that wasn't true. I was going to betray his trust sooner or later no matter what, but if I did it after getting to know him, it would be all the harder to go through with my mission.

Hearing about it all back in the administration building had been easy. I hadn't known any of the people I would be betraying, so it'd been a purely intellectual exercise. That wasn't the case any longer. The people I'd met so far since arriving in the city had been a definite mixed bag, everything from Piter and Bash to Beth, Billy and the trio from the fire brigade, but they were real people. They had hopes and dreams. They had worries and people they loved, people who loved them in return.

I forced out a yes, and made myself smile, but I wanted to scream. I was going to go through with the mission because that was what I'd been trained for—the reason that I'd been entrusted with my franchise and a set of nanites that were the next best thing to priceless. I agreed because it was what the Citizen-President would have wanted me to do, but the truth was that there was something about Brennan that made me want to believe in him.

The next couple of hours flew by in a blur. The various gang leaders and warlords wielded an incredible amount of power, but up until I saw Brennan, I hadn't really appreciated that power. Having the power to have someone killed was what the leaders like Piter used to keep their territories under control, but as terrifying as that could be for those caught in his territory, it was nothing compared to what I observed as Brennan got started with the repairs to the pipe room.

I'd half expected him to do everything himself—after all, he was supposed to be the boy genius who'd built this territory up to something worth noticing—but instead he called in the experts. A steady stream of people came through the control room shortly after Brennan sat down at the telegraph and began sending messages back up to the headquarters.

A pair of welders showed up asking to be shown the damaged pipe. I expected Brennan to show them to it—instead he had me do it. The same with the crew that arrived shortly after that with dozens of heavy steel bands for shoring up any pipes that looked like they had gotten hot enough to start deforming.

I had no idea if something like that would even work—the band that had given way and gone streaking across the room to embed itself in Del's chest hadn't been equal to the stresses our near catastrophe had placed on it, but then again, it had stopped the weld from giving way completely. If the pipe had completely burst open we all would have been burned alive.

Before he'd sat down at the telegraph, Brennan had led the rest of us through a complete survey of the pipes, so I had a pretty good idea where the problem spots were. I half expected to resent being told to go supervise the various teams being sent down to assist in the rebuild, but the exact opposite ended up happening. Pointing out the bulges we'd detected made me feel useful in ways I'd never experienced before.

It wasn't pleasant work. We'd gotten the valves all opened up to the point where the room had finally cooled back down, but I was suffering from steam burns and still nursing a broken hand. Under normal circumstances I would have been all too eager to head back home, turn on the vid display in my room and let the automated repair crews begin the cleanup, but that wasn't a possibility this time.

Here in the city there weren't any semi-autonomous robots to call in. There was no teenage supervisor—working the lowest of the low jobs in order to earn their franchise—with a hand-held processor to guide the robotic work crew. None of that existed here because Brennan's ancestors had bombed each other back almost to the Stone Age and we'd refused to let them advance technologically due to their history of weaponizing any and all advancements.

If something was going to get done here in the city, then it was going to be done with muscle power, and bulky, inefficient equipment that took twice as long to accomplish half as much as the automated systems back home.

Despite all of that, there was a satisfaction to working with my hands—or hand—that was undeniable. We surveyed the pipes with primitive bubble levels, and then we wrapped thick metal bands around every spot where the heat had permanently swelled the pipes. Once I'd pointed out all of the areas that Brennan and I had identified as being problems, I'd hit the limit of my knowledge, but rather than being shuffled back out of the way, someone handed me a wrench and I spent an hour tightening up the bolts that bound the bands around the pipes. I couldn't snug them down all of the way—not with one hand at least—but I made it so that the big guy who was responsible for bearing down on the wrench didn't have to waste as much time on the easy part.

Brennan came in partway through the process and reported that the foundry was a complete mess, and more than a dozen workers had received burns of some kind or another, but nobody had died. I half expected to end up down in the pipe room until well past when my shift was supposed to end, but Brennan gathered up his guards and waved for me to follow him as the people from the other shift arrived.

I waved goodbye to Beth and Billy, and then followed Brennan and the others up the tunnels. For a second I thought maybe he'd changed his mind about making me a guard—we seemed to be headed back to the worker dorms—but rather than going in through the main door like I'd been expecting, Brennan took a left and entered through another door, one that led underground.

There were no elevators, and we only went down four flights of stairs, but the similarities between Brennan's headquarters and the administration back home weren't lost on me. All other things being equal, most people would have picked the top floor of the new building for their command center just so that they could enjoy the view.

The basement wasn't any safer than the roof when it came to danger from the other warlords and gang leaders in the city—Brennan wasn't worried about them, he was worried about attack from the Society. It was one more sign that he was up to something that he shouldn't be.

The guards all started peeling off into different rooms as we started down the hall—all except for the big guy who'd shadowed Brennan the whole time we'd been inside of the pipe room.

"Jax, you've been on your feet for more than twelve hours and I know that you've got paperwork waiting for you back in your room. I'm fine here—if Skye wanted to hurt me she wouldn't have saved me from the bruiser earlier."

"Sir, with all due respect—"

"That's an order, Jax. In light of today's events, tomorrow's meeting is even more critical than we expected it to be. I need you at full strength while we're out there."

The guard—Jax—didn't look happy about the order, but he nodded and turned left when we turned right. Half a dozen steps later we stopped in front of a door and Brennan pulled a key out of his pocket and unlocked it. I wasn't sure what to expect as I followed him inside, but based on the tidy bunks from the worker dorms I knew it was at least going to be a step up from what the rest of the city's inhabitants were making do with.

It was nothing like what the franchised citizens back home had enjoyed, but it was surprisingly big. There was a hammock hanging from two oversized hooks in the ceiling, a variety of metal bookcases along the wall, and a shiny steel dresser not too far from the hammock.

"The bathroom is just through that door. Given that we've got all of the water pipes circulating at maximum speed, there's plenty of hot water to go around, but even when that's not the case, this floor still gets first dibs on the pipes."

I nodded slowly, still taking in my surroundings. There were weapons on the shelves, a variety of knives, a rifle and a handgun. It looked like there were boxes of ammunition there next to the firearms too.

Brennan followed my gaze and shrugged. "Sorry about that. Jax's orders—although he's probably regretting it right now. Everyone on this level is to keep an extra set of weapons in their rooms at all times. He's worried that two or more of the territories on our borders will end up combining against us and we'll have to fight our way out from down here. Being in charge isn't as much fun as you might think. We've also got rules about eating in our rooms. We've got a separate cafeteria down here so that we can keep a closer eye on the food from a safety standpoint, but you'll still be eating in a big room with everyone else."

"I understand. You're worried about rats and cockroaches—it makes sense."

My eyes continued to dart around the room, but I wasn't finding any kind of proof one way or the other as far as whether this was Brennan's room. It didn't look posh enough to belong to the owner of an entire sector of the city, but on the other hand it was much too big to be assigned to a junior guard. Not only that, there was also the fact that Brennan had been carrying the key to it around in his pocket. It strained belief to think that he did that for all of the empty rooms on this level.

Up until then, I'd been operating under the assumption that he'd actually meant it when he'd said that he wanted me to be one of his guards. If that wasn't the case, if he'd brought me here for something else, I was going to break both his arms, torture him until he told me where his prototype generator was being stored, and then kill him without feeling the slightest bit sorry about it.

Brennan looked around the room one last time and then pointed to the bookcase containing all of the guns. "Your key is over there on the third shelf. I know you've had a rough day, but I need you to come with me tomorrow. I'm meeting with Piter and he never lets me bring as many guards as I'd like. Given the fact that I'm not going to be able to make the deadline on my next shipment of rifles, things are likely to get testy."

"I don't understand. If you're going to be limited as to how many guards you can bring, wouldn't you want to bring someone with more training than me?"

For the first time I could remember, Brennan looked embarrassed. "Actually, that was the other thing I needed to talk to you about. I'd like to slip you into the group in such a way that he doesn't think you're a real guard."

I could feel my blood pressure skyrocket, but he held up his hands before I could say anything. "It's not like that. You'll dress in the same uniform as the rest of the guards, I just want you to talk to Jax about things you could do to make yourself look like you're not really what I'm trying to present you as."

"So this job, this promotion, is contingent on draping myself over you like some kind of—"

"Not at all. Look, I was serious about needing more guards, and the quickest way to get knifed is to get involved with the people who are supposed to be watching your back. Sneaking a guard into a meeting like this dressed up as a prostitute has been done to death, but I don't think that Piter will suspect anything if we come at it from the other direction. He'll see someone who's not competent pretending to be competent and never realize that there's a whole additional layer to the disguise."

I was silent for long enough that Brennan started edging towards the door. "If you're not comfortable you don't have to do it. In fact, it's probably best if you sleep on it. I wouldn't want—"

I cut him off, worried he was going to retract the offer to be part of his guards.

"I'll do it, but you should be aware that I was in Piter's territory before I slipped into yours. I wasn't there very long—I don't think any of his people will recognize me, but you should know it's a possibility."

"How long exactly were you in there?"

This was where things had the potential to get sticky. "About six hours. Through sheer dumb luck I managed to slip across the border a bit before the attack happened. I figured that it was going to take me weeks to get through his northern border, but then the bombing happened and I saw a chance to slip through an opening in all of the confusion."

Brennan considered my answer for several seconds, and the whole time he was silent I was worried that he was thinking about the guard I'd knocked unconscious when I'd crossed over into his territory. There was no avoiding the timing being so close—not given that I had no idea how most people slipped across the border.

"Okay. Like you say, there's a risk, but it's not an insurmountable one. I'll have someone come by with some clothes and other things to make sure that you don't look like the girl who passed through Piter's territory earlier this week. You're going to want to get to sleep right away—the knock on your door is going to come awfully early tomorrow."

After Brennan was gone, I locked the deadbolt and took a quick shower. As I went to bed all I could think about was that it would have been a lot easier to make sure Piter didn't recognize me if I hadn't used both of my faces while crossing his territory—that and if I could trust Brennan with the fact that I was a nanite-infused spy from the other side of the barrier, one who was supposed to destroy everything he'd spent the last several years working towards.

Chapter 11

The knock on the door that Brennan had warned me about came even earlier than I'd been worried it might. It turned out that was because it was Jax knocking and the last thing he had on his mind was clothes.

"Brennan told me he wants to take you into the meeting with Piter tomorrow."

"Yeah, that's what he said."

Jax frowned. "I told him that nobody goes with us who isn't a known quantity. I told him that I haven't seen you fight, don't know if you know how to use a rifle, none of that."

"What did he say to that?"

"That I'd better get up early enough to evaluate you."

I yawned and shrugged. "I guess you took him at his word."

"Brennan doesn't joke around—not about security. Put on some shoes, grab one of those rifles, and let's get moving. There's a range on the level below this one. We're starting with weapons training because I don't want you putting a round in my back by accident."

I grabbed a rifle—the magazines were already loaded, so I didn't have to act like I wasn't sure which bullets went with which gun—and less than five minutes later we were inside the firing range and Jax was running me through the basics of gun handling and safety.

I nodded in all of the right places, asked a couple of basic questions so that it wouldn't be obvious that I'd heard almost the exact same speech weeks ago when I'd been tapped to start training for this mission, and then took my spot on the firing line.

"Don't try to anticipate the shot, Skye. Just put the sights on the place you want to hit and start squeezing the trigger. When it actually goes off you want it to be a surprise."

I did as he asked and put several rounds downrange, being careful to put them all on the paper, but not group them too close together. After the first couple of shots I pretended to develop a flinch—just a mild one—and then let Jax train me out of it. Twenty minutes later Jax was satisfied that I knew which end of the gun was the dangerous one.

He took the rifle from me and looked over at the training pads and weights that took up most of the rest of the level.

"You hurt your hand yesterday?"

In reality, my nanites had completely repaired the broken bones while I'd been sleeping, but I'd been careful to favor my right hand ever since I'd opened the door to my room.

"It's just a sprain—nothing that won't be fine in another few days, but I'm trying to keep from making it worse before then."

"I guess we'll have to skip the hand-to-hand for now then. The fact that you took down Jerome yesterday speaks well to your capabilities in that area—that will just have to be enough for now."

"Does that mean I'm in?"

"For this meeting, yes. Whether you stay in the guard or not will depend on how good you are once your hand is all healed up, and how much progress you make after that."

"You seem awful sure of that considering that Brennan has the final say..."

Jax casually chambered a round into the rifle and snugged the stock up against his shoulder without actually pointing it at me.

"There's one thing that you and I had better get clear from the start. Brennan is the boss, but he's not an idiot, and I didn't get this job because I hit harder than the other guys. If I decide that you're out, then you're out. It might take a day or two for Brennan to come around to my way of thinking, but eventually he will. I'm going to be watching you like a hawk. Make sure that you don't do anything to make me regret letting you onto my team—even temporarily."

The weapons training I'd received from the Society military had been rudimentary simply because nobody had expected me to end up using a firearm since they were so scarce on this side of the barrier. I'd received a bit more training when it came to knives and other improvised weaponry, but none of that had received anywhere near the concentration that my basic hand-to-hand skills had.

Jax had an advantage because he was the one with the rifle, but he was standing too close to me. Not only that, he still thought that my right hand was the next best thing to useless. I'd never seen Jax fight, but I was reasonably confident that I could close the distance between us and take him down before he could get a shot off.

The fact that I was superhumanly fast and currently had the drop on Jax didn't mean he wasn't dangerous though. Part of me wanted to take him out right now just so that I wouldn't have to worry about him catching me in a lie later on. Jax was going to be a constant threat during my time inside of the compound, but eliminating him now would leave too many things to chance.

I was fairly certain that the generator was in the level below the firing range—assuming that there was another floor below us—but I hadn't confirmed that yet, and even if I was right, who knew what kind of security measures would have to be bypassed in order to get to it. No, I was going to have to leave Jax in play and just hope that I would be able to outsmart him for however long it took me to get a bead on the generator.

"I read you loud and clear, sir. I won't give you any problems."

"Good. Brennan briefed me on your cover. Don't go overboard on the physical contact, but make sure that you're always the one closest to him. Grip your weapon like you're not entirely comfortable with it, but keep it pointed at the ground. A real guard would be responsible for part of the three hundred and sixty degrees of space around us, but if I see you lift your rifle without a valid threat, you're going to be sorry once we get back here to the compound."

"Yes, sir."

"Good, get back upstairs and put on your uniform—you've got about ten minutes before Lexis will be arriving."

Jax turned out to be wrong. Lexis showed up less than five minutes after I got back to my room. In a move completely at odds with my normal habit, I'd forgotten to lock my door, and she burst into my room like a tornado of clothes-toting energy.

I was in the middle of slipping into my shirt when she came in and started shaking her head at me.

"That's never going to work—it's a good thing that I brought other options."

Lexis was a middle-aged woman with red hair and more energy than any two people should have had so early in the morning. The 'other options' she'd referenced turned out to be a cart full of clothes that exceeded anything I'd ever had back home—in quantity if not quality.

It was odd. For years I'd been told that I was living an existence that only the Society could provide, that I just needed to work hard enough to get my franchise and then I'd have everything I'd ever wanted, but my life back home hadn't been especially remarkable compared to what I'd seen so far in Brennan's compound.

The non-franchised citizens indeed lived better than the average grubber, but only the franchised citizens with their crazy parties lived better than Brennan's top people. If he could create a pocket of civilization at the very heart of this desolate city, maybe there was hope that he could eventually come around to following the precepts.

That thought sent a little thrill through me. Our Society had preached for more than a century that the point of everything we were doing was to bring those outside of the barrier to an understanding of the precepts. If Brennan was actually on the cusp of that kind of enlightenment then maybe I wouldn't have to destroy his invention after all. Maybe I could bring him and his entire compound back and join it to the Society.

I sternly told myself to focus on the matter at hand as Lexis handed me a length of fabric. "What's this for?"

"Brennan said that you're supposed to look like a member of the guard, but like a member who didn't really belong. He said to dress you up as fetchingly as possible given the constraints of the uniform Jax designed. A couple of centuries ago, our ancestors had special underclothes to accent their chests.

"Brennan has helped us make incredible strides when it comes to producing fabric, but for now this is the best I can do for you. Don't be bashful, the door is closed and you don't have anything I haven't seen a hundred times or more fitting up some girl or another for one of the gang leaders."

I tried not to blush as I started unbuttoning my shirt again. She was right, a couple hundred years ago nearly everyone who wanted one had owned half a dozen bras. Now only the Society still had those kinds of luxuries.

Even as an unfranchised juvenile, I'd had several—all functional garments designed to provide support for a range of different activities—but this was the first time I'd ever put on something with the sole intent of drawing attention to my body.

Franchised citizens—the most flighty at least—went about nearly naked when that was the style, but all of the shops for those kinds of apparel had been down in the middle of the social desirability index. Many of my dorm mates had spent some of their earnings on one or two pieces of seductive clothing, but for the most part everyone had desperately been saving all of their resource allotments in order to earn their franchises as quickly as possible.

Lexis wrapped the length of cloth around my back, up over my chest and then crossed it and tied it off behind my neck where it would likely show above my shirt collar once I was fully dressed.

"That's going to incense Jax, but that's okay, it's perfectly in keeping with what Brennan said the two of you are after. Let's try on some shirts."

"You seem like you've been doing this for a long time."

Lexis nodded as she held a shirt up to me and then went back to her cart for a different one. "Since I was a child. My mother was a seamstress, and hers before her—all the way back to the Desolation. The stories my nana told me said that this was just a hobby for the woman that survived the Desolation, but after the ants rained fire and destruction down on us, she managed to attach herself to one of the first warlords. Back then there was still lots of clothing to be looted, but even looted clothing looks better after it's been tailored to fit."

I shouldn't have been surprised that the grubbers thought that we had been the ones to cause the Desolation, but I was. It only made sense that they would blame us rather than each other, but that didn't stop me from having to suppress a flash of anger.

"Were you here before Brennan took over?"

Lexis frowned at a succession of three more shirts before finding one that passed muster. "No. I was in the territory to the east of here. The warlord I worked for kept a very tight lid on information flowing across the border—still does, I expect—but I was always working on clothes for him or his men or whatever girls had caught their fancy. They got so that they didn't even notice that I was there in the room with them. I heard all of the stories they told each other, stories about a crazy warlord who appeared out of nowhere with weapons and the know-how to make more.

"I listened to the stories for more than a month and then I reached out to someone I knew who specialized in smuggling people across the border and offered him everything I owned to get me through to Brennan's territory."

Once I'd finished buttoning the shirt, Lexis pulled out a small metal container full of safety pins and started pinning the fabric across the back, taking out what little slack there was around my waist.

"It's not as good as I could have done with a day or two of advance notice, but this isn't the first time that Brennan showed up in my office with some crazy idea and a timeline that's half of what any normal person would expect. I was up half the night altering these shirts in the hope that one of them would fit you."

I suddenly felt guilty. "I'm sorry—I had no idea..."

"Don't you fret—Skye, was it? If it had been up to me I would have made Brennan let me measure you last night so that I could turn out something that I knew would fit you, but he was right to insist that you get your sleep. He said that you saved his life last night—for that I'd give up a whole week of sleep and never utter a word of complaint. You did a good thing yesterday."

The blush that came over me then was even deeper than the one sparked by being shirtless around another person.

"I just did what anyone would have."

Lexis shook her head. "Humility is a good thing—it keeps the worst of the gang leaders and warlords from feeling threatened, but you'll be wanting not to take it too far here. Brennan isn't the kind to resent the worth of another, and you'll want to make sure that he values you like he should. Even the smartest man needs help sometimes seeing what's right in front of his face. There are lots of us who would have tried to save him—I dare say Beth did her best—but most of us would have failed miserably. Now, let's get you into some better-fitting pants."

This time Lexis turned her back to me while I pulled off my pants. It was a good thing too. The crude underwear I'd been provided back home had seemed like it wouldn't stand out in the city, but if anyone was going to know that it didn't fit with my backstory, it would be Lexis.

I pulled on the pants she passed back to me, and they were pronounced satisfactory, after which she started pulling black tactical vests out of her cart. I paused midway into one of them.

"What made you decide to leave home, Lexis? What about the stories made you think that you'd be better off here—penniless—than back where you'd started? It sounds like you had an okay thing going for you back there."

"There were a few weeks of violence shortly after Brennan made himself known. By and large, Jax's people wiped the floor with any of the enforcers they encountered, but one of the enforcers I tailored for managed to get the drop on a small, three-man squad and he and a few others killed all three. They were ecstatic about the weapons they captured—despite the fact that they were going to be nothing more than awkwardly-weighted clubs once the ammunition ran out—but it was the clothes the guardsmen had been wearing that convinced me to come here."

"The clothes?"

"Yes, the clothes. I'd never seen anything so fine. Most of what I dealt with back then was tailoring salvaged cloth from back before the Desolation, that or stuff that had been handwoven by someone who'd grown up learning to weave from their mother. This stuff was nothing like that. Even weaves, thread that was impossibly thin, and a uniformity that I knew wasn't humanly possible."

"It was manufactured."

"Indeed it was. I knew that I wanted to be a part of that."

I went to buckle up the last pair of straps, but she gently slapped my hands away.

"Leave that one undone—it makes you look like you're pretending at being a soldier. Jax would never stand for something like that in one of his actual guardsmen."

She reached back and started tightening straps working from the bottom up, and within a couple of seconds I could see why Jax wouldn't have approved. It felt like the vest had been designed with the sole purpose of framing my chest. If I actually ended up needing to fight I was going to have to remember to unbuckle a couple of straps or I wouldn't be able to breathe deeply enough to avoid getting winded.

"You're glad you came then?"

"Most definitely. Even the newest, most unskilled worker here gets paid better than most of our fellows out in the rest of the city. We don't all think of it that way, but having a warm place to sleep and steady meals is the most important pay there is."

"There has to be more to it than that though, right? I mean, people aren't going to work to improve themselves if there isn't a prospect of something more than just the same food and housing that they started out with, are they?"

Lexis tapped my vest. "You're wearing the reward. Brennan started the textile plant early on because it was a necessity if he was going to be able to give his people a shared identity and create identifiable uniforms so people knew who they were supposed to take orders from. These days, we aren't taking people in anywhere near quickly enough to strain our production abilities. That means that there are plenty of resources left over for us to make clothing other than just the work clothes that everyone is issued on their first day here. We have our little luxuries here, and with each month that passes they get a little better."

She finished adjusting the straps on my vest, and then pulled a long, slender stainless-steel spike out of one of her bags as she steered me over to the room's single metal chair.

"Speaking of luxuries, let's do your hair."

Lexis pulled my hair back, twisted it into a messy bun, and then slid the sliver of metal into place so that it wouldn't come undone. I'd been able to see everything else she'd done up to that point without a mirror, but I had no idea how I looked now. There was a mirror in the bathroom, but when I tried to turn that way, she gently pushed me back into my chair.

"We don't have time for that right now. Jax and Brennan both told me at least half a dozen times to make sure that you weren't late. We have just enough time to do your makeup, and not a minute extra."

"Makeup?"

Maybe my early existence had prepared me better than I'd realized for this life. I was quickly realizing just how much my acting skills left to be desired, but in this instance, my reaction was exactly right for my presumed backstory.

A girl raised inside of the city—someone who hadn't caught the eye of the gang leader in charge of the territory where she lived—would never have worn makeup. Actually, the grubbers didn't really have anything we would have termed back home as being makeup, but as Lexis pulled out a thin piece of charcoal, I realized that didn't mean they didn't have ways of changing their appearance.

"Yes, dear, makeup. I know this is something that you aren't accustomed to, but Piter is never going to believe that you are some kind of…escort…if you go there without doing any-thing to make yourself more fetching."

"I thought that was what the clothes and the hair were for."

The truth was that in the last ten minutes she'd done more to enhance my sex appeal than I'd ever attempted back home. Franchised citizens had no more limits when it came to makeup—for either gender—than they had in their choice of clothing, but that was another thing that I'd never experimented with.

"They are, Skye, but no woman in the role you're playing would forgo any possible weapon to wrap a man like Brennan more tightly around her finger. Now hold still while I darken your eyelids."

Remaining motionless while she'd approached me with the metal stake had been difficult. Having weathered that, I'd thought it was all going to be downhill from there. I hadn't counted on the fact that this time the pointy object was going to be headed towards my eye. My nanites were perfectly capable of regenerating muscular, skeletal, and vascular damage, but I wasn't so sure that they could do the same for a destroyed eye.

"Are you sure that's—"

"Skye, if you don't hold still I'm going to poke you by accident. You're going to have to trust me. I've done this hundreds of times when someone brought me some poor girl who needed a new set of clothes so they could be displayed on the arm of some top enforcer. There wasn't much I could do for those poor things, but I could at least teach them how to look their very best so that they didn't get cast aside a moment sooner than necessary."

I gritted my teeth and a few seconds later she set the charcoal back down and pulled out a small brush and a red mixture.

"It's just berries. The city has hundreds of times more space than we could possibly fill. In most territories the top floors of the buildings are converted into gardens to supplement the flow of food in from the border territories, but Brennan is the first warlord to throw his full weight behind those projects."

"How—" Even as I started to ask the question, I realized the answer. "Dirt. He's moving the dirt from the excavation up into the buildings inside of the compound and using that to grow crops. It solves two problems at once. If he didn't do that, he'd have piles of dirt inside the compound forty feet high."

Lexis gave me a smile. "Smart girl. That's exactly right. He's also built a system for collecting rainwater and then sending it down into floors that need water. When times get really rough I expect he'll dedicate some of the power being generated towards pumping additional water up to the cisterns, but so far it hasn't been a problem."

"Why haven't the rest of the warlords done something similar? They have to hate being forced to depend on the territories on the outskirts of the city for food."

"One of them tried. To hear Jax tell it, the fool was barely more than started on the project when his digging brought one of the nearby buildings down."

I shook my head in amazement as she stepped back and studied her handiwork. "How did Brennan manage it?"

"He systematically pulled down all of the buildings bordering the shaft so that he could build the wall around the compound. Don't ask me how he knew where to build this one. Apparently he's just that smart. Well, dear, would you like to see how you look?"

I nodded hesitantly, and then stood and walked over to the bathroom. The mirror wasn't long enough for me to see my entire body at once, but it sufficed to let me see the results of her handiwork.

I'd known that she was emphasizing my breasts, and I'd been expecting the pants to be just as flattering, but I was still surprised by the results. For the first time in my life I looked like an actual woman rather than a teenage girl who was too busy with training to worry about what other people thought of her.

I slowly allowed my eyes to drift upwards. Ironically it was my hair that I first noticed. For years I'd pulled it back into a simple ponytail—more than once I'd contemplated cutting it short. It would have made things a lot easier, but I'd never quite managed to convince myself to do it. Apparently I was more vain than I'd realized.

The messy knot at the back of my head looked both effortless and elegant in ways I wouldn't have believed possible. When combined with the startling shade of red she'd applied to my lips and the darkened eyelids that made my eyes much bigger than normal, I very much looked the part I'd agreed to play.

"What do you think?"

I turned and gave her a slow smile. "Would you be willing to teach me how to do this?"

Her grin made me feel like we were co-conspirators. "I'm sure we could work out a trade."

"In that case, I think I better get on my way or Jax and Brennan are going to have something to say to both of us."

I grabbed the rifle that I'd just finished shooting for the first time less than an hour before and slung it over my shoulder with the barrel pointing down the way I'd seen Jax and the others carry theirs. A few seconds later I'd filled the appropriate pockets in the vest with fresh magazines, and was following Lexis out the door.

Brennan and Jax rounded the corner before we'd taken two steps. Seeing the two of them, especially Brennan, pull up short—obviously shocked by the transformation I'd undergone—was surprisingly satisfying.

They'd obviously been on their way to find out what was taking so long, but rather than the dressing down I'd been expecting, Brennan gave me a smile and Jax simply nodded in approval. Two of Jax's men carried Lexis' cart up the flights of stairs, and minutes later we were jogging through the busy streets of the compound.

I'd been expecting Jax to ride me over some supposed infraction or another the entire way, but now that we were outside of the secure underground floors, he was completely focused on our surroundings. He and the other five guards spread out to form a circle around Brennan and me, each focused on a specific arc, scanning both high and low to make sure that we weren't surprised by any threats.

Everyone else had their weapons out and ready for action, but I remembered Jax's warning and kept mine pointed at the ground, carefully matching Brennan's pace.

As we exited the wall around the compound and entered the rest of Brennan's territory, I stumbled and Brennan reached out and steadied me, grabbing my arm with surprising strength. "We're making up for lost time right now, but Jax will have to slow down once we hit the boundary between our territory and Piter's territory. It's bad enough for us to move like this inside an area that is supposed to be secure. It won't matter how late we are—once we hit their territory we'll slow down."

"I'm sorry about that. We were trying to hurry—"

He shook his head. "You don't need to be sorry. Lexis is a talker, we knew that, which is why we stressed that she couldn't be late. I think it comes from spending so many years unable to say what she was really thinking. Now that she feels safe she sometimes has a hard time staying silent."

I looked around at the team of bodyguards running in a cordon around us and was suddenly struck by just how lethal they were. I'd seen plenty of military personnel during my training back home, but that had somehow been different. Most of the people I'd interacted with had been newly-franchised trainees who were even younger than I was. The few experienced individuals had all been instructors, and I'd never seen more than one or two of them in the same place at the same time.

Inside the barrier nobody carried anything heavier than a stun baton, and even when I'd been loaded into the plane for the drop into the city, there had been a different feel to everything. Pilots were a different breed. They fought and sometimes died, but they delivered death from miles away. Jax and the others were used to facing death from close range without flinching. This was the price of power here among the grubbers.

"Is she?"

"Is she what?"

"Safe. Is Lexis really safe?"

Brennan caught my eyes and something passed behind them that I couldn't identify. "She's as safe as any of the rest of us, Skye. We live in a dangerous, violent world. I take steps every day to try and secure the safety of my people—the ones inside the compound and the ones on the outside alike—but I'd be lying if I said that I had every base covered as well as I would like to."

We arrived at the southern barricade before I could respond, and Jax slowed us down to nothing more than a walk. I looked at the soldiers on our side of the makeshift wall, and was struck by the difference between them and the six guards with us.

The men along the barricade were well-trained and disciplined, but they didn't have the same air of deadliness that Brennan's personal guards had. They were soldiers, but they weren't hardened killers yet, not like the enforcers waiting on the other side of the opened gate, not like Jax and the others.

I'd taken down one of these soldiers while suffering from a broken leg. I wouldn't have had such an easy time of things if I'd been up against Jax. I was faster and stronger than any of the men and women around me, but I'd hesitated when I came up against the guard who'd tried to stop me after I'd jumped out of the building. I'd failed to kill him, and in doing so burned my only other face. If things went badly in

Brennan's territory I wasn't going to be able to just change my face and start over—all because I'd been unwilling to kill someone who'd just been doing their job.

"Are you sure you want me over there with you? I kept my head down while I was in Piter's territory, but that doesn't mean—"

That drew another smile out of Brennan. "Relax, Skye. Trust me when I say that he's not going to recognize you—not given how you look right now. Just try to look a little nervous and stand a little too close to me—like you're aware that your safety depends on my goodwill."

Nervous was easy. Standing close to him was something else altogether. Brennan was the threat that I'd been sent to make sure didn't cause the Society long-term problems. I should have been tallying up his strengths and weaknesses, should have been keeping track of the sidearm strapped to his right leg so that I could make sure he didn't get the drop on me. Instead, I found myself repetitively scanning my surroundings as though keeping him alive was just as much my job as it was Jax's.

We made it to the open gate, and a massive enforcer with a shaved head and crude tattoos looked us over.

"I was told you were only allowed to bring six guards."

Brennan didn't say anything. He just looked at me and then stared expectantly at Piter's man.

After only a few seconds the enforcer cleared his throat.

"I suppose you can go through. Piter has been waiting for you."

There were a lot more enforcers waiting for us than I'd been expecting, and the situation only got worse with each step we took past the barricade. Only a few of them had firearms of any kind, and those were mostly ancient weapons that looked like they were just as likely to explode as actually fire a bullet, but it was still nerve-racking to look around and see the better part of a hundred people with clubs, knives, swords and axes lining the streets ahead of us.

I didn't realize I was shaking until Brennan reached over and gave my hand a squeeze. When he spoke his voice was the next best thing to inaudible.

"He's making a show of force precisely because he knows that he's so badly outmatched. Jax and the others could easily wipe out dozens of these bullies in the course of just a few seconds. Don't worry though, we won't be going very far into his territory. We're just headed to that building right up there. The idea is that we'll go in through the door on our side, and meet him in the room right there on the ground floor."

I nodded as I finally realized the reason the guards on the wall had been sporting field glasses. "You'll station someone at the window and if things go south the guards on the wall will sortie out to save us."

Brennan didn't answer for a second, but it wasn't until I looked over and saw his raised eyebrow that I realized I was using words that the average grubber wouldn't know. I was still debating how to cover my lapse when Brennan shook himself and nodded.

"That's right. It's not perfect, but it gives Piter the illusion of control, and that matters quite a lot. Our forces could mow his men here down in short order, but this is less than a third of his men. If he really wanted to make things difficult, he would attack under cover of darkness when we don't have the guards on our side of the border bumped up to nearly twice their normal strength. The more concessions I give, the stronger he feels and the less likely he is to push for the stuff that really matters."

I nodded. What Brennan was really saying was that he was less worried about Piter attacking by himself than he was about the possibility Piter would choose to attack in concert with one or more of the other warlords surrounding our territory.

We arrived at the door Brennan had pointed out, and Jax and one of his other men threw it open as they glided inside the building, weapons at the ready in case this was all just one huge trap.

"Clear."

I followed Brennan inside, followed in turn by the rest of the bodyguards, and then I was looking at a scene out of some kind of medieval hell. Piter was there, top hat and all, and the room behind him was packed with enforcers.

It was hard to tear my eyes away from the dirty, threatening mass of heavily-armed individuals, but I knew I needed to take in the entire scene before I got fixated on one particular threat. The chair that Piter was using could more properly have been called a throne. It was set on a makeshift platform that made sure that he wouldn't have to look too far up in order to meet the eyes of anyone in the room.

The back of the chair was only inches from the ceiling, and the arms were massive platforms that were more than big enough to each support a person, which was exactly what they were doing. A pair of girls with big brown eyes and long dark hair were sitting on either side of Piter, bodies pressed up against him. That would have been bad enough all by itself, but they were obviously even younger than I was, scared, and wearing thin—almost sheer—dresses that left them shivering in the autumn chill.

They were terrified, and he was enjoying their fear. I'd known that many of the warlords were terrible men, but somehow after meeting Brennan the contrast was all the more shocking.

While I was still staring at Piter, the warlord stood and stepped towards us. "I was ready to order my man at the gate whipped for letting you through with too many guards, but I can see that this one's not a guard. I have to admit you almost had me convinced, Brennan. For months now you've maintained this front, it's nice to finally see the real you."

Brennan placed a hand on my arm as though to make sure that I wouldn't throw myself at Piter. "I don't like what you're insinuating. Skye is a member of my guards in good standing. You will please treat her as such."

Piter shrugged. "I couldn't care less what you call her. Now, are you going to sit down and have a drink with me or not?"

Brennan smiled broadly and stepped forward to meet Piter as the other man set his hat on his throne and then waved for some of his men to bring a small table and matching chairs forward.

"I thought you were never going to ask."

Piter poured some kind of milky-white liquid into a pair of earthen mugs, and then the two of them tossed back the contents of their respective cups.

"I'm guessing that it's a bad sign that you came here with nothing more than guards on a day that you were supposed to be bringing over a shipment of rifles."

Brennan leaned back in his chair. "I'm afraid so. We had an accident inside of our foundry. One of the regulators on the arcs that melt the metal gave way and we had an unregulated burst of heat that nearly killed several of my people. I'm going to spend at least the next week or two trying to get the foundry back up and running. Hopefully getting the secondary generator back online won't take weeks more in addition to that."

Piter belched. "That's what my spies said as well. It's a good thing, too; if you'd shown up empty-handed and my spies had been telling me that things were running smoothly over there, I would have been forced to assume you were running some kind of game on me. I need those weapons to keep the rabble on this side of the barricade down in the dirt where they belong."

Brennan waved the words away. "You know me better than that. The last thing I want is to be a bad neighbor. You'll have your guns—I'm just going to be behind schedule a little more than we'd discussed. Honestly, you should just create an inner compound like I've done—it does wonders when it comes to keeping the riffraff in their place."

"That's the thing that I like most about you, Brennan. You've been unnaturally celibate the entire time I've known you, but at least you don't have any illusions when it comes to the natural order of things. I hear about the recruitment speeches your man Tyrell rattles off, and I get reports about the motivational speeches you give the workers inside your compound, but in the end, you're just as much of a blasted pirate as I am."

I nearly saw red as Brennan raised his glass again. "To power and glorious profit, Piter. We're two of a kind; I've just figured out that the best way to get a man to work is to make him think it's his idea. Convince a slave that they're actually profiting from their labors by offering them some cheap trinkets, and you can run him twice as hard with nary a complaint until he drops over dead from the exertion."

If I hadn't been so angry I probably would have been sick. I'd been taken in by Brennan's handsome face and sincere, almost shy, manner. I'd thought that Lexis had been right, that Brennan was trying to build something better, that he was closer to living the precepts than he was to the greedy capitalist he appeared to be from the outside. I should have known that it was all an act.

He wasn't choked up about the deaths of his people, he just knew that he needed to appear that way in order to keep the ones inside of the compound working. He was building an empire on the backs of people who trusted him, people who were running risks that they never would have run for someone like Piter.

If I'd needed any more proof than what he'd just said, their earlier talk of weapons would have done it. Brennan would be a fool to arm someone he thought could eventually become a threat to him. He had to be doing it because he really did believe that the two of them were more alike than they were different.

Brennan let Piter fill his mug up again, and then downed it in one long drink. "What about those supplies that we agreed to trade?"

Piter shook his head. "I'd like to, Brennan, I really would, but without your side of the exchange I can't see my way towards providing you with the lumber."

Brennan looked back at me, and then rose unsteadily to his feet and headed my way. I wanted to slam the butt of my rifle into his nose, but doing that while surrounded by people who were loyal to both Piter and Brennan would have been a death sentence.

"What about this rifle? I'll give it and all of the magazines she's carrying to you. What will that get me?"

I slowly relinquished my hold on the weapon, mind racing. I could easily kill Brennan before anyone would be able to stop me. Jax and the others were still focused on Piter's men. I could snap Brennan's neck before anyone would be able to get a shot off, but that wouldn't guarantee the success of my mission.

The Citizen-President had been very specific regarding the necessity of finding the prototype generator at all costs. Simply eliminating Brennan would probably be enough to make sure that his research wouldn't continue, but it wouldn't be a guarantee. I needed to make sure that he led me to the prototype before I eliminated him.

Piter contemplated the offer for several seconds. "I can give you half of the shipment for that, and in doing so I'm letting you get away with far too much. If, however, you want to throw in the girl I'll give you the whole shipment—you can even have her back in a few weeks when you've got the rifles."

Brennan shook his head. "No, I'm rather attached to her. I'll take the half shipment that you're willing to trade and keep my people busy some other way—maybe I'll have them dig holes and fill them back in just to see if I can get away with it."

"If you're sure, but I think you're making a mistake. She looks like she's ready to strangle you with her bare hands."

"I know, that's why I like her so much."

Piter's smile made my skin crawl. "Ah, I see. It's not that you're celibate, your tastes are just stranger than I expected. To strange tastes."

It only took the two of them a few more minutes and three more glasses of alcohol each to close the negotiation, at which point Brennan unsteadily made his way back to me and wrapped his arm around my waist, using me for support.

I forced myself not to break his arm, and endured his loathsome touch as we walked back towards the barricade. It took us four times as long to get back to the headquarters building as it had to cross the same distance earlier, and by the time we arrived it was all I could do not to shove him away from me.

The last thing I expected once we were inside the secure area of the building, was for him to suddenly straighten up, release me, and resume walking as though he'd never had anything to drink at all.

"Congratulations, Skye. You passed."

The change was so shocking that I was having a hard time processing everything. "What do you mean I passed?"

"Either you're a much better actress than anyone I've ever come across, or you're exactly what you seem to be. It's important that Piter think I'm like him. As long as he feels like he has the upper hand, and that our interests align, he's happy to continue believing the intelligence we've been feeding him via the agents we've turned."

I shook my head. "You can't really expect me to believe that was all just an act. It's just as likely that was the truth and this is just an act. It's a lot easier to believe someone in power is really just in it for themselves rather than to create the utopia that you seem to have here."

It hadn't escaped my notice that Jax and the others still had their weapons up against their shoulders. It was entirely possible that handling the situation incorrectly would get me killed, but I just didn't know what the right answer was. All I could do was answer as honestly as possible and hope that would be good enough.

Brennan noticed me looking at his guards and waved as though to signal for them to lower their weapons, but none of them complied.

"She hasn't tried to kill me yet, Jax. Go ahead and dismiss the rest of the detail, it's time for you and me to show her what's really going on here."

Jax frowned, but finally lowered his weapon and then waved the rest of the team away. I had started fidgeting by the time one of the guards returned with a standard-issue vest and several balaclavas. Brennan quickly put on the vest, and one of the balaclavas, and then turned and looked expectantly at me.

"You're going to have to put it on, Skye. Some of our people can get away with walking around and not being recognized, but the three of us are much too noticeable for that."

I stepped back away from the three of them and let my hair down, pocketing the steel spike Lexis had used to put it up, and then pulled on the thin black material. I positioned the eyeholes so that they didn't impede my peripheral vision any more than necessary, and then did up the top buckle on my vest. Jax had taken the opportunity provided by the second guard's presence and me being several feet further away from Brennan to slip his on as well.

We were now indistinguishable from any of the other guards inside or outside of the compound. I got the feeling that Brennan was smiling, but there wasn't any way to be sure—not with his face covered like it was.

"Once we exit the secure floors, it's important that you don't speak, Skye. We don't want to give anyone reason to think that the building where we're headed is anything other than what everyone thinks it is. I'll lead the way, then you, then Jax. Try not to make him worry any more than you absolutely have to—his nerves are already awfully abused."

Brennan accepted a rifle from the guard who had brought him a vest, and then looked back at me as though planning on telling me to get a rifle as well. Jax cleared his throat as though to remind Brennan that I still didn't know which version of him to believe, and Brennan shrugged.

"Any questions?"

I shook my head wordlessly, and then the three of us headed back outside. I'd half expected him to lead us somewhere inside of the compound, but instead we once again headed out through one of the two gates between the compound and the rest of Brennan's territory.

We moved quickly—like we'd been dispatched on an important assignment—but not so quickly as to draw attention to ourselves. Less than fifteen minutes later we were standing outside of a high-rise building that had bars welded over the ground-floor windows in much the same manner as the building I'd been forced to jump out of just a few days before.

That was unique in my experience so far inside of Brennan's territory, but I didn't realize why that was until we made it around to the doors and saw the pair of guards standing just in front of the entryway to the building.

We were challenged, but rather than responding verbally, Brennan tapped out a complex rhythm on his own arm. The guards didn't relax at all, but they let us approach to within a couple of feet before challenging us again.

"It's me, boys. Can you please usher us in without making any fuss?"

The higher-ranking guard looked startled for a moment, but nodded, and a second later we were walking inside the building. There was another pair of guards waiting for us inside. They didn't relax until Brennan and Jax pulled off their balaclavas, and even then they still eyed me with distrust. Apparently Brennan wasn't in the habit of bringing new recruits with him on his clandestine missions.

"This is the southern guard facility. It's still undermanned compared to what I'd like to see, but it gives us a safe place to station our reserves, a place that is close enough to Piter's territory that they'll be able to respond if he sees through my charade and decides to attack."

Given the high cost of electricity and the endless demands on our very finite power generation facilities, I'd been expecting us to go upstairs. Back in the dormitories the bulk of the places people spent any time had all been along the exterior of the building so that they would have natural light and not have to turn on lightbulbs.

The underground floors I'd been introduced to the night before had been unusual, and the only reason for us to go down rather than up was that whatever we were going to see was as important as the safety of Brennan and his most trusted advisors.

I was surprised to find a quartet of soldiers waiting for us at the bottom of the stairs, but that was nothing compared to the astonishment of realizing that the entire basement had been sealed off with a massive steel door that looked like it could have withstood a nuclear bomb.

Brennan nodded to the guards, and then walked over to a rack of rifles and picked up two of the long weapons, both of which he handed to me.

"Don't give me that look, Jax. Neither of them is loaded, and it's not like I can carry them and all of the ammunition. This stuff is heavy enough that I should be using some kind of cart to move it around with."

I ran some quick math as he picked up a pair of big, steel boxes. He wasn't kidding. Based on how heavy the boxes of ammunition back in my room had been, and the volume of space inside of the boxes, and the probable weight of the boxes themselves, he was lifting more than seventy pounds of ammunition with each arm. That surprised me. He looked fit, but that kind of feat from someone without nanites was commendable.

Brennan wasn't some kind of useless egghead; he was apparently capable of keeping up with Jax and the rest of his guards.

The four guards who'd been stationed in front of the vault door swung it open, and I followed Brennan inside of the hallway that awaited us on the other side. The steel door swung shut behind us, and I tried not to flinch as the massive locking bolts slid into place. We wouldn't be getting out that way—at least not without someone on the outside opening it for us.

The hallway was lit only by a single bare bulb, and I spared a single thought to hope that it wouldn't go out on us while we were down there. Being trapped in the dark didn't sound like a very pleasant way to die.

We rounded a corner and were faced with another door, this one only marginally heavier than a normal exterior door. Jax stepped around Brennan and me, and unlocked it with a grimace. I got the feeling that it wasn't the act of unlocking the door that he didn't like—it was dislike of what he knew awaited us on the other side.

My jaw dropped as I took in the sight before me. We were standing in what appeared to be a massive underground parking garage, one that took up the entire area underneath the building, and even extended off to the south—underneath the barricade between Piter's territory and Brennan's territory.

The sound of high-velocity bullets brought me around to find a dozen people standing in lines, waiting for their chance to shoot one of a pair of rifles just like the ones I was carrying.

The sound was deafening, but one of the individuals waiting in the line happened to look over and see us. He got the attention of everyone else and they all backed away from the guns. I thought for a moment that they were scared of Jax, who had the muzzle of his weapon pointed at a spot midway between us and them, but that didn't gel with the smiles that broke out on their faces.

"We heard that you had a meeting with Piter, but the rumor mill was afire with news that you'd had problems with your production process."

The speaker was a thin woman in her late thirties. She looked like she'd had a hard life, but even the scar that ran from her right ear to the center of her chin couldn't dim the brilliance of her smile.

Brennan lugged the cases of ammunition over to the makeshift tables the group had been using as firing stations, and then stretched his back with a nod. "We did. We're going to be a lot further behind than I'd like by the time we get everything cleaned back up, but we've got a stock of weapons built up, and the foundry being down just means that we can't cast new cartridges—it doesn't do anything to stop us from casting lead bullets or reloading the rounds that you guys go through."

Lacking any clear instructions one way or the other, I let the woman take the two rifles I'd been carrying out of my hands. She handed one of them to a stocky kid who looked like he was probably a year younger than me. Back home he would have been fantasizing about earning his franchise and then picking up some hobby or another. Here he was handling a weapon like it was something that he'd done hundreds of times before.

Brennan looked around at the group and nodded to several of them before turning back to the lady who seemed to be in charge. "Victoria, this is Skye. Skye, this is Victoria. Skye is my newest bodyguard. Victoria is a big part of the reason I'm playing the games I'm playing with Piter."

I looked back and forth between the two of them, still not understanding, but Victoria didn't seem surprised by my confusion. "Strictly speaking, I'm not one of Brennan's people. When I leave here, I'm going back to Piter's territory and pretending to be a good little slave like everyone else."

"You're setting up an insurrection," I breathed.

Brennan nodded. "Piter is most concerned about getting his hands on more rifles—which is understandable considering they're the hardest part of the equation. I've been slowly satisfying his demand for rifles, but under-supplying him when it comes to the ammunition necessary to make the rifles useful. Victoria, on the other hand, has been forced to make do with just two rifles, but has nearly a hundred rounds for every single rifle I've given Piter."

I shook my head in awe. "You're planning on the rebels being able to take weapons from Piter's men."

"Yes, exactly that. There's still an unfortunate amount of risk, but Victoria's people will have had weeks to identify which of Piter's men have rifles and the best ways to take them out, which means they should have a decent chance of succeeding. If at all possible, we'll support them with an attack by the guardsmen from inside the compound, but that's predicated on Jax's people not being needed to combat one or more of the other gang leaders."

I looked over at the closest target, noting the tight cluster of shots through the center of the paper. They were still shooting from close range, so it was hard to be sure, but it looked like whoever had just finished shooting was a better shot than me. "Even if you succeed, your people could take terrible losses."

Victoria shrugged. "We're all aware of the risks; none of us wants to die, but each of us has lost somebody we care about to Piter or one of his men. Death is better than having to continue living as a slave."

Brennan gave her a sad smile. "As much as I'd like to spend hours down here with all of you, we won't keep you from your practice—I know that you can't linger here without running even greater risks than you're already running."

We all said our goodbyes and the three of us headed back towards the surface. My original appraisal of Brennan had been correct.

There was a lot more going on in this city than I'd realized.

Chapter 12

I hadn't been quite sure what to expect when we got back to the headquarters building and doffed our balaclavas again. It was awfully early in the day to be calling it quits, but for once Jax and Brennan seemed unified regarding what needed to happen.

"You need time to process all of this."

"What's to process? I thought you were awesome, then I thought that you were just as bad as Piter and the rest, then only a few minutes after that I found out that you're even more committed to helping out everyone else in the city than I thought you were. It seems to me like we've just come full-circle."

Brennan shook his head. "It's not that simple, Skye. I wish it were, but it's not. Everything I just showed you was the truth, but that doesn't mean that there aren't gray areas that you're going to have to trust me to navigate."

I shrugged. "My world doesn't have much gray in it, Brennan. Everything is pretty much black and white. People like Piter need to be stopped, and you're the only one who's willing to do it. I'm in. Let's get to work."

"Just like that you're willing to take a bullet for me?"

"The odds of someone shooting at you are pretty slim. We own most of the guns, remember?"

Brennan looked down at his watch, an antique timepiece that had to be more than a hundred and fifty years old, and then turned back to Jax.

"Tyrell is going to need to supervise rebuilding the foundry without me. Can you please head down the bore and let him know that I've been unavoidably detained?"

"Let's go over to Chell's room and see if he's there. He can run the message down."

Jax looked like he was digging in for a fight, but Brennan stopped him with a look. "If I'd wanted Chell to run the message, I would have told you to go ask Chell to do it, old friend. I know that you're nervous about leaving me here by myself, but Skye has had several chances already to kill me if that's what she really wanted to do."

"With all due respect, Brennan, now isn't the time to be risking everything on your gut. With the progress you're making towards completing the prototype it's almost certain that the an—"

"That's enough, Jax. When you signed onto my service you agreed that there were going to be times that I couldn't share the whole picture with you. Sometimes that means that you have to take my decisions on faith—just like everyone else. You're the next most technically skilled person after Tyrell and me in the entire compound. If I can't be down there with him, then I need you to be down there serving as his strong right hand. Trust me on this; Skye isn't going to hurt me."

Jax's lips tightened into a thin line, but after several seconds he nodded and headed back towards the stairs, and it was just Brennan and me. Brennan studied me for a heartbeat or two, and then waved for me to follow him. A short time later we were standing in front of another door, this one made out of heavier steel than mine.

Once the door was unlocked, I followed Brennan inside and realized just how naive I'd been to think that someone like Brennan would live in a room like mine. I'd thought that the amount of space I'd been given here in the compound was excessive, but my room was less than half as big as Brennan's.

That was just the start though. The far end of Brennan's room was filled with a variety of firearms, most of which appeared to be working prototypes that he'd abandoned somewhere along the process. One set of shelves was taken up by a set of rifles that clearly showed the progression he'd gone through in arriving at the current issue weapon that Jax and all of the rest of the guards carried, an all-steel utilitarian weapon that was capable of laying down a devastating hail of bullets from a variety of distances.

I was more interested in the shelf next to it which held a monstrous rifle that was obviously designed for use by snipers. Judging by its appearance, it easily weighed more than thirty-five pounds, and was probably capable of delivering a bullet the better part of a mile away from wherever the shooter was located.

Nobody had briefed me that this was even a possibility. A weapon like that would be only moderately useful without precision optics, but if Brennan could get that part of the system ironed out, he could conceivably kill people across a distance of two or three territories. He'd carved out his territory on the strength of his guards and their fully-automatic rifles, but the weapon I was looking at would be an incredible force multiplier. A small group of snipers could kill dozens—maybe even hundreds—of enforcers while the opposing force was still well outside of the range of the rifles Brennan was slowly letting his enemies get their hands on.

The space between the prototype weapons and us was filled with a startling array of tools and projects, everything from hundred-year-old computer equipment to high-speed lathes. For a moment I felt a flare of hope that Brennan had just taken me to his prototype generator, but nothing in the room looked like a good fit for what the scientists back on the other side of the barrier had theorized the generator would look like. There were no bulky power cables running from any of the machines I couldn't identify, which meant that it wasn't here.

The area closest to us had several chairs and a couch which was little more than a stainless steel frame that supported large swathes of sturdy fabric. None of the furniture looked particularly comfortable, but it was a clear attempt at giving visitors a place to sit and converse. It made me wonder how frequently he entertained in his room, which brought my eyes over to the thing that I'd been steadfastly trying to ignore.

Surprisingly, his bed wasn't any different from mine. It was a simple gray hammock dangling from two bolts in the ceiling, and I was relieved to see that it was much too small to accommodate a second person. The Society in general was relaxed when it came to people sleeping together, but not for people still in the juvenile dormitories, and even once someone left the juvenile dorms, it still was frowned upon until after they'd earned their franchise.

I hadn't really thought that Brennan was bringing me into his room so that he could seduce me, but as odd as he was acting, almost anything was possible.

"Go ahead and sit down, Skye."

I took a seat in one of the chairs, worried that picking the couch might give Brennan the wrong idea. "You're acting a little crazy, Brennan—more so even than usual. What's going on?"

Brennan dropped down onto the couch and sighed. "You're in, Skye. You passed the test. You were angry that I was helping Piter out—I could tell—and it wasn't because you wanted vengeance of some kind or another. You sincerely thought it was terrible that anyone would help him keep all of those people subjugated."

I shook my head in astonishment. It was hard to keep up with Brennan. "I thought you felt like I needed time."

"I do, but that's not because I don't trust you."

"Really? Because it kind of feels like you don't. If you really trust me, then let's get back to work."

My voice had gotten a little...testy. I was trying not to let the situation get to me, but I was undeniably uncomfortable. This mission was supposed to have been a simple information-gathering project. I was supposed to figure out where the generator was being built, and then radio back in for additional instructions. I'd known going in that I was going to have to deceive people, but I'd been mentally preparing to deceive people like Beth, Jerome, Billy and Del.

THE SOCIETY

The people I'd dealt with so far hadn't been idiots exactly—although, that was a pretty good description of Jerome and Del—but convincing a team leader, or even a foreman like Tyrell, that I was nothing more than just another teenage grubber girl was a completely different undertaking than lying to someone as intelligent as Brennan.

All of my test scores had indicated that I was possessed of above average intelligence, but I was still a ways below genius level, and the more time I spent around Brennan the more convinced I was that he was the real deal. He was the kind of mind that only came along once in a century.

If he'd been born two hundred years ago he would have probably spent all of his time sitting in front of a computer screen. He would have been skinny and so focused on his chosen profession that he probably wouldn't have noticed if a bomb went off a block away from wherever he was working. Maybe if he'd been born back then he could have invented some-thing that could have stopped the Desolation, but he hadn't been born two hundred years ago.

He'd been born now—within a year or so of me. That meant that he'd survived—and even prospered—in a lethal environment. It meant that he had the broad shoulders and hard muscles of someone who'd spent long hours doing the manual labor required to begin rebuilding the technology base that had been destroyed in every part of the world not protected by the barrier.

It meant that he wasn't oblivious. He was sharp as a whip and more than capable of ferreting out my secrets—only he seemed to have some kind of odd blind spot where I was concerned.

Somehow along the way he'd decided that I was to be trusted—decided that off of very flimsy evidence. All of my training said that this was the time to jump in and see how far his trust extended, but a tiny voice in the back of my mind was screaming it was a trap. A man capable of rediscovering lost processes and technology that was little more than myth to the rest of the grubbers wasn't the kind of person who would accept things at face value like this.

That kind of person would relentlessly question everything he believed, seeking for discrepancies between the way he *thought* the world worked and the way it *actually* worked.

"I know how this must sound, Skye, but I believe that once you agree the broad principles in life, all of the little stuff eventually takes care of itself. If you can get people headed in the same direction because they agree about the most important stuff, then everything else is just minor details.

"I saw that you care about how people are treated, that you have an innate sense of justice. I talked to Beth and she said that you were a good worker. Not just smart, but that you seemed to enjoy the satisfaction of a job well-done. I can work with someone like that. The only question is whether you can work with someone like me."

I shrugged. "I'd say yes, but you're obviously not convinced. Go ahead and let the other shoe drop."

"Okay, that's a fair challenge. The long and the short of it is that I believe everything Tyrell says in his recruitment speech—that's why I let him give it the way he does rather than focusing on something else. I'm going to take the fight to the ants, Skye. What do you think about that?"

All of my instincts screamed at me to jump him right then and there. The Citizen-President had said that Brennan was a threat to our way of life—to the precepts. I'd nearly been taken in by the facade, nearly believed him to be some kind of harmless inventor, but this was unarguable proof that my briefings had been right all along. Brennan was dangerous.

I'd spent enough time among the Society's military recruits to understand that there were real, serious threats to our Society. Our population was less than a fraction of one percent of that of the rest of the world. Conservative estimates indicated that there were more than two billion people out there on this side of the barrier who wanted nothing more than to kill every last franchised citizen.

If every single franchised citizen had been willing to take up a weapon in our defense, we still would have been outnumbered. When you compared all of the grubbers to the small number of men and women who chose to enlist in the military, the ratios were even further against us.

If all of the billions of people in the world were able to assemble themselves into one giant body and throw themselves against the barrier, it would come down, overloaded from the effort of holding back an inexorable tide.

The last thing the world needed was for the masses of grubbers to be led by someone like Brennan, someone capable of molding the world around him with nothing more than the brilliance of his mind and the unrelenting power of his will. If left unchecked, Brennan would destroy hundreds of years of civilization and progress simply to see our Society—my Society—burn.

I wanted to slam my fist into his throat, but I forced all of that down where it couldn't make it out to my eyes and responded with what I knew he wanted to hear.

"I have no problem with that, Brennan. The ants all deserve to die. If Piter is evil, they are evil boiled down to its purest form. Point me at the right target, give me a weapon, and I'll gladly help you set their world aflame."

"That is what I was afraid you would say, Skye. The sentiment you just expressed is all too common here in the city—both inside my territory and out. It's not the right way to be thinking about things though, and if you're going to be part of my inner circle, then you're going to have to get past that."

"I don't understand."

"Do you know that most of the people inside the barrier believe that they weren't responsible for the Desolation? Hundreds of millions of us on the outside of their energy field have been taught our entire lives that they started the Desolation, that they destroyed our ancestors in an effort to make sure that we would never get to the point where we could challenge them, but they believe something entirely different there.

"They believe that the world was on the brink of a great invention, something that would change the lives of every man, woman and child who would ever be born on this planet, and then that invention was stolen away from them by someone called the Destroyer. They believe that was the trigger that caused the rest of the world to attack them, and then when we couldn't get past their barrier, we turned on each other, bombing ourselves halfway back to oblivion."

Something deep inside of me was shaking, but I refused to let any sign of that out onto my face. This was as critical a conversation as I was ever going to have with Brennan.

"So they are just pawns? Does that mean that you aren't going to go to war with them after all?"

"Yes, most of them are nothing more than pawns, but I'll still be going to war with them. I don't want to kill any innocents—as unlikely as it is that anyone can make it to adulthood in such a depraved place and still retain any claim to innocence—but they have to be stopped, Skye."

I nearly opened my mouth and asked him why, but that would have been the real Skye asking, the one who had grown up on the other side of the barrier. The version of me that Brennan knew wouldn't ask that kind of question. Luckily Brennan answered the question without any prodding from me.

"They bomb us on a regular basis, not because we represent a threat, but because they want to make sure that we never have a chance to become one. Each year they kill hundreds of thousands, maybe even millions, of people who have done nothing more than be born and manage to survive inside a place like this. That would be bad enough, but the truth is that the ants are a societal dead end—they just don't realize it."

"How so?"

I was pleased that my voice came out without any of the passion I was feeling. If Brennan had been on top of his game it still might not have been enough to fool him, but he was staring off into space—seemingly overcome by whatever vista he was imagining.

"In the last hundred and fifty years, the ants haven't managed to achieve more than one or two significant advances. Before the Desolation, it wasn't uncommon for a single year to see the realization of dozens of amazing discoveries. The ants have sat at the very top of the pyramid for so long that it's easy—even for them—to forget that they have ceased growing and changing.

"They have a stranglehold on progress. They won't let us advance, and they refuse—or are incapable—of doing it on their own."

He looked back at me and shrugged. "I know that makes it sound like I worship at the altar of progress, but the truth is that I do. I disapprove of the slothful, worthless lives that most of the ants live, but that wouldn't be enough to make me destroy them. Even them bombing the cities doesn't necessarily mean that they are evil individually. Reasonable people can disagree, and sometimes those disagreements escalate, but this is something else."

"Slothful?"

That drew a chuckle out of him. "Ant society is the very definition of sloth. They have unimaginable resources at their fingertips. Nearly every inorganic substance they could want is created by one of their automated factories, and their food is grown and harvested by semi-autonomous robots that allow a single human to supervise a force capable of providing food for thousands.

"Down here we slave away for thirteen hours a day in an effort to feed and clothe ourselves while making the capital investments that will allow our children to somehow live better lives than what we've known. The ants could change the very face of the world if they worked those kinds of hours. Instead they lie around, wasting their time with drugs, gambling, and worse.

"The only time that isn't the case is when they are working to become full citizens—to earn their franchise—but even then what they do barely qualifies as work. Once they become full citizens they might work an hour or two in total during any given week. That's all it takes to provide them with food, clothes and everything else they might want."

I felt like I'd been slapped. Hearing someone paint such a terrible picture of the people back home was hard to take—especially because there wasn't any way to really argue with his assessment of life on the other side of the barrier without admitting that I was a spy.

The precepts taught that life was about people realizing the best possible versions of themselves, and art was held as the highest of accomplishments. From the time I'd been born, I'd been taught that the pressure of providing for oneself was a negative influence, one that impeded people in their quest for excellence.

Looking back at my time in the city, I could easily see half a dozen examples where that wasn't the case. Brennan and his people were attacking the work before them—work that had little if anything to do with art—with incredible energy.

They were accomplishing phenomenal things, and Lexis was a perfect example of someone who'd arrived at the compound with a useful set of skills and then gone on to make something even more amazing out of herself. She was helping Brennan build a textile operation that was capable of producing a hundred times more per person than she'd ever been able to make back when she'd been doing everything by hand.

I'd talked to Lexis and I was convinced that she had the soul of an artist, but that soul was being governed by the mind of a business woman, one who was accomplishing something with more permanence than would ever have been possible with hair-pins and charcoal pencils.

Instead of arguing with Brennan and blowing my cover, I asked the only logical question—the question that my trainers would have wanted me to ask.

"Why haven't I ever heard this before? If everything you just told me is true, how did you learn it?"

Brennan suddenly looked very tired. "It's impossible to fight a war without intelligence, Skye. It's like I mentioned earlier. Tyrell is very good at this kind of stuff. The ants would never believe that anyone could pierce their barrier and spy on them, but he's managed to do it. We have a…source on the other side of the barrier.

"As for the first half of your question, you've never heard any of this before because it's never been in the best interest of the people you reported to for you to know. A despot like Piter would never tell you the truth of someone he viewed as his enemy because he wouldn't want you thinking of them as human beings. In wars, the side with the best propaganda is often the side that wins."

"If that's true, then there's even more reason for you not to tell me this, Brennan. You just finished telling me that you're going to war with the ants…"

"Yes, but I'm not some kind of amoral despot. We're going to beat the ants because they've backed us into a corner where we don't have any choice, but I don't want any of us to lose our souls along the way.

"I know this is a lot to ask, but I need you to remember that the average ant—the average franchised citizen—isn't necessarily bad. Lazy? Yes. Dreadfully—even criminally—ignorant? Yes. They aren't evil though, the real evil is in the leadership of their people. When this is all over, I'm not going to run around executing the innocent.

"I'm going to rip down the barrier, destroy their military, and steal away their factories, but

I'm not going to kill anyone I don't have to. I'm going to just let nature take its course. If they're willing to work as hard as the rest of us, then there isn't any reason for them to starve. The question for you right now though is whether that's something you can get behind."

I swallowed to buy myself time, and then nodded. "Yeah. I can oppose something—actively fight even—without demonizing everyone on the other side. I'll help you bring the ants down, and when the smoke clears, I'll help you save whoever can be saved."

Chapter 13

After my talk with Brennan, my head hadn't stopped spinning. His take on life inside of the barrier—and the revelation that he and Tyrell had somehow managed to slip a spy into the Society—would have been enough to keep me off balance for hours, but things didn't stop there.

Once I'd satisfied Brennan that I could be the person he needed me to be, he'd dropped another bomb. Tyrell had reports that the Society was working on infiltrating his organization—this time with an operative rather than with the semi-autonomous micro drones they usually used.

Both Brennan and Tyrell were convinced that this operative was going to try to assassinate Brennan before he could implement his plan to take over the city. It was almost ironic that they'd somehow stumbled onto information about me that had been known only to the Citizen-President and a few others, but still managed to misinterpret the intelligence so badly that they didn't realize that I was the operative.

As a result, Brennan had decided his best chance of surviving was to lure the assassin into a false sense of security. During significant blocks of time Brennan's team was going to be cut back from the normal complement of five or six bodyguards to just two people...and me. I was going to continue to receive the best instruction Jax could provide—hopefully turning me into one of the most effective guards Brennan had—but by all outward appearances I would be nothing more than what Piter had taken me for at the meeting in his territory.

Even before he'd finished describing the situation, I'd realized I was going to be spending a lot of time with Brennan.

I could feel Brennan's discomfort as he laid out the plan—a plan that he'd apparently been putting together with Tyrell while Lexis had been dolling me up. It read like every guy's fantasy. Take one pretty girl, dress her up to emphasize her sexuality, and then order her to spend nearly every waking minute with you. He stopped short of telling me that I was going to have to sleep in his room every night, but I could tell that it was a possibility if he and Tyrell started worrying that the assassin was going to be able to get inside of the secure floors underneath the headquarters building.

I half expected Brennan to tell me that I was going to have to spend the night with him right then, but after I agreed to keep up my charade of being nothing more than a pretty face, he walked me back to my room and wished me good night.

I fell asleep worrying about how I was going to get away from everyone for long enough to report back to the Citizen-President. One thing was certain—it was only going to be a matter of days before I would know exactly where the generator was being stored.

Brennan didn't strike me as the kind of guy who was capable of letting a project like that sit neglected for weeks on end. Even around all of the work of cleaning up the wreckage in the foundry, he was going to find a way to dedicate some time to his pet project, and when he did that, I would be at his side.

Morning came all too soon. My nanites made me faster and stronger—they were even capable of healing most life-threatening wounds in short order—but they didn't do that much to reduce the amount of sleep I needed. I was awakened by a knock on my door that was far too soft to be Jax.

I should have known that it would be Lexis. She came bearing gifts again—more clothes—and this time everything had been tailored so that it didn't need additional modifications to emphasize the fact that I was female.

She wished me a good morning, handed me a complete change of clothing, and then waited while I changed in the bathroom. Everything fit snugly—just like she'd intended—but she still fussed over me once I left the bathroom and let her see how it all fit.

"It's not much, but this will get you through today and tomorrow, and I'll take the stuff you wore yesterday and tailor it in based on the way that this set fits. This entire floor has laundry service three times a week, so that should be enough to keep you from running around naked until I can get through a few other projects and get back to working on the rest of your wardrobe."

"I can get by with three sets of clothing, Lexis. You don't need to work on more stuff for me."

She shook her head at me. "You're getting a full range of outfits, dear. With what you'll get paid as a guard you could afford most of this on your own within a few weeks, but Brennan is paying for all of it—the tailoring too. He said that you need clothes that let you look like something other than a guard when the time is right."

I wasn't sure just how in the loop she was with regards to the assassin that Tyrell and Brennan were worried about. Brennan seemed to trust her—he wouldn't have her running the textile factory if he didn't—but it was always best to play privileged information close to one's chest.

It made sense though that Brennan was going to want me in stuff that downplayed any association with the guard. It was too bad, I'd just been starting to get used to the uniform Jax had designed.

Lexis looked at me expectantly, so I nodded. "I'm completely in your hands, Lexis."

"Of course you are—that's been the case for more than twenty-four hours now—but it's nice of you to acknowledge the fact."

She showed me how to do my hair up in the messy bun she'd teased it into the morning before, instructed me in the use of the rudimentary cosmetics that were the only thing available so deep inside of the city, and then left me with what seemed to be her entire supply of charcoal and paint.

Within a minute or two of her departure, Jax was pounding on my door. He handed me a rifle as soon as I opened it and then led me back to the shooting range, where I let myself demonstrate a small but significant degree of improvement with my marksmanship.

Weapons training was followed by some careful hand-to-hand testing. Jax took it easy on me in light of my 'injured' hand, which was a good thing. He was a lot bigger than me, and his muscular bulk made him deceptively quick.

THE SOCIETY

When those advantages were added to his superior training and experience, I wasn't a match for him—at least not without the benefits provided by my nanites. If I'd actually been trying to kill Jax, that wouldn't necessarily have been a problem, but given that it wasn't the case, I had to be careful about exposing the true extent of my abilities.

The strength and speed my nanites provided on a constant basis could be explained away as the result of training and practice, but I knew as soon as my adrenaline kicked in that my reaction time would become quite literally super human. Fortunately, as long as Jax wasn't going all out and I kept reminding myself that the fight wasn't for real, I was able to keep the nanites from bypassing parts of my nervous system in order to speed up my reaction time.

Even so, there were several times where it was obvious that Jax sensed something was off. I was fortunate that my trainers from back home had designed a distinctive fighting style for me based on my size and strength. If they'd tried to cram me into the same fighting style used by the Society's military personnel, I would've had an even greater chance of having my cover blown.

Once Jax released me from training, I headed back to my room, showered, ran to the private cafeteria just off of the headquarters area for some food, and then reported to Brennan's room freshly dressed with my hair and makeup done.

Brennan answered the door on my second knock. I'd known that we were going to be spending a lot of time together, but somehow that knowledge hadn't translated into realizing that he was going to be answering his door shirtless.

"Hi, Skye. I need just a moment to finish getting dressed and then we can go check on the progress down in the foundry."

I shifted my rifle around uncomfortably as he walked over to his dresser and pulled out a light gray shirt. I'd known that he had a muscular build just based on the way he'd picked up the ammunition when we'd gone to meet with the insurgents in the parking garage, but I was astonished at just how tightly ripped he actually was.

I found myself torn between staring and looking away as he pulled the garment over his head. I ended up trying to stare until the last possible moment when I could look away without him realizing what I'd been doing. My timing was off and he chuckled as he met my gaze.

"You can sit down, Skye. You're going to be spending enough time here that you might as well make yourself comfortable. Even once I'm dressed we won't be going anywhere until Jax shows up. He tends to get more than a little irate when I leave my room without my full guard detail. I can only imagine that he's going to be even more touchy now that the normal detachment has been reduced in size."

"Do you ever get tired of it?"

The question seemed to have taken him by surprise. "I think you're the first person who's ever asked me that. For most of the new arrivals inside the compound, bodyguards for a gang leader or warlord are just a fact of life. Truth be told, I'd like nothing more than to be able to walk around without worrying about someone taking a shot at me, but this is the world we live in. If I have to be surrounded by bodyguards, I couldn't ask for a better security chief than Jax."

"It sounds like he's been with you for a long time."

"Yes, basically from the beginning—but that's a different story."

It wasn't like Brennan to be so evasive, but before I could pin him down, a knock at the door signaled the arrival of Jax and the other bodyguard who would be shadowing Brennan for the next ten hours. Jax frowned when he saw me there waiting inside Brennan's room.

"Typically we meet up at my room and then all proceed to Brennan's room together."

Brennan turned to the other guard. "Alan, could you please wait outside for just a moment?"

After Alan had left the room and the door was closed, Brennan turned to Jax. "We talked about this. If Skye is going to be able to play the part we've assigned her, then she can't act like all the rest of your men. If the ants have really placed an operative inside the compound then every part of this illusion must be perfect."

It was obvious to me that Jax still wasn't happy with Brennan's decision to lure the assassin out with a show of weakness, but he nodded. "Very well, I won't raise any more objections around my men, but I'm still not sure this is a very good idea."

"Maybe not, but it's the way I want to handle it. Go ahead and be your usual surly self around your men though—the point is for everyone to think that you're convinced this is a mistake and I'm leaving myself uncovered. It shouldn't be too hard for you given that it's exactly how you feel."

The next few hours passed in a blur. We spent a good chunk of the day down in the foundry helping clean up the damage from having the circuit breakers fail and the resultant overheating of the arc furnace.

I knew very little about electricity or smelting iron either one, but as nearly as I could tell, the furnace was a big circular bowl lined with bricks and topped off with three electrodes at the top that actually did the work of melting everything down. It wasn't that there weren't any moving parts—the lid containing the electrodes was designed to move up and down—but there were so few moving parts that

I initially had a hard time understanding what needed to be fixed.

That deficiency in my understanding didn't last long. Given that we were down to just three guards, Brennan didn't expect any of his bodyguards to help with the actual work of rebuilding the foundry, but I still got to watch as he and Tyrell directed a crew of more than two dozen people as they ripped overloaded wiring out of the wall and began the process of running replacement electrodes through the lid of the furnace.

The foundry was actually quite a bit smaller than I'd envisioned—the furnace was only capable of pouring a few tons of metal at a time—but repairing it was still just as big of a job as Brennan had told Piter it would be.

I split my time between watching the foundry crews work—because it was fascinating to see how everything came together—and watching our surroundings to make sure that Brennan was safe. It was silly—*I* was the assassin whom Brennan and Tyrell were so worried about—but that didn't stop me from tensing up each time one of the workers approached Brennan with a tool that was big enough to be used as a weapon.

Partly that was because maintaining my cover required me to look like I was doing my job as a bodyguard, and partly it was because Brennan was a mystery. Some combination of his dark good looks, drool-worthy body, impossible knowledge of my home, and towering brilliance had allowed him to get under my skin. I'd been sent to stop him from weaponizing his new generator—which I was going to do—but before I left I also wanted to know for myself which version of Brennan was the real one.

Keeping such a close eye on him meant that I noticed things that the regular workers didn't. Brennan kept a smile on his face during each interaction with the people around him, but I could see that he was growing restless.

When he'd sent Jax away the day before to go help Tyrell supervise the cleanup, he'd implied that the two of them could get the foundry back up and running without him, but that was only half true.

The work of replacing overheated pipes and electrical wiring wasn't rocket science, but none of the workers really understood how all of the pieces fit together. Just because someone was capable of welding two lengths of pipe together didn't mean that they understood the complex weave of pipes required to cool the scorching temperatures involved in melting steel.

Singly, each and every task involved in the rebuild was only barely more than trivial, but keeping all of the pieces moving smoothly forward took something very close to genius. Tyrell was obviously competent. He was directing his team with a skill that I never could have hoped to equal, but he was still missing something—some spark of genius that Brennan possessed.

Some guys would have lorded their intelligence over the rest of us. Knowing that you were the smartest person in any given room was the kind of thing that could inflate a person's ego, but that didn't seem to be the case with Brennan.

He appreciated each and every person working at his side. He seemed to understand that they were absolutely indispensable in a world without computers to monitor and control processes, but that didn't stop him from resenting the fact that he had to be down there supervising the cleanup efforts.

For the rest of us, the foundry—including the systems that delivered electricity into the smelter, and the pipes that kept the ambient temperature down to where humans could stand to be inside the cavern—was straining the edge of what we could comprehend. Getting the foundry back up and running was a worthwhile endeavor for us, but for Brennan it was nothing more than an unfortunate means to an end.

Brennan didn't want to be the power-generation czar inside the city any more than he wanted to be the steel-pouring savant who was slowly reclaiming all of the useless steel inside of the battered skyscrapers that towered over us.

When you got right down to it, Brennan probably didn't even want to be the man who was going to wage a war against the Society.

Those things were all peripheral. They were nothing more than a means to an end. Brennan wanted to be the man to discover a new energy source—he was just going to have to rediscover all of the foundational technologies that had been lost in order to reach his real goal.

He kept a smile on his face and remained polite to everyone he interacted with, but by the time we all broke for lunch, I could see it pulling at him. He wanted to be away from the foundry, wanted to be working on his generator.

Brennan waved Tyrell over as everyone trickled out of the man-made cavern where the foundry equipment was located.

"I need to get away and clear my head. I'll swing back by the guard post and grab a replacement for Jax so that he can come back here after lunch and help supervise things."

Tyrell sighed. "Okay, but you're going to have to spend most of the day here tomorrow if we're going to keep things moving along."

Jax wasn't quite as resigned to the plan, but he looked around to confirm that we were alone before voicing his frustrations. "Brennan, I scheduled myself and Alan during this shift for a reason. If we're going to be down to two guards, then it only makes sense to make sure that we've got two of our best."

Brennan rubbed his temples. "Fortunately, even once you are back here helping Tyrell, I'll still have two of your finest people with me. I know you don't like it, but it's not like I'm leaving the compound. The workshop level is the most secure location anywhere inside the city. If I'm not safe there with three guards, then we've got much bigger problems than any of us are willing to entertain."

Alan and I exchanged embarrassed looks as Brennan turned on his heel and walked away, leaving the rest of us to follow along behind him. Jax only let him get a few steps away before breaking into a run to catch up. The two of them exchanged words—too quiet for me to make out—and then Jax took the point position, leaving Alan to take rearguard and me to walk alongside Brennan.

Making our way out of the bore and picking up a new guard to relieve Jax took only a few minutes, and then Brennan headed off to the secondary entrance that led down to the secure living quarters and the headquarters level. We passed a pair of Jax's handpicked guards just inside of the doorway, and then another set as we went past the headquarters level.

My stomach was growling that breakfast was nothing more than a distant memory, but I was too nervous to pay it much notice. I was finally going to see the workshop area where Brennan was working on his generator.

Once we hit the housing area, we crossed the entire length of the building before Brennan finally stopped in front of a nondescript door. He fished out his master key, and slowly opened the door—apparently so as not to spook the two guards stationed just inside of the room.

Brennan turned to Alan and the other guy and pointed to a pair of chairs against the wall. "The two of you aren't off duty, but you might as well take a load off—I'll be at least an hour or two."

Alan flinched. We all knew Jax was going to be furious when he heard that Brennan had taken me into the workshop rather than one of the 'trustworthy' guards, but Brennan didn't seem to care. He simply walked over to the large, vault-like door set into the outside wall and entered a combination—screening the dial he was turning with his body.

The master key from around his neck completed the unlocking process, and then the vault door was swinging open and Brennan was waving for me to follow him down the dimly-lit stairs that had just been revealed.

My attention split between watching Brennan and keeping track of my surroundings, I misjudged one of the steps and stumbled, but Brennan caught me with surprising ease.

"I'm sorry about that. We wired this level up before we had the secondary generation facility up and running. Getting more lighting in the stairway has been on my to-do list for months now, but there's always a dozen other things that are higher up."

I struggled for a moment with what to say—not because I was worried about blowing my cover, but because I'd never had a guy wrap his arms around my waist like that before. It was all innocent—nothing more than him trying to save me from a broken leg—but that didn't change the fact that I had industrial-sized butterflies rampaging around inside my midsection.

He was all hard planes—that were somehow still noticeable through the heavy material of my vest—and he was surprisingly warm. Back home I'd never had time to let anyone pursue me, but I'd still thought about it sometimes. In my imagination the first encounter never took place in a dim stairway dozens of feet underground, and the male lead had always been played by someone wearing some kind of cologne, and a dark suit.

Brennan wasn't wearing any kind of designer scent, but he didn't need one any more than he needed a suit. He smelled like himself. Like harsh soap, hot metal and machine oil. He smelled like industry, and that was a much headier scent than I'd expected it to be. With anyone else I would have immediately pulled back as soon as I had my feet back underneath me, but this time I let myself linger there as he slowly withdrew his arms.

When contact between us finally broke, I shook myself. "It's fine. I should have been paying closer attention to the stairs. I can't be a very good bodyguard if I can't even keep my feet under me."

We resumed walking down the stairs, hit the first landing, and doubled back several times before arriving at the bottom floor. I tapped the concrete wall next to me and tried to get back into character.

"What is this place? Your workshop? Doesn't having it so far underground make it hard to bring supplies down?"

Brennan nodded. "Yeah, it can't be helped though. This is the only way to make sure that nobody can spy on my work."

We were standing before another door. Brennan unlocked it, and then we were inside his workshop and I was having a hard time breathing. So many months of training, years of proving myself loyal to the Society, and it was finally happening. I could see the generator dominating the center of the space in front of me.

Luckily Brennan attributed my speechlessness to something else.

"I always feel the same way when I come down here. So many pre-Desolation artifacts gathered in one place. It's awe-inspiring."

"I don't understand. Where did you find all of this stuff, Brennan? I thought that nearly everything from before the Desolation had been destroyed."

"Nearly everything *was* destroyed. Electromagnetic pulses took out almost all of the electronics, but some stuff survived. Things that were buried far enough underground, or that were stored in Faraday cages were safe from the EMP, but even then most of those installations were destroyed by the high-altitude bombs. The ants had near-perfect penetration of the military organizations of all of the major powers of the day, but there were still some small countries that stockpiled supplies and equipment in locations that the ants didn't know about."

I shook my head, still not understanding. "But how did you find them? More importantly, how did you get them transported here? Everyone knows that the ants have completely shut down travel outside of the cities."

"I wish I could answer all of your questions, Skye, but that isn't my secret to tell. Suffice it to say that I'm the heir to a priceless legacy. More effort than I can comprehend went into hunting down this machinery, and enormous risks were taken to get it all moved here."

"It's impossible. I know that I'm seeing it with my own eyes, but it still feels impossible. Are you sure that you didn't just invent all of this yourself?"

That earned me another smile. "I know how you feel, but no, I didn't create most of the contents of this room. This is what I'm working towards though. The tools down here are letting me progress much faster than I otherwise could have, but every time I fire them up I know there's a chance that they're going to break on me. That's why I'm working so hard to create a decent tech base."

"No wonder you have so much security in place. The other warlords could never hope to utilize the stuff you have down here, but they wouldn't be above destroying it just so that their rivals couldn't get their hands on it."

"Yeah. To be honest though, the other warlords and gang leaders are the least of my worries in that area. If the ants knew I had all of this they would probably level the entire city if that's what it took to make sure this tech can't be used."

I wanted to keep walking, wanted to get closer to the generator, but I wasn't sure the person I was pretending to be would realize that was Brennan's crown jewel.

"Brennan, why am I down here? I mean doesn't this violate every security protocol you have? Wouldn't you have just been better off leaving me upstairs with the other two?"

"Yeah, but I'm not the one who instigated the protocols. Tyrell and Jax aren't going to be particularly happy about me bringing you down here, but they were the ones who insisted that I always have at least one other person down here with me. I could've brought Alan down. He's been with me almost as long as Jax, so he is the next logical person to be brought into the inner circle, but that wouldn't have been in keeping with the front we're trying to present to the outside world. If you and I were...dating...then I wouldn't have left you up there with the others."

He gave me a nervous shrug and then started off towards the generator, motioning for me to follow. "This is what I've been thinking about almost non-stop for the last two days."

"What is it?"

"Something new. Everything else I've accomplished here so far has just been rediscovering something somebody else invented centuries ago. This, though, this is something that has the potential to change everything. It's a new kind of generator, one that will make energy the next best thing to free."

It was time to play dumb. "Don't you already have that? I mean, with the geothermal plants that you've built here? Now that they are up and running the ongoing maintenance is basically zero."

"No, it's not comparable. There are only a few places on this continent where the ground gets hot enough quickly enough to make drilling for geothermal energy feasible. Even here, it took us months to get even just the first-stage power generation working. When you add in all of the raw materials for the pipes and everything else, our phase one generator was a ridiculous investment that we made only because there wasn't any other way to get the power we needed. This will use a fraction of the resources to build, and once it's up and running will produce four hundred times as much power."

"How is that even possible?"

"It's an antimatter generator. The math is ridiculously complex, but the basic idea is that under the right circumstances certain elements will break down into matter and antimatter. When that happens free energy is sucked out of the surrounding environment. That cooling effect will form one stage of the power generation. Kind of the opposite of what we're doing with the geothermal installation in the bore. The real kicker, though, is that it should be possible to channel the antimatter into a special chamber with magnetic fields where it can then be annihilated against regular matter."

I had to force my mouth closed. The Skye whom Brennan thought I was never could have understood what he was talking about, but the one from the Society could almost grasp the edges of what he was trying to tell me.

If the reactions he was talking about all happened inside of a small enough space, there would be no net energy generated because the heat sucked out of the surrounding environment when the matter and antimatter were split would just be put back into the environment when antimatter collided with some other bit of matter.

By doing what he was doing, Brennan was creating a temperature difference between the two stages of power generation, which would allow him to generate something that for all intents and purposes looked like free energy. No wonder the Citizen-President had been so worried about this device.

Once again, Brennan misinterpreted my silence. He turned around and grabbed my hands like a little boy who'd just been told that Christmas was arriving twice this year.

"This will change everything, Skye. Energy is a cost, an input, into everything we do. The food we grow, the clothes we wear, the steel required to build this building, it all required energy to bring it to pass—often at multiple stages of the creation process. If energy gets cheaper, then everything else gets cheaper too. Rebuilding civilization is going to be unimaginably expensive, but this generator is going to reduce the costs in a major way. It will cut decades, or maybe even more, out of the process."

I looked into his eyes and smiled, faking an excitement that I didn't actually feel. I was no closer to unlocking the secret of Brennan's real intentions, but I finally understood just how high the stakes really were.

Chapter 14

Brennan pulled a chair up for me next to his work area and got started fitting something round to an arm-like protrusion on the top of the machine. I watched him work for two hours and was astonished by two observations.

The first was just how lost he became in his work. It was like nothing else but the generator existed.

He finished fitting the round part onto the generator and then went over to some of the machinery mounted against the wall and began fabricating a long copper coil. I was pretty sure that was going to end up with a current running through it so that it could serve as a magnetic conduit for the antimatter, but I couldn't ask—not without betraying too much interest.

The second observation was the fact that Brennan didn't seem to be working from any written notes. It seemed incredible that he could construct something so complex from memory, but it was hard to argue with my own eyes.

It wasn't until he sighed and set down the copper coil that I finally dared ask. "Are you really doing all of this from memory?"

"Not exactly." He pointed over at a heavy steel cabinet. "I've got plans locked away over there, but they are all encoded, so I tend not to use them unless I don't have any other choice."

"You're worried about someone stealing your idea?"

He double-checked that the machines he'd been using were powered down, and then nodded. "Yes, but even if someone managed to make it through all of my security it still wouldn't do them any good. My notes are useless unless you know the set of rotating constants that I multiply my calculations by."

I faked a smile and nodded. "That's good. So all you have to worry about is someone stealing the generator itself."

"Yeah, only that's going to be a lot harder than it sounds. It's going to take a lot of disassembly to get it through the door at this point, and once it's up and running it's going to be full of anti-matter, so disassembling it without knowing what you're doing will result in an explosion big enough to take out the entire city block."

Brennan gave the generator one last pat. "As much as I'd like to stay down here all day and make more progress on this beast, we'd better go back upstairs. There isn't a ton more I can do on it without the rest of the steel and copper I still need from the foundry. If I want to finish the generator, I'll need to put in the time to get the foundry back up and running."

I followed Brennan over to the door, and then waited as he shut off the lights inside of the workshop before leading me into the dim stairwell. I was trying to be more careful, but despite that I still misjudged one of the steps halfway up and stumbled again. Brennan's arm once again snaked around my waist, offering support at the same time that it pulled me in closer to him.

I didn't complain, even though he didn't release me until we were all the way up to the top of the stairs. It was odd—I was the one with cutting-edge nanites flowing through my bloodstream and an assault rifle hanging from a sling, but he somehow made me feel safer with just his touch.

We picked up Alan and Chell—the other guy waiting for us—and then headed upstairs. I was surprised when our destination turned out to be one of the older buildings in the compound. I'd been expecting Brennan to lead us back into the bore so that we could go help with the foundry, but instead he'd led us to the textiles factory.

A tired-looking Lexis met us a few feet inside of the door. "Her clothes aren't ready for you yet, Brennan, if that's what you're here for."

The words could have been taken as an insult—some of Lexis' previous employers no dobt would have taken them that way—but Brennan didn't seem to mind.

"You know me better than that. I'm not here to bust your chops over a new outfit."

"Do I? If you wanted to get right down to it, all I do here is make new outfits, so every time you've come over here to bust my chops it has been over a new outfit of some kind or another. Technically speaking."

Brennan stopped looking around at the factory floor and focused on Lexis. "What's going on, Lexis? This isn't like you."

"The main drive belt is weeks overdue getting replaced. The power outage when the foundry blew put us behind schedule, which means that we're going to miss our delivery window for the latest shipment of textiles, and there isn't anything I can do about it."

"Damn it, I should have remembered that was one of the things that Piter didn't deliver. You should have said something, Lexis."

She shook her head at him, and then pulled him towards a small office over in the corner of the building. "Saying something wouldn't have made any difference, Brennan, and you know it. This whole thing is one giant, rickety cart with four loose wheels that might come off at any moment.

"The foundry being down means that we've got fewer goods to export to the surrounding territories. We are a long way from being self-sufficient, which means that the rest of us have to pick up the slack. If we shut down textiles production then you're not going to have anything left to trade Piter and the rest, which means that you're not going to be able to get me a replacement drive belt."

Brennan was starting to get angry—maybe the only time I'd seen him angry since I'd arrived. His anger wasn't a hot flash, it was a slow, white-hot force of nature that I could tell he was having a hard time containing.

"Lexis, you don't get to make that call. If that belt goes it could destroy the surrounding machinery—or even worse, it could kill someone. I know you're concerned, but it's my job to make these kinds of calls, not yours. If we're that far past the scheduled replacement date, then Tyrell or I need to be over here at least twice a day to check on things and make sure that the belt is still holding up."

"And then you'll shut me down, at which point you'll be out of trade goods."

"There's still fresh produce—hell, if necessary I can probably just go ahead and trade Piter more ammunition. I'm not losing another person to a needless accident. We lose too many to the ones we can't avoid as it is. Shut the production floor down."

Lexis looked like she was going to keep arguing, but the fact that her workers were at risk seemed to finally sink in.

"Okay. Go ahead and examine it. If you say it needs to be shut down then we'll shut it down, but at least check that it's really that far gone."

Brennan looked for a second like he was going to respond with something biting, but instead he took a deep breath and nodded. "Okay, let's go take a look."

The drive belt turned out to be all the way over on the other side of the production floor. The far corner of the building housed a massive electrical motor that used a heavy rubber belt to drive a series of long, slender steel shafts that each powered more than a dozen sewing machines.

The pipe room had seemed incredibly dangerous to me back when I'd first arrived in the compound. It was nothing like the sterile, shiny machines that had provided for all of our needs on the other side of the barrier. Maybe the Society's heavy industry installations—which were mostly hidden underground—had been a different matter, but I suspected that even those hadn't looked much like the pipe room or even the foundry.

As dangerous as the pipe room had been, the foundry had felt like it was an order of magnitude worse. I'd thought that the foundry was as bad as things were going to get danger wise, but the textile factory was even worse. Spinning shafts and whirling belts were in operation all over the floor with only the most rudimentary of physical guards to keep someone from being pulled into the machinery.

The corner next to the motor housed a massive weaving machine that looked like it would cut a person in half if they wandered too close to it, but there wasn't any wall of safety glass encircling the dangerous machine, only a bright orange line painted around it to warn people to keep their distance.

I was so caught up in analyzing the dangers all around me that it took me several seconds to realize that Lexis had fallen back to the tail end of the group. I'd expected for her to lead the way to the drive belt—full of spit and fire—but instead she was lagging behind everyone else. I belatedly remembered that she'd been slaving over clothes for me when she should have been working on much more important stuff.

"I'm sorry, Lexis. If I'd realized how critical things were, I never would have let you waste time on stuff for me."

She waved away my concern. "You weren't the one who asked me to do it, child. The truth is that I welcomed the distraction. I've known for days now that we were headed into an impossible situation, but I just didn't know how to fix things.

"I've had all of the machines manned and going full-tilt ever since the power came back up. We extended our normal two shifts so that the machines are going round the clock, which means that Brennan's going to shut us down because the belt has a lot more wear on it than he realizes. Tailoring your outfits down—mostly by hand—was a break from worrying about everything else, but even if it hadn't been, none of this is your fault."

I shrugged uncomfortably. "Actually, it probably is. I was in the pipe room inside the secondary power generation facility when the regulators down in the foundry burned out. If I'd been faster realizing what was going on, the damage down in the foundry wouldn't be anywhere near as bad as it is right now."

Lexis snorted. "I'm one of Brennan's direct reports, Skye. I heard the whole story. You were inside the pipe room rather than out monitoring the communications from the foundry. You realizing what was going on when you did was an outright miracle. Besides, if you hadn't saved Brennan from that bruiser, none of this would have any point whatsoever. Don't be so hard on yourself."

The group had stopped, Brennan at the front where he could see the spinning driveline, and the other two bodyguards flanking him so that they could watch the factory floor. Lexis sighed and started forward so that she could hear Brennan's verdict on the belt. Based on the way he was shaking his head, it didn't look good.

"You've been running longer shifts, haven't you?"

"Yeah, the girls agreed not to draw any kind of overtime though, just their normal wage."

"That's not what I'm concerned about, Lexis, and you know it. This belt could go any day now. We need to shut everything down before it snaps and we end up with real damage to fix."

"You're sure it can't last another day or two? That won't be enough to let us get through the stock of fabric that we have built up, but it will let us spin and weave the last of the cotton that the farms have produced. That way we can at least continue sewing the raw fabric by hand."

"I said it needs to be shut down, Lexis. Now are you going to get up there and turn it off, or do I have to do it myself?"

Under other circumstances it probably would have been humorous to watch Lexis struggling to keep her calm, but somehow the stakes involved sucked all of the amusement out of the situation. I'd been going along blindly for the last few days completely unaware of the pressures building up inside of the compound.

Brennan's creations had made the compound feel like some kind of massive, indestructible monolith, but the truth was that the stresses being placed upon his organization from the outside were incomprehensible to anyone who wasn't part of his inside circle. The territories around Brennan's domain were only one step away from open hostility, and he was being forced to navigate a razor's edge with his efforts to keep goods and materials flowing in without giving up his sovereignty.

Rather than laugh at Lexis, I moved closer to Brennan's side to get a better look at the drive belt. I didn't really know what I was looking for, but it did appear that the belt was frayed in spots.

"Don't get too close, Skye. If your clothes brush up against the belt it could pull you into the drive mechanism."

I nodded absently, already having moved as close as I was planning on getting. A dozen feet away, up on the platform containing the motors controls, I heard Lexis swear.

"The controls are stuck. I'm going to try speeding the motor up slightly to see if that will break things loose."

Brennan turned towards Lexis, mouth open as though to stop her, and then all hell broke loose.

Everything happened so incredibly fast that the adrenaline didn't even manage to hit my system and activate my nanites before I was in mortal danger.

A split second after the pitch of the motor changed, there was a clunking sound, and then something slammed into me. I was falling to the ground still trying to understand what had happened when I saw Brennan slammed into the ground, thrown there by the titanic impact of the massive rubber belt that had just broken loose from the drive mechanism.

The rest of the belt whipped past me, clipping the new guard and throwing him into

Alan—crushing his chest as bad or worse than it had just crushed Brennan's chest, but I barely registered that. My attention was on Brennan and I was already crawling towards him, desperate to find out if he was still breathing.

Brennan, the man whose life's work I'd been sent to sabotage, had just thrown himself in front of me in an effort to save my life.

Chapter 15

My training included some minimal first-aid courses, but they had all been targeted at treating the wounds of someone with military-grade nanites in their system. When trying to save the life of someone from the Society, you generally didn't have to do much more than stop the bleeding and occasionally perform rescue breathing.

If you could keep their blood pressure up, their blood circulating, and keep them breathing, then usually you were only hours from having them make a full recovery from anything that didn't destroy an organ outright. What I knew about keeping someone alive beyond that wouldn't have filled up a very tiny book, but I was very much aware that things didn't work that way for someone who wasn't carrying several trillion nanites inside of them.

I made it to Brennan's side to find him gasping in a vain effort to fill his lungs, and thought for a moment that I might be sick. The way the entire right side of his chest had been caved in was nothing less than grotesque—it was no wonder he was having such a hard time breathing.

There was surprisingly little blood given the force with which he'd been struck. As fast as the belt had been moving, I would have half expected it to shear through human flesh, but instead it had manifested primarily as blunt-force trauma.

I tipped Brennan's head back, clearing his airway, and then placed my mouth on his and pushed air into his lungs. I broke contact to get a fresh breath of air, and saw tears running down his face, but despite the pain as his ribs ground against each other, he didn't fight me.

Alan reached me as I bent back down to give Brennan another breath, dropping down next to me as Lexis was still making her way down from the control platform. Alan evaluated the situation with surprising composure and then started yelling for someone to go get Tyrell. As Lexis joined us, Alan turned back to me.

"How much training do you have? Can you stabilize him?"

"Next to none, if we have access to anyone else we need to get them." I spoke quickly, between breaths as I continued to try to keep Brennan conscious.

Alan grabbed Brennan's wrist, taking his pulse. "His heart is still beating. Tyrell's the only person I know who might be able to keep him alive, but every second counts. We need to get Brennan to the hospital."

Lexis sprang back up to her feet. "Sammy, Marcy, Pam, grab the big stretcher. We have to move him and Skye at the same time."

The next few minutes were a blur of activity. Lexis and Alan marshaled the workers and got us moving towards the headquarters building. Brennan went completely white when they moved him onto the stretcher, and I thought we were going to lose him then and there, but I continued to perform rescue breathing and Alan continued to report that Brennan's heart was still beating.

The trip out of the factory made my skin crawl. The eight women carrying the stretcher were doing their best to provide a smooth ride, but they weren't perfect and I could feel his ribs grinding together each time one of them missed a step.

I was so focused on trying to keep Brennan alive that I didn't notice when Tyrell joined us. It wasn't until we started down the stairs that I realized he'd altered our destination, and even then I only realized things had changed because the guards who'd taken over carrying the stretcher moved much more smoothly than the workers had been managing.

By that point I was starting to get light-headed from the strain of breathing for both of us, so I didn't even question when we were ushered into a bedroom rather than the hospital

I thought we were headed to. Jax had to say my name several times before I registered the fact that he was trying to talk to me.

"Skye, I'm taking over, you need to move out of the way."

I started to comply, still punchy from giving Brennan mouth to mouth, but I apparently wasn't moving fast enough because a second later strong hands picked me up. Tyrell and Jax moved Brennan onto a padded table and then Jax began rescue breathing while I stood there trying not to pass out.

Despite my concern for Brennan, months of training reasserted itself and I found myself scanning my surroundings in an effort to identify any possible threats. The hammock hanging in the corner of the room gave testament to the fact that we were in someone's bedroom, and the sheer size of the room told me that its owner had to be in Brennan's inner circle.

Given the way that Tyrell was taking over treatment of Brennan, it was only reasonable to assume that we were in his room, but I found myself startled at the sheer amount of medical equipment crammed into the space. None of the paraphernalia in the room was as advanced as the equipment in Brennan's workshop. All of it looked like it had been constructed using the compound's current technology, but there was a surprising amount of tubing, a dozen glass syringes, and what looked like a hand-powered centrifuge.

I'd known that Tyrell was smart, but I hadn't realized that his expertise was anywhere near that broad. The act of educating oneself in one discipline given the almost complete loss of knowledge due to the Desolation was impressive enough. The fact that Tyrell had also managed to become conversant with medical practices was the next best thing to miraculous. I didn't question our good fortune though, I was too busy hoping that his skills and rudimentary implements would be enough to keep Brennan alive.

Tyrell looked up, searching for some piece of equipment, and I moved forward so I'd be able to hand him whatever he needed, but as soon as he met my eyes, he frowned.

"Clear the room. Alan, get everyone out—the last thing I need right now is someone distracting me at a key moment. Jax and I will see to Brennan."

I'd lost my weapon at some point along the way, which was a good thing, because when Alan tried to pull me out of the room I started to fight him and it was only the sound of someone chambering a round that brought me back to myself. I looked up to see that Tyrell had a rifle trained on me.

"If you really care about him, you'll get out of my way and let me get started trying to save him."

I nodded shakily and allowed myself to be conducted out of the room, but that didn't stop me from leaning to the side in an effort to see around the door as it swung shut. I would've stood there, desperate for some news, but Alan gently grabbed my arm and ushered me down the hall.

"I know you're worried, but you can't stand there. If I let you stay, all you're going to do is wear yourself out and make whoever is assigned to guard the door nervous."

"They should be nervous—we should all be nervous!"

Alan shook his head. "We are, but the simple fact of the matter is that you making everyone more nervous than they already are isn't going to help Brennan. Go to your room and do something to take your mind off of what's happened."

"Great idea, except for the fact that there's nothing to do in my room."

Alan ran his hands through his hair. "I don't know what you want me to tell you, Skye. I'd send you to the shooting range, but I'm not sure it's a good idea to give you a rifle right now. Hand-to-hand is out too because we're going to need every available body out there patrolling the compound to make sure nobody uses the accident to create some kind of incident."

I shook my head. "Don't make me stay down here, Alan. I'll go crazy."

He looked back towards Tyrell's room, obviously desperate to get back to the rest of the guards. "Okay, it's not like I can force you to stay here—even Jax doesn't win against you half of the time. You want to go up to the surface, then go up to the surface. Just please promise me that you'll stay inside the compound and that you won't start any fights. If you get killed on my watch, Brennan is never going to forgive me."

"Assuming he survives."

That earned me a frown. "Don't talk like that or you'll start a panic. It's bad enough to say things like that down here. Don't you dare say something like that up on the surface. I've seen Tyrell bring people back that I never expected to make it. Brennan is tough—he's going to be okay.

I nodded in agreement, but my heart wasn't in it.

A few minutes later I was standing outside the headquarters building wondering what to do with myself. I didn't know very many people inside the compound. Jerome and Del had probably been kicked out after Del had nearly got us all killed and Jerome had tried to kill Brennan. Billy never said more than four words together at a time, which kind of precluded him from carrying on a real conversation, and the guards were all going to be circulating through the compound in an effort to calm everyone down.

That just left Lexis and Beth. Lexis was probably back inside the factory throwing herself into her work in an effort to distract herself from the accident. If I'd been a real friend, I probably would have gone to her and tried to reassure her, but I needed some kind of distraction myself.

I turned toward the bore and a few minutes later found myself inside of the foundry. Somehow I'd assumed that everyone would be working rather than just standing around. I should have realized that they'd all been present when Tyrell had received the news that Brennan had been injured. Even if that hadn't been the case, the rumor mill had probably spread the bad news through the entire compound within minutes of Brennan being hurt.

The foreman, a short, boxy man whose name I'd never caught, hurried over as soon as I stepped into the cavern that contained the foundry. "What news, miss? Is Brennan going to be okay?"

I shook my head. "It's too soon to tell. Tyrell is with him, but when I left Brennan was still breathing and there wasn't a whole lot of blood at least."

It wasn't quite a lie. Brennan had been breathing—just not without help. I could see more questions coming, see them on the tip of the foreman's tongue, but I was already uncomfortable with what I'd said so far.

My duty to the Society was getting cloudier by the moment. I was supposed to stop Brennan and make sure that his generator couldn't ever be used to pierce the barrier. Now was the perfect time to strike if I wanted to destabilize

Brennan's operations, but I hadn't gone into the mission thinking in those terms, which meant I wasn't prepared to instigate some kind of coup. Even worse, if I tried something like that and failed, I would be found out and never have another chance at the generator.

Besides, my orders had been to find the generator and then radio in. The only way forward I could see was to continue to play the role of dutiful bodyguard, but it made me wonder if the Citizen-President had realized just how convoluted things were going to get on this mission. Probably not—the Society didn't have a history of using human assets to infiltrate the cities.

My questing gaze finally found something that would serve to distract everyone—me included—from the question of what was going to happen next. I pointed at the piles of bricks just inside the entrance to the foundry.

"What's the situation with the rebuild? Are we to the point where we can start putting the new layer of bricks in?"

"I...I think so. It seemed like Tyrell was nearly to the point of having us tear out the old bricks when he got called away."

"You don't know?"

"Look, lady, I can melt metal, but that doesn't mean that I know how to build the machines that make it all possible."

I took a deep breath and then nodded. "That's fair—I don't actually know how my gun works, but that doesn't stop me from pulling the trigger. Well, we'd better get started."

"Right now? What's the hurry? We don't even know if Brennan is going to make it."

That woke an unexpected flash of anger inside of me. "The hurry is that we've got metal that needs to be poured and shipped off to the surrounding territories so that we can trade for all of the stuff that we can't make or grow ourselves. With the textiles factory down, that puts even more pressure on us to get the foundry back up and running."

The foreman was backing away now—almost like he was afraid I was going to physically assault him. I didn't help the situation by stepping forward into his personal space, but I was too furious to care.

"Brennan is going to be fine, but even if he doesn't pull through, that doesn't mean that everything he's built—that all of you have helped build—needs to disappear. He's done something amazing, and even if the rest of us aren't good enough to push it forward like he would have, we're still good enough to continue doing the stuff that he's already taught us how to do.

"This couldn't have happened without Brennan, but it's bigger than just him now. We have a chance to live lives that matter, to experience an existence that is more than just barely getting by. So either help me rip out the old bricks or get out of my way, because when

Brennan is finally back on his feet I don't want to have to look at him and admit that I jeopardized everything he's worked towards because I wasn't smart enough to know that piles of new bricks all around the furnace mean that we need to tear the old bricks out to make room for them."

It was like I ran a current through the entire crew. They all jumped into action, and within seconds we were all beating on the refractory material inside of the furnace. It turned out that the bricks inside of the furnace had been coated with something that was the same consistency as the bricks, but which formed a relatively smooth face which was presumably what kept the molten metal from running out through the cracks in the bricks.

The coating meant that we couldn't just lift the bricks out, we had to take hammers and chisels to the lining and break it up into pieces that were small enough to be lifted out of the furnace. It was much more work than I'd realized it was going to be going into the project, but I quickly lost myself in the task, and after several hours—long past when my shift was supposed to be done with—we finally pulled the last of the bricks out and decided to call it a night.

Somewhere along the way, I realized that I'd meant every word I'd said to the foundry crew. The presence of the generator complicated things, but once the possibility of weaponizing it was removed, the things that Brennan had accomplished were nothing but admirable.

The precepts spoke again and again about the need to shepherd those on the outside of the barrier to a life of self-sufficiency and progress, but Brennan was the first of the warlords with any interest in doing that. I just needed to make sure that the Citizen-President understood that.

The Society couldn't stand idly by while Brennan finished up the first phase in a weapon designed to bring down the barrier, but there wasn't anything to say that Brennan's compound needed to be leveled. We just needed to find a way to make sure that Brennan wouldn't weaponize the generator. Once that happened, we could leave the rest of what he'd built in place to serve as a guiding light to the rest of the city's inhabitants.

Maybe we could kidnap Brennan and show him all of the good inherent in the Society. Surely once he and the Citizen-President sat down and talked about their concerns it would be possible to come to some kind of understanding.

It might even be as simple as showing Brennan the archives showing the different nations attacking each other in spite of the Founder's best efforts to stop the war. Even as I thought it, I knew just how unlikely that scenario was, but I ignored the tiny voice in the back of my head that was screaming that Brennan would die before he would agree to work with a culture he found so repugnant. I had to try, had to at least attempt to find a way to satisfy all parties before it turned into a war that Brennan couldn't possibly win.

All of that ran through my head during the long hours it took to tear out the furnace's lining, and by the time I watched the rest of the crew head back towards the surface, I'd decided that it was time to report back to the Citizen-President.

I told the foreman that I wanted to swing by the pipe room before going back home, and turned left when he turned right, working my way towards the location where I'd stashed my radio transmitter. I breathed a sigh of relief when I arrived and it was still where I'd stashed it. I'd affixed it to one of the pipes that came out of the pipe room and then jogged back horizontally for several dozen feet—all the way to a neighboring tunnel—before making a right angle upwards again.

The fact that it was still there meant that I could still call back to my superiors—could still exert some small influence on events—and it also meant that there was a good chance nobody had stumbled across the transmitter yet.

I turned on the radio, took a deep breath and then pressed the transmit button as I spoke into the hush mic, hoping that my transmitter really was strong enough to penetrate the jamming that Brennan and Tyrell were using to stop the Society from spying on their operations.

"This is Skinwalker calling Home Base. Come in, Home Base."

The response was almost instantaneous, which meant that they had someone monitoring the frequency around the clock.

"This is Home Base; you're a go, Skinwalker. Have you found the present?"

"Yes, I've located the present—it still needs some assembly before it will be ready for gifting."

"Is there an instruction manual, Skinwalker?"

"Yes, but it's not a threat—it's in another language, one that nobody else can speak."

There was a pause while whoever was on the other end of the conversation digested the fact that Brennan had encrypted his notes. I was still working my courage up to the point of suggesting a kidnapping when the voice resumed.

"Understood, Skinwalker. How long before the present will be ready for gifting?"

"I'm not sure, several weeks probably. Recent events mean that assembly will take a lot longer than the toymaker originally planned. We have time to analyze the situation."

"Your brief is being changed, Skinwalker. For now, you need to protect the toy and the toymaker at all costs. The Architect wants the present; you're to begin gathering intel to allow us to get our hands on it."

The abrupt change confused me. I was relieved that the Citizen-President wasn't going to order me to kill Brennan, but it didn't make sense for the mission to shift objectives so quickly.

"Skinwalker copies the order. It's going to take some doing to find a way to get both the toymaker and the toy out without causing massive collateral damage."

"Neither of those issues are your concern, Skinwalker. You find a way to get the present, Home Base will worry about everything else. Home Base out."

My world seemed to be spinning around me as I reached out and turned off the transmitter. They hadn't explicitly said that they were going to burn the compound down and kill Brennan in the course of grabbing the generator, but I couldn't get away from the feeling that they were planning on doing exactly that.

Chapter 16

I woke less than six hours later to the sound of someone pounding on my bedroom door. Lexis understandably hadn't had time to deliver any of the rest of the outfits Brennan had commissioned, so I was sleeping in my underwear.

I grabbed my blanket as I rolled out of my hammock and wrapped it around myself as I stumbled towards the door. It turned out that it was Tyrell knocking. He took in my blanket and messy hair with a frown.

I rubbed my eyes as I looked for the simple, wind-up clock on one of my shelves. "What time is it?"

"Nine a.m. You had the entire afternoon off and you couldn't be bothered to do laundry or go to bed at a decent hour?"

"I went down to the foundry and helped them rip the lining to the furnace out. I only made it back here a little before three this morning."

His manner softened slightly. "Go ahead and get dressed—Brennan is asking for you. He's back in his room."

Tyrell turned and walked away before I could process the information enough to respond, and after standing there in my doorway for several seconds I swung my door shut and ran over to my last clean set of clothes.

I didn't stop to take a shower or do my hair, I just threw on my clothes and sprinted from my bedroom to Brennan's. Once I arrived, I was torn between knocking or just opening the door, but before I could make a decision one way or the other, Jax opened the door.

He waved me inside, where I found Brennan resting on the same table he'd been on in Tyrell's room. Brennan's eyes were open and he managed a faint smile when he saw me, but other than that he looked like he was half a step from death's door.

Tyrell had put a metal frame around Brennan's torso, which was obviously designed to both immobilize him and provide traction to his ribs where necessary. Brennan was shirtless, which meant I could see both extensive bruising up and down the right side of his chest wherever the bandages weren't covering and the metal rods that ran between the framework and Brennan's bandages.

I'd seen my share of battlefield injuries, but this one made me queasier than I'd expected. Maybe it was the way the rods disappeared into the bloody bandages, or maybe it was just the fact that it was Brennan rather than someone I didn't know or care about, but it was all I could do to stop from being sick. I resolved to stay focused on his face so as not to embarrass myself or let on to him how badly he'd been injured.

"You have a terrible poker face, Skye."

"I'm not sure if that's a compliment or an insult."

That earned me another smile. "Definitely a compliment. The last thing someone in my position needs is more people he can't trust."

I hid a wince at the reminder that I wasn't who he thought I was.

"In that case, I accept your compliment. How are you feeling?"

"Like I was hit by a truck—don't worry though, that's an upgrade from earlier when I felt like I'd been hit by a plane. I'm just glad you're okay."

Now it's my turn to smile. "Isn't that my line? I still can't believe you pushed me out of the way of that belt. I thought it was the bodyguard's obligation to take a bullet for the principal, not the other way around."

Tyrell stepped forward with a syringe full of clear liquid and injected it into Brennan's arm. Brennan winced slightly and then turned his head back towards me.

"Yeah, well, I'm just trying to keep up the act. If I really wanted everyone to believe that

I'm head over heels for you then I really had no choice but to step in front of the belt."

I shook my head at him. "The whole point of the act was to keep you safe. If you get yourself killed protecting me then the exercise was pointless."

"That's where you're wrong, Skye. It's only pointless to get myself killed protecting you if it's really just an act."

I opened my mouth and then closed it again, unsure what to say, but Tyrell stepped over and patted me on the arm.

"That's the morphine talking. He was about to come down from the last dose, so I gave him another. Given the state of his ribs and lungs, we can't afford to let him get to the point where his breathing gets ragged or he'll do even more damage to himself."

Tyrell sighed, and I suddenly realized that he looked terrible. He had dark circles under his eyes and was moving like someone twice his age.

"Are you okay?"

"Jax and I were up all night trying to put Brennan back together. I think I've got all of the major rib fragments stabilized, but it's going to be a little while before we know for sure."

I tried to do some quick math in my head, but gave up when I got past twenty-four hours. "You should go get some sleep. I'll keep an eye on Brennan."

Tyrell looked at me for several seconds before nodding. "I'd argue with you, but at this point if I tried to open him back up I'd probably do more harm than good. If you can watch him for the next twelve hours or so, then I'll have Alan come by and spell you. I wouldn't ask you to run such long shifts, but if Jax and I can't get the foundry back up and running, we're going to have even worse problems than we already have."

I waved away his concern. "I owe Brennan my life; I'm hardly going to complain about playing nurse for a few hours. If you can just make sure that there is a guard or two around so that I can yell for help if he takes a turn for the worse, I'll be fine. What do I need to watch out for?"

"Changes to his breathing mostly. If he starts struggling have someone come get me. If he stops breathing altogether, then start mouth-to-mouth. Beyond that give him morphine whenever he needs it, and check his pulse every twenty minutes or so and let me know if it seems like it's getting weaker. That's our best way of telling if he's got internal bleeding."

"Okay, I can do that."

Tyrell turned to go, and then stopped. "You're an odd one, Skye. Where did you learn mouth-to-mouth? There can't be more than a handful of people in the entire city who would have known what to do in a situation like that. Most of the gang leaders are being cared for by people who've regressed back to believing that leeching someone is good for them."

I reached for an explanation that would make him less suspicious rather than more.

"There was a man in my building growing up who took me under his wing. He...well, he was unlike anyone I've ever met before or since. I guess he was kind of like a warrior monk. He taught me how to fight, and he taught me a very little bit about stopping bleeding and keeping someone breathing."

Tyrell cocked his head to the side. "I can't think of very many warlords who would be comfortable with the idea of a fighting man inside their territory who didn't have any kind of allegiance to them."

I reached for a feeling of sadness, and let it crash over me. It made my lip quiver and tears start to pool in my eyes.

"He—he tried to keep a low profile. We trained early in the morning at the very top of our building so that nobody would see us. A couple of years ago one of the enforcers noticed me and started hanging around. I told him no—that I wasn't interested—but that only seemed to make it a game for him. I would try to make sure that I was never off by myself and he would try to catch me alone so that he could force his attentions on me."

Tyrell held a hand up. "I'm sorry, I didn't mean to pry. You don't have to share anything you're not comfortable sharing."

I nodded, relieved that he wasn't going to make me spell out the gory details. It wasn't until Tyrell had left and closed the door behind him that I finally allowed myself to admit where the sadness had come from.

The sadness, the story, it had all come from the same place, from an experience I'd walled away for years now.

Chapter 17

Four years ago

"The Destroyer take you, Skye. Aren't you ever going to have any fun?"

"Don't curse, Styles. It has a low social desirability index."

Styles shook his head at me, wavy red hair flopping from side to side. "That's kind of the point, Skye. We aren't children now. One more year of school and we can drop out and start working toward earning our franchise full-time. Now that we don't have crèche nannies following us around everywhere we go, there isn't any reason to worry about social desirability. Live a little."

I opened my mouth to tell him that he was being short-sighted, that service would lead to a bigger payout than just a franchise, but then the voice of one of my nannies ran through my head again reminding me to keep my desires secret.

"Rules are rules for a reason, Styles. If they aren't important then they would have been changed ages ago."

Sammy rolled her eyes. "That or they are just there to separate out the children from the adults. Didn't you ever consider the possibility that the rules are meant to be broken, that we're meant to outgrow them as we get older?"

I didn't have an answer to that—not really. I'd spent too many years with the same voice in the back of my head, the endless parade of nannies telling me that it was vital I never break any of the rules.

Styles waited for a second to see if I would manage a comeback and then smiled. "Does that mean you're ready to venture out of the Destroyer-taken green zones finally, Skye?"

I shook my head. My crèche mates and I had only been living in the juvenile dorms for a few weeks, but most of them had already ventured as far away from the green zones as it was possible to get without a franchise. A few of them had even snuck into restricted areas and been caught.

They'd been fined and confined back in the detention area of the children's dorms. Of the two punishments, the fine was by far the worst. They were going to have to spend dozens of extra hours working to earn their franchises.

It didn't make much sense to me. Everything was still so new and exciting right now. When we'd been in the children's dorms we'd been lucky to make it outside for field trips once or twice a year. Now we could go out to parks and the tamer eating establishments whenever our studies were done. It was exactly the kind of stuff that we'd all spent the last few years talking about, but as soon as it had stopped being forbidden, everyone had stopped wanting it.

Styles frowned. "Just by being around me you're being exposed to socially undesirable influences, Skye. It's not like you're going to get hauled off in chains for stepping across the street."

"Give it up, Styles. She's not going to come and we're wasting time. I want to get into that new reality simulator before the lines start forming up and we have to waste half our night waiting for a turn."

Sammy pulled on Styles' arm, but he stubbornly refused to move. "What about if I stop swearing for the night? Then everything will even out."

"I think you're overlooking the fact that once you leave I won't have to listen to you glorify the man who nearly destroyed civilization as we know it."

"Swearing by the Destroyer isn't glorifying him, Skye. Besides, we're supposed to remember what he did so that we're never tempted to repeat his mistakes."

Sammy blew a bubble with her gum. "I hardly think that any of us are going to sabotage the development of a new technology that could have granted mankind immortality."

Styles puffed his chest out. "It could happen. I'm getting really high marks in our technology courses. If that turns out to be my life's purpose, then there isn't any reason to believe that I couldn't help create a new strain of nanites that could stop the aging process."

"Nobody really believes the precepts, Styles. They are just there to convince us to buckle down and work on something after we earn our franchise. Anyone with brains knows that there's no real reason to work after you earn your franchise. An hour a week is more than enough to keep you in all the games and stimulants you could want."

I shook my head again as Sammy let go of Styles' arm. For whatever reason Styles finally decided I was serious about not going. He watched Sammy take several steps toward the arcade and then finally shrugged and headed after her.

I watched the two of them until they'd disappeared, and then headed toward one of the nearby parks. I had my running shoes on—remaining physically healthy had a high social desirability index—but once I arrived I found that I wasn't in the mood for a run. Instead, I walked over to a bench and sat down.

In theory the high social desirability index of the park served as a deterrent for any of the behaviors that were considered unsuitable for someone my age. In reality, franchised adults were very nearly a law unto themselves. Particularly egregious behaviors could result in a fine, but even then it was rare for someone not to be able to work their way out of the obligation within a few weeks.

By and large, the fact that there weren't any of the more exotic entertainments available at the park meant that there was nothing to draw franchised adults there, but as with any rule there were plenty of exceptions. As I watched, a trio of women wearing little more than body paint walked by with the unsteady gait of people who'd had several doses of one of the designer drugs that all of my dorm mates were so eager to try out.

The three of them stopped at the bench a few dozen yards away from me, giggling as they tried to catch their breath. I thought the giggling was a side effect of the drug until I saw two guys stroll into view. Both of them wore little more than a complex array of straps that covered up only slightly more than the body paint the women were wearing. One of the guys had the soft, overweight build of a sim junkie while the other guy had the aggressive muscles of someone taking steroids supplements.

Neither of the new arrivals were as far gone as the three women, but they both had the bright eyes and jerky movements of people who'd had a dose or two of something to take the edge off.

This was the first time that I'd seen such a large group of franchised adults in the park at one time and I slid forward to the edge of my bench, uneasy at the prospect of being exposed to something that properly belonged in another area with a much lower social desirability index. Unfortunately, my movement caught the attention of the bigger, more muscular guy and he turned and started walking toward me.

I stood, planning on hurrying back to my dorm room, but he called out to me. "Hey, what's your name?"

Before I could decide whether to answer him, another woman came walking quickly around the corner of the path. Unlike the other five franchised adults, she walked with the sure steps of someone who was completely sober, and it took only seconds to interpose herself between the muscular guy and me.

He tried to move around her, but she easily maintained her position in front of him. "Go home now, and don't come back to this park."

It was obvious that she was talking to me, and I did exactly as instructed, running the entire way back, relieved that I'd managed to avoid interacting with any of the other franchised adults.

I foolishly thought that was going to be the end of things, but over the following weeks it seemed like any time I left the dormitories the same muscular guy was waiting for me. I tried staying in the dormitories, but unlike the children's dorms, our new housing was designed with the intent of nudging us outside. There were no games or books or movies, and I quickly became bored.

It seemed as though he was less willing to approach me when I was with friends, so I did what I could to convince some of my other dorm mates to spend time with me in one or more of the green zones, but that too was a losing battle. At first Styles or one of the others were willing to walk me back to the dorms when they decided they wanted to go somewhere with a lower social desirability index, but after a few days where the muscular guy failed to appear, the other kids my age became more and more reluctant to take time away from what they really wanted to be doing.

I told myself it would be okay, that I was in much better shape than someone who maintained his physique by way of steroids. I figured as long as I could see him coming I wouldn't have any problem outrunning him and therefore it was okay for me to go to the green zones with my friends and then turn around and run home when they were ready to move on.

Another week went by before I'd used up all of the favors I could call in from helping my dorm mates with their studies, at which point I was once again faced with the prospect of staying in my room by myself or venturing back outside without the protection of a crowd. I debated for nearly half an hour before finally deciding to go out on a short run.

I was less than ten minutes from home when it happened. As I ran past a tree, the muscular guy stepped out from behind it and grabbed me by the arm.

"Why have you been playing hard to get? I just wanted to know your name."

My heart was hammering away in my chest and my mouth was dry. I didn't know what to do other than answer him.

"Skye, my name is Skye."

"Today's your lucky day, Skye. I can get you into any place you want to go."

I shook my head desperately as I tried to pry my arm out of his grasp. "I don't want to go anywhere, please just let me go."

He frowned as though unable to believe what he was hearing. "It's okay, there's nobody to overhear you telling me what you really want. I know how girls your age are—desperate, willing to do anything to get into the really dirty restricted areas. I'll take you there, I just need a little something in return."

His free hand had drifted over to my shoulder, tugging on the neckline of my shirt as he pulled me across the street obviously intending on hauling me to whatever low-desirability area he most liked to frequent. There was a brightness to his eyes that seemed to say he was on something again, but his speech was too clear and his movements too crisp for that.

I was so shocked at what was happening that I couldn't do anything more than passively resist as he pulled me out of the park and two steps across the border to a neighboring, undesirable zone.

I opened my mouth to scream, and then suddenly we weren't alone anymore. It was the same woman from the time before in the park. I would've said that she just chanced upon us, but as she came around the tree it was obvious that she was looking for something, and she didn't hesitate in the slightest when she saw the two of us.

The muscular guy had started to let go of me, moving with a suddenness that all but screamed he'd been doing something wrong, but he wasn't moving fast enough. The woman stepped in close and slammed her fist into his gut.

I'd been expecting the guy to drop like a ton of bricks, but apparently there was more to him than just steroid-grown muscles. He grunted from the blow and then lashed out with a backhand that would've taken off her head if it had landed.

Luckily she was even faster than he was. She ducked under the blow and slammed her foot into his knee. This time he didn't just grunt, he screamed out in agony as he collapsed to the ground.

I expected her to stop now that she had neutralized the threat, but instead she kicked him in the throat. I watched in shock as the man clawed at his throat in a futile effort to draw breath.

"What are you doing?"

"Depriving the military of one of their finest."

I shook my head, not understanding. The military didn't interact with the regular franchised citizens. They had their own facilities for training as well as a separate section of land carved out and stocked with all of the normal diversions.

"He can't be military if he is here."

"He wasn't military yet, but it was only a matter of time."

The woman had been calmly watching the man die, but now she turned toward me with a passion that was shocking. She grabbed my arm and shook me. "You need to go back to your dormitory and pretend like none of this ever happened. Do you understand me? Never admit to anyone that you left the green zones."

I nodded numbly, more because I knew that was what I needed to do in order to get away from her, than out of actual understanding.

She released me, and then picked up the body and hurried further down the path. It wasn't until I was back in my room with the door locked that I finally realized what about the woman had seemed so familiar.

Her face, the way she stood, the sudden violence that she had unleashed upon my attacker, it all pointed towards her being someone I'd never met before she'd saved me the first time in the park, but I couldn't get past the feeling that the cadence of her speech was exactly the same as the way my first nanny had talked.

Chapter 18

Tyrell and Jax took turns stopping by Brennan's room every few hours to inject him with morphine, and as a result, Brennan passed the rest of my shift without ever waking up. Alan showed up to relieve me right on schedule, and I went to sleep within minutes of making it back to my room.

My dreams were disturbing, an odd collage of old experiences mixed together with faces from my current life. I relived the episode where I'd nearly been raped, but this time it was Piter who was after me, and Jax was the one who saved me by killing the franchised citizen.

Everything about the dream felt odd, but it especially felt wrong for Jax to be saving me. If I'd had my preference I would have saved myself—that was a big part of why I'd spent so much time learning unarmed combat—but failing that, I would have at least preferred for Brennan to be the one saving me.

I woke feeling tired and wrung out, but when my alarm went off I forced myself out of my hammock and stumbled over to the shower. Bless Brennan for making sure that I would have a plentiful supply of hot water for as long as I stayed in the compound.

My briefings had included plenty of warnings about the deprivations I was going to be forced to endure, but regardless of what I'd thought when I jumped out of that plane, I hadn't really been ready to spend weeks between showers.

I was standing in front of my clothes wearing nothing more than a towel as I tried to decide which of my two uniforms was less filthy when someone knocked on my door. Worry over Brennan drove me to open the door despite my state of near undress.

I'd half expected to find Jax or Tyrell scowling at me, but instead it was Lexis. Even better, she came bearing gifts.

"It looks like I came just in time."

I grabbed my towel more securely as I stepped back out of the way so that she could enter. "Yeah, I guess you did. Nobody has explained how the laundry works yet, so I was just trying to choose between two uniforms that both look like they would stand up in a corner by themselves."

Lexis shook her head at me. "There's a brown linen bag in the bathroom. If you put your dirty things in it and then hang it on your doorknob before you go to bed, someone will take it to the laundry during the night. It will show back up on your doorknob within a day or two, but that doesn't help you right now."

She patted her cart as she wheeled it into my room. "Luckily I've brought something to tide you over until you can get your things cleaned."

"You didn't need to do that, Lexis."

"Yes, I did. I was the foolish old woman who tried to push that chunk of rubber further than it had ever been designed to be pushed. I nearly got Brennan killed, and if he hadn't pushed you out of the way I probably would have gotten you killed in his place."

"I appreciate the thought—I really do—but with all of the other stuff that needs to be done, I'm the last thing that you should be worrying about. Your whole crew must be killing themselves trying to get a shipment of clothes out despite the fact that you don't have any of your machines anymore."

Lexis ducked her head like a schoolgirl who'd been caught doing something she shouldn't have. "It turns out that I'm more of a fool than I realized. Tyrell probably told you that he was headed to his room to sleep when he left you with Brennan—maybe he was even planning on it when he left there—but instead he ended up in my factory building a device to keep the sewing machines running without power."

I gave her a confused look. "How is that even possible?"

"He rigged up a big metal wheel on a vertical base that lets it turn without touching the ground, and then ran a chain from the wheel to the shaft that actually powers the sewing machines. It's not smooth—the new recruits from outside of the compound who are turning the wheel can't seem to walk an even pace to save their lives—but it's working. Our seams look like they were done by a novice who'd never touched a machine before, but they still look better than the stuff I used to manage when I did it all by hand. The long and short of it is that we've got a team of three ladies on the sewing machines at all times, and the compound has a score of new residents who have no skill but that of being able to walk at something approaching an even cadence.

"Right now I've got all my girls who are not on a sewing machine cutting out pieces for more work clothes—simple stuff that we can either use here in the compound or trade to one of the other territories—but Tyrell has promised to have another three machines up and running before the end of the day tomorrow. That'll still put us behind where we were supposed to be, but not so far behind that I couldn't see my way to finishing up a few proper outfits for you."

I shook my head, but it was in astonishment rather than in disagreement. "I definitely don't deserve everything you've done for me, Lexis, but I appreciate it nevertheless."

She patted my arm and then started laying out the contents of her cart on a nearby shelf. There was another bodyguard uniform—the original one I'd worn to the meeting with Piter, now tailored so that it would fit without all the pins holding everything in place, and joined by one of the unique, broad-brimmed hats that I'd seen Jax and the other bodyguards occasionally wear—but that was just the beginning of what she'd brought. The uniform was quickly followed by several dresses of varying lengths that ranged from knee-length up to mid-thigh and some loose trousers that combined with a pair of breathable tops to provide me with workout clothes similar to what I'd seen some of Jax's men using for hand-to-hand training.

"I started the dresses before I knew we were going to have problems inside the factory. That'll teach me to put pleasure before business; I should've done a fourth uniform, but I didn't realize you hadn't been told how the laundry service works."

"I'm glad you chose to do the dresses, they're beautiful—more so than anything else I've ever owned."

As seemed to be happening more and more, that wasn't me pretending. All of the people my age had complained for years that they were being mistreated in the course of earning their franchise, but even the most vocal had accepted that that was just the way things were.

THE SOCIETY

In comparison to the people in the city—even in comparison to the people living in Brennan's compound—we'd all had it incredibly easy, but I'd never owned a dress. We'd worked only a few hours each day, which sounded like heaven to someone who was used to routinely putting in twelve-hour days, but until we earned our franchises it didn't matter how hard we worked—in public non-franchised citizens were only allowed to wear the drab utilitarian uniforms that the computerized textile factories turned out by the thousands.

The dresses that Lexis had made me were simple things in comparison to the complicated garments worn by franchised citizens, but they were well made and the material was surprisingly soft. Most importantly, they were mine. The number of times that I'd been able to say that in my life had been vanishingly small, and I'd never been able to say that about something that hadn't been a necessity.

It was hard to believe that the Skye from behind the barrier had something so basic in common with the Skye that Lexis and the rest thought I was.

Lexis patted my arm again as she turned her now-empty cart around. "No need to get sentimental, dear. You'll have this old woman crying if you're not careful."

I went to get the door for her and then realized I'd forgotten something very important.

"I don't have anything to pay you with, Lexis. I know you said I would get paid eventually, but it's never come up with Brennan."

That earned me a frown. "I told you that Brennan was paying for all of this. That hasn't changed, but if it had I'd still be making all of this as a gift to you. You just go on keeping our Brennan safe and happy and I'd gladly make you a new outfit each week and consider myself to have gotten the better end of the bargain."

It felt like I'd been punched in the stomach. I'd gotten surprisingly good at compartmentalizing my feelings towards the other people in the compound and the mission that I'd been sent to do, but every so often those conflicting priorities snuck up and ambushed me.

I could see that my response had taken Lexis by surprise, and I desperately looked for another explanation that would throw her off the scent.

"I don't think you're nearly the shrewd trader that you like to think you are. Over the last few days I haven't done a very good job of protecting Brennan or making him happy either one."

Lexis shook her head. "You youngsters are all the same—Brennan too, although I tend to forget that he's as young as he really is. You kept him safe when it mattered most, from that ogre down in the power plant. As for the other, you haven't seen the way that Brennan looks at you when you're focused on something else. If I hadn't seen it with my own eyes, I would've said that nothing but some engineering problem could make him light up like that. Do an old woman a favor and don't tell him that I was the one who let that particular cat out of the bag, but trust me when I say that Brennan is getting very attached to you."

Chapter 19

After Lexis had left my room, I spent so long staring dumbly at the door that I almost missed the start of my shift. By the time I realized how late it was, there wasn't time to put my hair up. Instead, I tied it back with a length of ribbon that Lexis had been using to keep the outfits she had brought separate, and then slipped on one of the dresses.

I knew that Jax—and probably Tyrell as well—wouldn't approve of me being out of uniform, but it seemed foolish to wear my one remaining clean guard uniform on a day when I knew that I wouldn't be leaving Brennan's bedroom. With any luck Brennan would be off the morphine and I would be able to avoid seeing either of his minders.

It wasn't until I was close enough to Brennan's room to see the two guards stationed outside that I realized it wouldn't matter whether I saw Jax today or not. The guards outside of Brennan's door were sure to tell Jax that I'd been out of uniform, but it was too late to do anything about that.

I squared my shoulders and gave each of the men a nod as they let me into Brennan's room. What I saw as I stepped through the door drove all other concerns from my mind. I'd thought it would be the next best thing to a miracle if Brennan had progressed enough to be off most of the morphine. I'd never even considered the possibility that he would be conscious and sitting up when I walked into the room, but that was exactly the sight that met my eyes.

"What are you doing? You're going to make things worse."

Brennan gave me a shaky smile. "I'm fine. Tyrell has me so immobilized from the waist to the neck that I couldn't reinjure myself even if I tried."

I shot Alan a questioning look, but he held his hands up as if to say the decision had been made without his input. "Tyrell was in here half an hour ago and he approved limited movement as long as Brennan was careful. I'm not sure that this is quite what he had in mind though."

Brennan weakly waved away the objection. "He told me not to do anything to increase my pain level. Sitting up isn't causing me any more discomfort than what I was already feeling lying down."

Alan shrugged. "Far be it from me to keep arguing with the boss. Skye, there's more morphine on that shelf. I know you don't know how to do injections, but apparently Brennan's expertise extends into this kind of thing as well. Tyrell wrote down dosages on that sheet of paper next to the morphine—your job is to keep an eye on him to make sure he doesn't overdo it, give him the morphine when he needs more, and make sure that he doesn't overdose himself, probably as a result of overdoing it. I'm past due for a date with my bunk."

Once Alan was gone, Brennan turned back towards me. "I see that Lexis found time to finish up the outfits I ordered for you."

My face went hot with embarrassment. "I'm sorry I'm not in uniform today. I figured you'd still be down for at least a few more days, and since I didn't have anything else clean to wear, I was hoping to get away with wearing my non-official clothes until the laundry had a chance to catch back up with everything I haven't been putting out for them to collect."

"You misunderstand me, Skye. That wasn't meant as a criticism. I think you look quite lovely today—even more so than normal."

I wasn't sure what the proper response was. Lexis' words from earlier were still echoing through my mind. If she was right, then Brennan's feelings for me were very much starting to mirror what I was feeling for him.

That was amazing and terrible all at once. If she was right, then things were even more complex than I'd realized. The last thing I needed was to add complexity to a situation that already had me so conflicted, but despite all of that I found myself hoping that my feelings were being reciprocated.

It was going to take a lot more than just hope though before I was going to be willing to act upon any perceived interest on his part. Even apart from the fact that I was supposed to sabotage his life's work, I had zero experience when it came to interacting with guys in a romantic sense. Back home the idea of dating had made me uncomfortable; making a pass at my boss—the guy who controlled a few dozen city blocks—was downright terrifying.

Brennan seemed to sense my uneasiness—that or maybe he felt at least a shadow of the same awkwardness. "Well, since I'm awake and at least partially lucid, how about you bring me up to speed on how things are going inside the compound?"

"I'm sorry, I wish I knew, but I haven't left this floor of the building in more than twenty-four hours. Any information I have is dreadfully out of date by now."

Brennan's smile somehow made all of the awkwardness go away. "Let's just start with what you know—it at least has the benefit of being more recent than anything I know."

"I guess you have a point there. For starters, I did talk to Lexis, and she indicated that Tyrell has them at least partially back up and running."

Brennan nodded. "He must've hooked up some kind of alternate power source to the drive shafts that power the sewing machines."

"Yeah, it sounds like he's actually using people to generate the power required to turn the drive shafts. Lexis said that he's promised to get another three sewing machines up and running very soon."

"Good. It's not a perfect solution, but it will keep things moving there while we hunt down the raw materials we'll need to create another drive belt. What about the foundry?"

"I haven't heard anything about the foundry since just after you were hurt. Tyrell and Jax kicked the rest of us out while they were working on you, so I ended up down in the foundry looking for something useful to do."

"Were you successful?"

There was a teasing tone in Brennan's voice that belied the pain I knew he had to be in. Without thinking about it, I stuck my tongue out at him. Someone like Piter would've been yelling to have his enforcers beat me unconscious, but Brennan just chuckled and then grimaced in pain.

"I was going to tell you good job—I don't think I've seen you that unguarded since you arrived—but I probably shouldn't encourage you when the results make me hurt so much."

I started to apologize, but he rolled his eyes at me. "Don't worry about it, it's my fault for teasing you in the first place. In all seriousness, what did you do while you were there?"

"There were piles of fired bricks stacked inside the cavern, so I told everyone to get started ripping the old bricks out of the furnace. I hope that's okay, it seemed like the kind of thing we couldn't screw up."

"Absolutely. I was saving that step for a time when I couldn't be around to supervise. How far did you guys get?"

Despite Brennan's words, I was still nervous. We'd had to hit the bricks pretty hard to break them up enough to get them out of the furnace. The fact that he'd asked how far we'd made it indicated that we shouldn't have finished up in just one session.

"We…ah, we got it all."

Brennan's smile got even bigger. "That's great news, Skye. I was expecting it to take a shift and a half to get that all out."

"Oh, then we weren't as far off as I was thinking we were. The day shift stayed around to help the night shift work on it, so we probably put the better part of eighteen hours into the project."

Brennan looked off into the distance, considering for several seconds, before he took an experimental breath as though testing how bad his chest was going to hurt.

"Inside the cabinet on the west wall—the taller one—there's a wheelchair. Could you please go get it?"

I put my hands on my hips and did my best impression of a crèche nanny who'd just found one of her charges misbehaving. "Yes, I'm perfectly capable of walking over and getting a wheelchair out of that cabinet, but if you think I'm going to get it so that you can leave this room, then you're still on way too much morphine."

I hadn't realized I'd started moving toward Brennan until he held up his hand to ward me off. "Tyrell said that I could determine what was and wasn't safe for me to do based on how I was feeling. I'm not kidding when I say that he's got me wired to this frame so tightly that I couldn't move if I wanted to."

"There's a reason for that. The entire right side of your chest was crushed, Brennan. I'm no doctor, but I can't believe you're even awake already, let alone wanting to move around."

Brennan was still smiling, but I could see the stubbornness that had allowed him to begin rebuilding civilization starting to manifest in his gaze. "You're right, Skye, you're not a doctor. All of the people you grew up with probably suffered from malnutrition, which means their bodies weren't operating the way they should have been. I, on the other hand, have been getting three square meals a day for years now. I'm not malnourished any more than I'm one of those useless ants who spend every hour of every day high on some substance that the human body was never meant to take in. I'll take it easy, but I need to be out there."

I was ready to keep arguing, but his comment about people from the Society being high all of the time struck too close to home. He was right—I had no real idea what the human body was capable of under normal circumstances. I'd seen military personnel injured, but they weren't a good yardstick because their bodies were chock-full of nanites.

I'd spent my early years around kids who were nanite-free and well-nourished, but the crèche nannies had been very careful to make sure that none of us got seriously injured. It boggled belief that Brennan could actually be healed enough to tour the compound, but if there was one thing I'd learned in my time in the city so far, it was not to underestimate Brennan. He was already sitting up, and Tyrell had been okay with that. Being pushed around in a wheelchair wasn't that much different than sitting motionless on a table like he was already doing.

"Okay, I'll get your wheelchair, but you'd better be right about this. Everything depends on you pulling through this."

"Yes, but if I spend too much time down here nursing my wounds then everything will come crashing down just as surely as if I'd been killed by Jerome the first day that we met."

He was talking about Piter and the others. Under other circumstances, a delay of a week or two wouldn't matter for someone who was rolling out technologies that hadn't been seen outside of the barrier for more than a century, but that wasn't the world that Brennan and his people lived in. There was a limit to how long Brennan could stall his customers, and once that limit was reached people were going to die.

I found the wheelchair and brought it over to the table as Brennan slowly turned himself so that his legs were hanging off the table. Part of me wanted to lift him all by myself. My nanite-infused muscles could easily accomplish the task, and I desperately wanted to touch him, but that would blow my cover.

It was that urge that finally made me realize just how bad my situation was. Brennan had saved my life—saved it when he'd had every reason not to. I didn't want anything to come between us, but my very presence there in his room was a lie. There was no course forward where Brennan and I ended up together. The best I could hope for was that he wouldn't hate me forever, but in order for that to happen I was going to have to betray everything that I'd arrived in the city believing.

I wasn't sure I could do that, but the thought of killing Brennan hurt me in ways I'd never been hurt before. I was stuck between a rock and a hard place with no idea how to get out.

Brennan was too focused on holding himself still so that he wouldn't be in pain to notice my internal battles, and by the time he looked up I'd pulled myself back together enough to pretend that everything was okay. Once I was sure that he hadn't overdone it just rotating on the table, I went out and asked the two guards at the door for assistance.

The two of them were just as doubtful at the prospect of moving Brennan as I'd been, but they'd had even more experience with the futility of denying him anything he wanted. Working carefully, the three of us slid Brennan off the table and got him situated inside the wheelchair, which looked like a hundred-and-fifty-year-old model that he'd had Lexis refurbish with a new seat made out of material from the textile factory.

It was obvious that Brennan was in a lot of pain, and for a moment I thought he was going to ask for more morphine, but he didn't. Maybe he knew that would be the straw that convinced me he wasn't fit to leave the room.

At some point during Alan's shift, Tyrell had added to Brennan's bandages, covering his chest so completely in white that there was no trace of visible skin left. It almost seemed pointless to cover him up with additional layers, but I wanted to make sure he didn't get chilled, so I grabbed the blanket off of his hammock and wrapped it around him as we left his room.

The first obstacle to be faced was the stairs, but none of us were foolish enough to try to carry him up them without more help. I stayed with one of the guards, a weathered black man in his early forties, while the other guard started knocking on doors looking for additional help.

A few minutes later we had four more guards, all sleepy, all in various states of undress, assembled to help carry Brennan up the stairs. I watched from the side until they'd managed to convey him up to the ground floor, and then resumed my spot behind the wheelchair so I could be the one to push him. It was obvious that all four of the new arrivals were torn between going back downstairs to catch up on their sleep and staying with Brennan to make sure he was adequately protected.

We all knew what Jax would've demanded, but Brennan gently but firmly insisted that he would be fine with just three guards. I wanted to argue with him. There was an awful lot that Jax and I hadn't been seeing eye to eye on lately. I knew that Jax wouldn't consider me an adequate guard in my current state. Even when I'd been armed and in uniform, Jax hadn't been thrilled at the idea of Brennan moving around the compound with only three of us for protection.

He was right—if not for quite the reason he thought—but this time I was inclined to agree with him. Brennan needed more protection than I could provide.

I was a heartbeat away from verbalizing my concerns when Brennan turned to me with a serious look on his face. "I know what you're thinking, Skye, but there isn't anybody else who can be spared right now. I was the one who came up with a contingency plan for this situation. All of my normal bodyguards are currently working sixteen hour days trying to make sure that nobody—inside the compound or out—decides to stage some kind of coup while I'm too injured to rally our forces."

"Do you hear what you're saying? That's all the more reason that you shouldn't be running around with only two bodyguards."

Brennan shook his head. "First of all, there are three of you—just like Jax and I agreed days ago. Second of all, given how many people we've got out on patrol right now, anyone who wants to hurt me will have only seconds before the three of you are joined by half a dozen other guards. I'm as safe as I'm ever going to be and it's vitally important that I'm seen moving around so enemies don't get any ideas."

I looked at the other two guards hoping for help, but neither of them seemed willing to argue with Brennan like Jax would have.

"Fine, but you tell us before you start hurting so we can get you back to your room without further aggravating the damage to your ribs."

Brennan held up his hand. "I solemnly swear to do exactly that."

For all that I knew Brennan was vitally important to the future of the compound, part of me had been convinced he was overstating the importance of him being out where everyone could see him. I realized just how wrong I was when Tyrell came hurrying out of the bore less than five minutes after we left the headquarters building. Either someone in the headquarters had sent a message down to the foundry, or runners had set out as soon as Brennan had been spotted.

Tyrell was obviously angry as he walked towards us. The two guards looked like they'd rather be anywhere else, and I didn't blame them, but Brennan appeared supremely unconcerned.

"What do you think you're doing?"

"Well, I had considered taking a trip down to the foundry to see how you were getting on, but given the roughness of the terrain we have to cross over, that didn't seem particularly prudent. Instead, I thought maybe I could go check on Lexis."

"You're playing a very dangerous game, Brennan. You are very well aware of the risks—I know because I explained them to you at length. Isn't there anything I can say to convince you to leave off this folly?"

Brennan made as though he was going to shrug, and then winced when his body refused to cooperate. "You're right, I'm aware of the risks—all of them—but we're running out of time."

I'd seen Tyrell disagree with Brennan several times since I'd arrived in the compound, but this time was different. It felt like there was a subtext to the conversation that I wasn't understanding. My impression of their relationship had always been that Brennan was the driving force and Tyrell was the trustworthy, competent right hand that every genius needed to make his dreams a reality.

It only lasted for an instant, but in that moment Tyrell felt like something other than the subordinate he'd always seemed before. His manner was more that of a mentor than anything else, and I found myself wondering if there was more history between the two of them than I'd suspected previously.

Even more unusual was the way that Tyrell looked up at the sky a moment later. It was as though Brennan had acknowledged more danger than just the gang leaders from the other territories.

Tyrell sighed. "Very well, you're right that it will take some of the pressure off once people have seen with their own eyes that the accident didn't kill you, but don't push so hard that you create another set of problems for yourself."

Brennan sketched a choppy salute and then the four of us were off to the textile factory.

I wasn't sure quite what to expect when we arrived. The big wheel was much as Lexis had described it, but I was surprised at just how far along construction had come on the second of the human-powered generators that Tyrell had promised her.

Brennan made as if to take over supervision of the team that was building the second wheel, but it was obvious even to me that his presence wasn't needed. If they'd been building something from scratch that might not have been the case, but the team Tyrell had sent was experienced enough that they weren't having any problems copying the design he'd used for the initial mechanism.

We stayed inside the textile factory for twenty minutes until it became obvious that even Lexis was getting antsy for us to leave so that her people would go back to focusing on their work.

After we left the textile factory, Brennan seemed content to wander about aimlessly. We visited some buildings and passed by others, but as time went on I was finally able to detect something of a pattern to our movements. Brennan behaved as though he wasn't at all concerned about the security arrangements Jax tried to keep in place around him, but he was actually being very careful to make sure that we didn't go anywhere too full of people unless there was a patrol there at the same time.

It was ingenious. A warlord like Piter never would've circulated among the inhabitants of his territory without at least a dozen guards. That went a long ways towards guaranteeing their safety, but tended to increase alienation felt by the rank-and-file inhabitants of their section of the city.

Brennan, on the other hand, was taking great pains to appear approachable and confident, while also minimizing the amount of danger he was exposing himself to. He was once again walking a very thin line in an effort to avoid one problem without causing another.

By the time that we'd been out for an hour, I could see that the trip was starting to take its toll on Brennan. He was bearing up under the effort better than I would've expected for someone without my advantages, but I felt a wave of relief as we approached the far end of the compound and I realized we would soon be able to turn around and head back to the headquarters building.

As we exited another high-rise building that had been converted over primarily to growing foodstuffs, the remnants of a twelve-story burnt-out shell of a building caught my eye.

"What do you use that one for, Brennan?"

"Hmm? Oh, that. We use it mostly as a source of raw materials. Originally the compound walls didn't include that particular building, but we recently started running low on the structural steel we need to feed into the foundry. That was one of our big projects last month. We went room to room inside the building to make sure it was completely unoccupied, and then we extended the walls out so that they brought the building inside our secure perimeter."

"How much steel are we going through? I wouldn't have believed you could melt down so much of that building in such a short time."

Brennan shook his head. "It's hard to see from here, but big chunks of the superstructure have decayed to the point where they collapsed into the center of the building. The inside is a real mess, which creates other problems for us. It's hard to know whether we're better off trying to clean out the interior first, or if that's just going to result in the upper floors caving in on us. If I had my way, we would leave that building alone until we can take it down with cranes, but Tyrell was right to push for that to be the one we brought inside the perimeter.

"All the other candidates were in much better shape, which would've made them easier to tear down, but it also would have meant evicting the people who were already living there. There are risks with what we decided to do, but going this way generates a lot less ill will among the rest of the people in our territory."

I mulled over his answer for several seconds. "You really are something, you know? I think most other men in your position would view the area outside the compound as nothing more than a buffer between them and their enemies. You, on the other hand, actually have guards out there trying to keep the peace and protect those people."

"In all fairness, my reasons aren't completely altruistic. We recruit from the people outside the compound. It's easy to think of the investment in machinery and infrastructure as being the most important undertaking that we're involved in right now, but that would be a mistake. It's just as critical that we continue to develop the human capital side of the equation.

"Half of our problem over the last few weeks hasn't been in deficiencies in equipment or machinery, it's been failures on the part of the people manning the equipment. I'd give just about anything right now to have a school up and running, but we just can't afford it yet. It's far more efficient to train people only on the tasks they deal with on a day-to-day basis."

I nodded. "But then they have such a narrow focus, they can't see how all the pieces fit together."

"Right, which ultimately just creates more work for the few people I do have who are capable of seeing the big picture. It's one more piece that has to be juggled at the same time we worry about what the other territories are busy doing."

As we'd been talking, we'd continued forward and we were now less than a dozen yards from the shell of the building that had caught my eye. I started to turn Brennan's wheelchair back the direction we'd come from, but he stopped me.

"Did any of you hear that?"

I exchanged looks with the two guards and then shook my head. "No, what was it?"

"I'm not sure, it almost sounded like a child."

I tried to remember if I'd seen any children during my time inside the compound. I didn't think so, but that didn't necessarily mean anything. I was starting to realize that only a fraction of the compound's population lived inside of the headquarters building. Dozens upon dozens of people worked farms on the upper floors of the buildings which hadn't yet been torn down to make way for new construction. For the most part, the farmers seemed to eat and sleep on the floors where they worked.

It didn't seem like much of an existence to me—at least not compared to daily warm showers and food that I didn't have to cook myself—but I couldn't entirely blame them for not wanting to climb fifteen or twenty flights of stairs multiple times per day. The fact that Brennan had managed to get running water up to all of the farm levels meant that it wasn't strictly necessary for many of those farmers to mix with the rest of the inhabitants of the compound.

"Is that even possible? Do we have kids inside the compound?"

Brennan nodded. "Not many—we don't actively recruit anyone younger than fifteen and we don't tend to get a lot of recruits with kids joining up—but we do get some, and the compound has been here long enough that people are starting to get married and have kids of their own. This building is a restricted area—it's too dangerous even for most of the adults—but it's entirely possible that someone felt like that was all the more reason they wouldn't be bothered out here."

If any other seventeen-year-old had told me he was concerned there were kids using a condemned building as their own personal playground, I probably would've laughed, but I wasn't even tempted to do so when it was Brennan making the statement. He peered at the building, moving his head back and forth in an effort to locate where the sound was coming from, but didn't seem to be having any more luck than I was.

"Can you wheel me around the side of the building, please?"

Williams, the older guard, put his hand on my arm when I started to comply with Brennan's request. "I don't think it's a good idea for us to get that close to the wall—not when there are only three of us to keep an eye on him."

We were close enough now to the building that I thought I could hear the same thing that Brennan had heard. He was right, it sounded like a child was in pain and crying.

I could see Brennan getting ready to dig his heels in, but I put my hand on his shoulder. "He's right, Brennan. We can't afford to have you hurt if the building comes down, and there's no reason to get any closer to the compound wall than we have to. Let's head back to the headquarters building. Once we get back there, you can assign a squad of guards to come check out the building."

Brennan turned his head to look at me and I could see his desire to help warring with the common sense that told him we were right. "All right, I won't force the issue and make you guys push me over to the other side of the building, but could one of you go check on it now? I would hate to send a squad out here and have them arrive ten minutes too late to save whoever's trapped inside the building."

Williams and the other guard both obviously didn't like that idea much better, but I was afraid if they dug in their heels that Brennan would change his mind and say we all had to go.

"I'll go. It only makes sense, since I'm the one who's going to be least able to protect you if something happens."

Brennan frowned. "Absolutely not, Skye. This is silly—we'll all go and everything will be just fine."

Williams still didn't look happy, but he motioned for the other guard to go check out the noise. We watched as the younger guard disappeared around the corner of the building, and then Brennan suddenly sat up straighter in his wheelchair.

"Something just happened."

I started forward, but Williams grabbed my arm before I could take a second step. "No, I'll go. You take Brennan back and get another team headed this direction."

THE SOCIETY

I opened my mouth, planning on arguing, but Williams was already moving towards the corner of the building. There was no way to stop him unless I was either willing to leave Brennan on his own, or wheel him closer to the potential danger.

I had just taken a step back towards Brennan when a strange hissing sound brought me around just in time to see an arrow take Williams through the throat. A second later more than a dozen men stepped out of the shadows inside the building.

Only two of them had rifles, but all of them were armed with some kind of melee weapon. There were too many of them to fight. My only option was to try to get Brennan deeper inside the compound in the hopes we would stumble onto a patrol before the enforcers caught up to us.

I grabbed Brennan's wheelchair, spun it around, and took off like a shot back towards the north.

I should have been faster than any normal human, but the forty-pound wheelchair that had seemed like a minor burden at walking speeds was suddenly a much bigger deal now that I was trying to push it and run at the same time. I only made it half a dozen steps before something crashed into the back of my leg with enough force to slam me face first into the ground.

Brennan's wheelchair hit a pothole in the road and sent him sprawling onto the blacktop. I scrambled back to my feet and spun around just in time to block a knife that otherwise would have taken me in the ribs.

My right leg was a solid mass of pain, but it still seemed structurally sound enough to provide me the base I needed. I swept my attacker's right leg, and then used my hold on his arm to destroy his elbow as he headed towards the ground.

The entire exchange had taken less than a second, but it still bought the enforcer's companions time to close with me, and the next two attacked at the same time. The one on the right was wielding a short sword, while the one on the left was swinging some kind of collapsible baton.

Even my nanites wouldn't allow me to regenerate a severed limb, so I prioritized the attacker on the right. He came at me with a low slashing attack, so I stepped forward to put myself inside the arc of his swing. He tried to backpedal and buy himself room to get his weapon back in play, but my nanite-infused muscles propelled me forward with the speed he couldn't hope to match.

I slammed the point of my elbow into the top of his throat and then spun around hoping that I'd been fast enough to avoid being clubbed in the back of the head by the second enforcer. I caught a flash of motion out of the corner of my eye, but even with the adrenaline in my system causing my nanites to take up station along my spinal cord, there just wasn't time to avoid the end of the baton as it slammed into my collarbone.

The pain as the slender bone that connected my right shoulder to the rest of my skeletal system shattered was excruciating, but I threw myself forward and slammed my forehead into the baton-wielder's face. I felt a moment of satisfaction as the third man collapsed to the ground, but I'd once again turned my back on the main body of enforcers.

The sound of footsteps behind me was all the warning I got, but I made the most I could out of what I had. My right arm was useless now. I spun to my left hoping I was fast enough to beat my next attacker, only to gasp a split second later as a knife entered my stomach and skidded off one of my vertebrae.

I slammed my knee into the fourth guy's crotch, but the guy behind him hit me in the chest with a rusty mace and I hit the ground. I meant to bounce right back up and continue fighting, but I was having a hard time breathing. No matter how hard I tried, my body refused to obey my frantic orders. I tried to roll out of the way of the kick I saw coming, but the enforcers had me surrounded by that point and there was nowhere else for me to go.

I counted four kicks before someone connected with my head and I lost consciousness.

Chapter 20

I probably should have died—I would have if not for my nanites. We were far enough off of the beaten path that nobody found me, but I woke up just as the sun started to go down.

For the briefest of moments I was confused by my surroundings, but then everything came rushing back. Williams and the other guard were both dead, and when I'd last seen Brennan he'd been on the ground, vulnerable and quite possibly dying from having his ribs re-injured.

I pulled myself up to my feet, and then almost fell back down as a wave of dizziness assaulted me. My nanites had managed to fuse my bones back into place so that I could use all of my limbs, and they'd repaired enough of the rest of the damage to allow me to regain consciousness, but I was still probably suffering from a concussion.

I took in my surroundings, and nearly threw up as I turned my head. Williams' body was still lying there where he'd fallen after being shot, but his rifle was gone. It was a good bet that the other guard was just around the corner, but I was too weak to drag either of them back to the headquarters building, and there was no point searching for him when I already knew that Piter's people had grabbed his rifle.

Brennan's wheelchair was still lying on its side, but there was no sign of the enforcers I'd taken down—no corpses to prove that I'd put up a fight—and there was no sign of Brennan.

The trip back to the headquarters building was a nightmare. There were several times when I thought I was going to fall over and puke my guts out, but the further I got away from the scene of the ambush the better I felt.

As I walked, I checked myself over. My dress was ripped and dirty, but all of the blood on it looked like it belonged to the guys who'd jumped me. That was good because it meant that I wouldn't have to explain away stab wounds that had healed in a fraction of the time they should have required.

My face was puffy—apparently the nanites had been too busy dealing with more severe wounds to get to the surface damage—but that was the least of my worries. I needed a reason why the enforcers who'd attacked us would leave me alive, a reason better than just sloppiness.

They should have taken me along with Brennan. If they were really smart, they would have taken Williams' and the other guy's bodies too. That would have left Tyrell and Jax with no real idea what had happened to us.

I tried to remember how many enemies I'd been up against there at the end, but it was all too fuzzy for me to be sure. There were flashes of things that were crystal clear, but the blows to my head had rendered most of the experience unusable.

Maybe they'd simply brought too few people to get the job done. They would have needed a couple of guys to carry Brennan, and another two guys to retrieve anyone I'd killed or severely injured. I remembered crushing the throat of at least one guy.

I stumbled back to the headquarters building as Tyrell arrived—obviously returning from the bore.

"Skye! What happened?"

"It's Brennan. We went to the condemned building on the south side of the compound, and we got jumped. There were enforcers who'd been hiding inside of it—they lured us close by making it sound like a child had been trapped inside."

Jax had also arrived while I was talking, and his face went white as he realized what had happened. He started to run towards the secure entrance—obviously planning on rounding up a group of guards to go after Brennan—but then stopped as he realized that leaving would mean he wouldn't hear the rest of my debriefing.

Tyrell followed my gaze. "Go get your men—I'll find out the rest of what you need to know."

Jax didn't need to be told twice. I watched him leave, and then realized that I was having trouble maintaining my focus. By the time I came back to myself, Jax had disappeared and there wasn't any way to know for sure how long I'd zoned out, but it was long enough that Tyrell noticed.

"Are you okay, Skye?"

"I—I took a pretty bad blow to the head, but I think I'll be okay. I'm just having a hard time keeping my thoughts headed down a single track. That doesn't matter though. They have Brennan. We need to get him back."

"Who has him? Do you have any idea who attacked you?"

I shook my head slowly, relieved that I didn't feel an overpowering urge to throw up. "They were armed, and most of them were big. I think a couple of them had rifles, but mostly they looked like enforcers from the other territories. They took out Williams with an arrow. No...first they killed the other guy. They waited until he was out of sight around the corner of the building, and then they took him out. Williams was next so that there wouldn't be any gunshots, and then they rushed Brennan and me.

"I tried to get him out of there, but the wheelchair was too slow. They hit me with a rock—knocked me down—and then it was too late to run. I killed one of them—I think I crushed his throat. I might have managed to get another couple of hits in, but there were too many of them. They knocked me to the ground and then the last thing I remember is being kicked in the head.

"I'm sorry, Tyrell. I tried to save him. Jax was right—we never should have let Brennan run around without more cover. I didn't even have a weapon."

Tyrell shook his head. "This isn't your fault, Skye. You did the best you could. To be honest, none of us thought that Brennan was really in danger inside of the compound—not that kind of danger, at least—not even Jax. Our precautions were mostly meant to deal with a disgruntled worker or a single agent from one of the other territories. The compound was supposed to be secure."

"It's still my fault. I should have been armed. I need a rifle—need to be a part of the rescue mission."

"No, Skye, that would be a very bad idea. You're obviously hurt and you've probably got a concussion. Jax and the others will handle this—we'll pull people off of the barricades if we have to. The last thing that Brennan would want right now is for you to risk your life for no reason."

He'd gently grabbed my arm while he'd been talking, and was pulling me in the direction of the secure entrance to the headquarters building, but I twisted my body and tore my arm free.

"No. With your blessing or without it, I'm going along."

The sound of a slide being racked behind me brought me around to find that Jax and Alan had just exited the building and Jax had his weapon pointed at me.

"I'm sorry if I'm not giving you enough credit, Skye, but you aren't going anywhere. At this point all we know is that Brennan is missing and you're the last person to have seen him. You're going to go down to your room and let Tyrell check your injuries while we go investigate the scene of the attack."

The desperate worry that had been driving me up until that moment didn't disappear, but it slid into the back seat as I stared coldly at Jax. The distance was right on the edge of doable. My adrenals were dumping adrenaline into my system by the bucketful, and I was going to be inhumanly fast. There was at least a sixty-percent chance that I could close and neutralize Jax before he could get an aimed shot off.

The tightly-controlled part of me that had sworn I would never be a victim again, that I would always maintain control of my environment, was screaming at me to do it, to take him down and then tear through the rest of the compound if that was what it took to get what I wanted. It was a seductive song, but I forced it out of my mind. Beating Jax to within an inch of his life wouldn't save Brennan.

There was only one other card left for me to play. I turned to Tyrell. "Please, this is a big mistake. I need to be out there helping bring Brennan back."

He considered for several seconds before shaking his head. "No, Jax is right. You need to be patched up, and it would be foolish for us to put a weapon in your hands before figuring out what really happened. I'm sorry, Skye, but you're going to have to let Jax and the others do their job."

I was shaking from the effort of overruling my desire to lash out, but I bowed my head in surrender. There wasn't any other choice—not really. If I wanted Brennan saved as quickly as possible, then I was going to have to let them lock me up.

"Fine. Confine me to my quarters, but I didn't have anything to do with him disappearing—I nearly got my head bashed in trying to protect him."

Jax looked like he wanted to gun me down right there and avoid the problems he'd been convinced I was going to create from the first day he'd seen me, but he just motioned for me to head inside.

"You'd better be telling the truth—about everything that's happened since the first day you arrived—or I'll execute you myself."

Chapter 21

Five minutes later I was sitting in my room wincing as Tyrell prodded the bone-deep bruises that were all that was left of the broken bones after several hours of my nanites doing their thing. He concluded the examination by using a small mirror to reflect light into my eyes.

"You're fortunate that you have such a hard head. You seem to have a mild concussion, but I think you're going to be okay once you've had a couple of days to rest."

I didn't respond. Jax and Tyrell could lock me up, but they couldn't make me like it, not while Brennan was out there needing every person we had to rescue him.

"If you can stomach it, you should probably get some food into you. You're hungry, aren't you?"

The truth was that I was famished. Lexis' visit earlier that morning had resulted in me missing breakfast, and I'd been unconscious for both lunch and dinner. I didn't want to give Tyrell the satisfaction of being right, but I also knew that I needed to keep my strength up. The nanites had been forced to gather building materials from elsewhere in my body to make their most recent round of repairs, and if I wasn't careful to keep up with the rate at which they were cannibalizing the rest of my body, I could end up in real trouble.

I nodded fractionally and Tyrell left to get me something from the cafeteria. As my door swung shut I confirmed what I'd been suspecting—a pair of guards had been stationed outside of my room to make sure that I stayed put.

It took Tyrell longer than I expected to return, but when he did, he was carrying a big loaf of bread so hot that it was still steaming. Back home plain bread would have been some kind of punishment, but I was so hungry I didn't even care that it didn't have any butter on it. I ripped big chunks off of the loaf and stuffed them into my mouth as quickly as I could chew and swallow.

Tyrell watched me eat for several seconds before moving away from the wall where he'd been leaning.

"There is a lot more to you than meets the eye, Skye. Don't think I haven't started noticing some discrepancies where you're concerned."

"I don't know what you're talking about."

"Don't you? I'm overjoyed that you saved Brennan that first day outside of the pipe room, but nobody your age should be able to take down someone twice their size that easily."

"I never said that it was easy."

That earned me a cold smile. "You didn't have to. I talked to Beth about what happened. She said that you moved like—and I quote—'greased lightning'."

I shrugged, moving gingerly to maintain the illusion that I hadn't yet recovered from the beating I'd just received.

"I have to be fast. When you're my size, everyone is bigger and stronger than you. If I don't move quick and make sure that my first blow or two counts, then I don't stand a chance."

I smiled as I said that, trying to lighten the mood, but Tyrell didn't return my grin.

"I didn't just talk to Beth, Skye. Jax tested your skills out a couple of days ago and is convinced that you were holding back on him. He says that there's something about your fighting style that reminds him of something, but he hasn't been able to place it quite yet. Don't worry though, Jax is like a pit bull once he has ahold of something like this. He'll eventually figure out where you learned how to fight."

I was still debating the best way to respond when Jax entered without knocking and saved me from having to answer. Jax looked at me and frowned.

"If you're through with her, we should go talk."

Tyrell shook his head. "She's not going anywhere, so even if your fears prove right and it turns out that she was behind the abduction, she still won't be able to get word out to whoever she's working for. Go ahead and report—her reaction may just give us a clue as to her real intentions."

Jax still didn't look happy, but he nodded. The line of succession inside of a group like this was rarely very cut and dried, but apparently Tyrell had the lines of power all sewed up.

"It doesn't look good, Tyrell. We found the spot where the ambush occurred. The wheelchair was pretty beat up, and there were blood spots where they took down our people. I've got a team keeping an eye on the building, but I can't believe that they would take Brennan unless they figured they had a way back out of the compound—probably the same way they got in. I've got two more teams walking the perimeter of the compound, but I can't imagine that they'll find anything."

Tyrell pursed his lips. "No, I expect you're right. Our standing patrols and guard posts would have noticed if someone had cut a hole through the compound fence. The only logical explanation is that there's some kind of under-ground passage accessible by way of that particular building.

"I truly wish that some kind of map had survived all of these years—knowledge of all of the tunnels that crisscross the city would be invaluable, but I suppose there isn't any use asking for things that we know we can't have. The real question is where they'll come back up. If their tunnel runs all of the way outside of our territory then we'll never track them down."

Jax had been pacing, but now he stopped and stuck his head outside of my room. "Alan, get teams of two guards each headed out to the guard posts on the outer edges of our territory, I want teams walking the perimeter looking for anywhere a group of people could use to get past the barricade. Make sure the guards walking the perimeter go in teams of at least three, and that they keep their eyes peeled—the last thing we need right now is to lose a bunch more people trying and failing to stop the grab team if they haven't already made it out of our territory."

Tyrell had been lost in thought—his fingers tapping on his leg—while Jax talked to Alan, but now he looked up.

"That's a good start, but we should get someone to take a read on each of our neighbors before we do anything that can be noticed from the other side of the barricades. If any of the other territories are functioning under a higher state of readiness than normal, that will give us a pretty good idea which of the local despots ordered the grab. Let's go—I'll take a read on one of the neighboring territories myself."

I stood, desperately hoping against hope that they would let me go out there and help, but Jax brought his rifle up against his shoulder in one smooth motion.

"If you take another step, I'll shoot you myself."

Chapter 22

The next twelve hours crawled by. Despite the risk involved in opening my door, I only made it an hour before desperation for some kind of update drove me to do so. By that point I'd conjured up ten thousand different fates for Brennan, and each of them was worse than the one before.

The doors weren't made to lock from the outside—apparently none of the doors in the compound were or Jax would have convinced Tyrell to lock me up somewhere more secure—but if Jax had left orders for my guards to shoot me on sight, I was lucky that the two he'd assigned me weren't as cold-blooded as he was.

They brought their rifles up and trained them on me, but when I made no motion to step over the threshold to my room, they didn't actually pull their triggers. The one on the left, a massive red-headed guy whose rifle looked like some kind of toy in his bulky arms, scowled at me.

"You're not supposed to be out here."

"I know—I'm sorry—but I just have to know what's happening with Brennan. Have they found him yet? It's bad enough that I can't be out there helping look for him, it's a hundred times worse not even knowing what's going on."

"I said get back into your room."

I backed up, hands still in the air. "You guys have to know something—all I'm asking is for you to keep me in the loop."

Both guards moved forward, the smaller one covering the redhead as he grabbed the handle to my door and pulled it closed.

"If you open that door again, we'll shoot you."

The words were faint with the heavy metal door between us, but there was no mistaking the tone to them. I'd just burned up any credit with my captors.

I made a good-faith effort to obey, but things didn't get any easier as time passed. An hour or two later I yelled through the door, asking them if they'd heard anything else. All I got back in exchange was curses. I tried again after another hour or so, and this time someone slammed the butt of their rifle against my door.

My money was on the redhead again. He was going to ruin his rifle before he would put a hole in the door, but there wasn't any guarantee that he would stop at threats and yelling. I debated egging him on in the hopes of forcing some kind of confrontation, but as badly as I wanted to do just that, I couldn't come up with a good reason to act on the urge.

In close quarters, with the element of surprise on my side, there was a very good chance that I could take both of them out, but all that would do was make Jax positive that I was involved in the grab. I would be free, but I'd be smack dab in the middle of hostile territory, surrounded by guards who were on high alert, and completely without the resources I would need to stage any kind of rescue for Brennan.

I locked my door, yelled through the metal one last time that I wanted to help—or at least to know what was going on—and then forced myself to lie down in my hammock. It was late enough that I should have been asleep, but I knew I wouldn't be able to nod off. Instead, I was conserving my energy and giving my nanites a chance to finish repairing the damage I'd sustained when Brennan had been kidnapped.

When I finally heard a knock on my door hours later, it felt like days had passed, but the alarm clock in my room told a different story.

"Who is it?"

"Alan. I've brought you something to eat—can you unlock the door, please?"

I'd been hoping for Tyrell, but I should have known that Brennan's number two wouldn't have the time to come visit me while he was trying to figure out which of the neighboring warlords had Brennan. I padded over to the door and unlocked it.

"I would have expected Tyrell to give you the master key before sending you here."

Alan had a tray full of food balanced in one hand. He nodded as he waited for me to back up far enough that I couldn't be any kind of threat.

"They did, but it didn't seem polite to just unlock it without at least giving you a chance to answer the door first. I brought dinner and Tyrell's apology for not getting you something to eat hours ago."

As he set the tray down on the floor just inside of my room, I nearly made some kind of wisecrack about the danger of letting me eat food down here where I'd just attract cockroaches, but there wasn't time for that.

"What do you know, Alan? Have they figured out where Brennan is yet? Is Jax putting together a rescue mission?"

He looked at me hesitantly. He probably didn't have explicit orders not to talk to me, but it didn't take a genius to know that Jax thought I was the reason Brennan had been captured. There were plenty of reasons for him not to trust me, but there was one reason for him to believe me.

He'd been there when Brennan had stepped in front of that belt to save me. He'd seen how badly it had shaken me up, and he'd watched as I did everything I could to care for Brennan when he'd been unconscious.

I looked him in the eyes and willed him to see just how worried I was about Brennan.

"It's—it's not good, Skye. We've got a team inside of the building looking for the tunnel that they used to get in and out of the compound, but so far we haven't found anything. We'll find it eventually, but it could take days—days that Brennan might not have."

I started pacing, desperate to come up with a solution. "There hasn't been any kind of ransom demand then? What about the efforts to dig up a way in and out of our territory?"

"No ransom demands yet. We've found half a dozen different spots where people could have crossed over. We already know about a couple, but we had trustworthy people stationed there watching to see who used them."

"How is that possible?"

"The city is riddled with tunnels. Everybody knows it, we just don't know where to find most of them, or how many there really are. Brennan had people tasked with identifying the smuggling routes, but a lot of the time it's our own people who are the most eager to keep that kind of stuff hidden. Smuggling is profitable for both sides of the operation. Tyrell and Jax put the screws on some people we knew had to be involved in the unsanctioned activities on our side of the border and that is the only reason that we found the paths we did, but everyone is swearing that they didn't have anything to do with Brennan's capture."

"Which is exactly what they'd do if Jax was torturing them. If they admit to something like that they'll be dead within the hour."

Alan nodded. "Yeah."

"So what are Tyrell and Jax going to do? They aren't just going to sit around and hope for a ransom demand, are they?"

"I don't think so. The jury is still out. All of the territories that border us were on high alert by the time you got back here."

"They're all involved?"

"That or they were just tipped off by whoever grabbed Brennan. The territory to the north of us—the one controlled by a gang called the Muertos—seems to be the most edgy though. Jax thinks that's where we should start. Either they have Brennan or they know that they are the most vulnerable."

"So what, he's just going to lead a group in and start killing people until he's convinced that Brennan isn't there?"

Alan refused to meet my eyes, but he nodded. "We don't have many options, Skye. If we just sit here without doing anything, then we look weak. We can't afford that—not right now, not when we don't have Brennan. It's not ideal, but going into the Muertos' territory and executing the entire gang will make things better for an awful lot of people."

"And it could get Brennan killed. A rescue operation doesn't work unless you've got solid information regarding where the hostage is being held, and even then it's a long shot."

"Like I said, we don't have any choice."

It hit me all of a sudden. All of the pieces that hadn't been making sense clicked into place.

"There isn't going to be a ransom demand, Alan. This was never about extorting guns or technology out of us. Someone predicted that Jax and Tyrell would do exactly what they are about to do. They don't want Brennan, not really—they just want to push us into taking down our neighbors. Grabbing Brennan was just the push that started the dominos falling."

Alan looked at me strangely. "How would you know that, Skye?"

"Because it's the only thing that makes sense. Tyrell and Jax are going at this all wrong. They should be trying to identify the territory that looks least like a threat, the one that they would leave for last. If they go in after the Muertos, all they'll be doing is weakening our forces at precisely the time when we can least afford to lose people. One of our other neighbors is massing forces at our border so that they can move in and take us down as soon as our people are worn out from fighting the Muertos."

I moved toward Alan, planning on shaking him if that was what it took to make him listen, but the guards behind him—including the redhead who'd given me such a hard time nearly twenty-four hours earlier—brought their weapons the rest of the way up and trained them on me. I stopped, teeth grinding at the fact that after everything I'd learned, after all of the training and the nanites, I was still helpless, still unable to make a difference when it mattered most.

"Please, Alan. You have to tell Tyrell and Jax. I'm not a spy, I don't know anything more than what you've told me, but it's the only logical explanation for all of this. Holding Brennan hostage is a losing proposition for our neighbors. Brennan has been trading them guns and ammo at an incredibly favorable rate of exchange. The longer things continue on as they are, the stronger they get in relation to everyone else on *their* borders.

"Nothing Piter or any of the others could hope to get out of taking Brennan is enough to justify losing their ongoing access to our guns—nothing but a chance to take over our territory altogether. They don't care about the textiles factory or the farms, or anything else, they want the ability to make more guns and guarantee themselves an infinite supply of ammunition. If Jax and Tyrell go in against the wrong target, they'll be handing our territory and everything Brennan has been working for over to whoever is behind the grab."

Alan had been slowly backing away the entire time I'd been talking. He was at the threshold now, still shaking his head.

"Is this why you were sent here? So you could prep for the kidnapping and then sow doubt into our ranks? Is that the last piece of your mission, to paralyze us while Brennan is worked over for the knowledge inside of his head?"

"No, Alan. I'm on your side, I'm—"

He cut me off with a gesture and then shut the door before I could cross the distance between us. I put my ear up to the door and listened as he walked away.

They were all looking in the wrong place, and I was the only one who had the tools necessary to save Brennan, Lexis and everyone else inside of the compound. I just had to be willing to pay the price and betray my Society along the way.

Chapter 23

I knew that time was short, but that didn't stop me from stripping out of my ruined dress and showering. Brennan could already be dead, and if he wasn't, every minute counted, but I couldn't pull off my plan looking like I'd just been beaten to within an inch of my life.

Once I was clean, I dressed in my last clean guard uniform and ate some of the food that Alan had left for me—not enough to slow me down, but enough to give my nanites something other than my muscles and connective tissue to break down. Then there was nothing left to do but hope that the redhead hadn't gotten to the end of his shift while I was showering.

I got right up next to my door and called out. "Please tell me that Alan took my concerns to Tyrell! I'm just as worried about Brennan as the rest of you."

It took the redhead exactly one second to cross the hall and slam the butt of his rifle into my door. A fraction of a second later I threw my door open with every ounce of my nanite-infused strength. Timing was everything. I needed to get him while his weight was still shifted forward, before he recovered and set himself.

I could probably match up with him on even footing just based on pure muscle power, but I couldn't keep up when it came to weight. Luckily I didn't have to.

I stepped to the side and pulled my door open as he fell inward towards my room. I couldn't directly oppose someone with as much inertia as he had, so I didn't even try. Instead, I cupped my hand behind his neck and gave him a strong tug just before I blew past him.

I heard the redhead's rifle hit the ground a second before he ran face first into the door jamb I'd just pulled him towards, but I didn't have time to finish him off yet. I shot across the hallway as the second guard struggled to get his weapon up, but adrenaline was pouring into my system and my nanites had turned me into something superhuman.

I grabbed the barrel of the smaller guard's gun and slammed the butt of his rifle back into him with enough force to snap his collarbone. He opened his mouth to scream out in pain, but I slammed my fist into the base of his neck and he went down in a boneless heap as I spun around and went back to deal with the redhead.

The bigger guard was nearly as tough as he thought he was, but even he needed a second to adjust from a collision like the one he'd just experienced. My job was to make sure that he didn't get that second.

I hit him with a palm strike to the stomach, knocking the wind out of him, and then launched a rising elbow into his chin as he doubled over from the pain of the first strike. I purposefully pulled the blow—he'd been a jerk, but I didn't actually want to kill him. Even so, the shock transmitted up through his teeth into his brain put his lights out.

I grabbed one of the rifles and then loaded my vest up with all of the ammunition the pair had been carrying before liberating a double-edged knife that slid nicely into the top of my boot. The easy part of my mission was over—things were only going to get more risky with every passing second, but there was no other way to know for sure where Brennan was being held.

I hadn't been in the compound for very long, but I'd seen a few female guards. None of them had been assigned to guard Brennan directly, but so far I'd counted two who guarded the headquarters building and therefore lived down on the secure level. One of them was even roughly my height and coloring. It wasn't much to work with, but it would just have to be enough.

I approached the guard post just inside the doors with my head down, rifle pointed at the ground, but fidgeting with it as though troubleshooting a problem with my sling. The adrenaline cursing through my system had my nanites on high alert. It was the only thing that gave me even a sliver of a chance of success, but it meant that my approach to the two guards seemed to take forever.

The closer guard, a skinny blond guy only a few years older than me, challenged me when I was still five steps away from the two of them. I sprang into action without hesitation and slammed the butt of my rifle into his temple a split second before he would've been able to get a shot off.

My rifle was out of position to deal with the second guard, so I spun around and slammed my heel into his ribs with enough force that I heard his ribs crack. He collided with the wall hard enough that he bounced back in my direction as I stepped forward and slammed my forearm into the side of his neck.

He dropped to the ground a split-second later, unconscious but still breathing despite the damage to his ribs. I slipped out the door fully aware that I had only minutes—possibly even just seconds—before someone would find the guards I'd taken out and raise an alarm.

Every instinct in my body screamed at me to head directly toward the compound wall, but escaping wouldn't be enough to save Brennan. I needed intelligence, intelligence that I could only get from one place. I headed straight towards the bore.

I was moving at something only slightly less than a dead run—as fast as I felt like I could get away with if I didn't want to draw attention to myself—but it still seemed to take forever to get down to where I'd left my transmitter. I was desperately worried that it wouldn't be there when I arrived, but as soon as I saw it that fear was replaced by worries that the frequency wasn't being monitored anymore.

I turned the transmitter on and felt my knees go weak when I saw the green light that indicated the transmitter was working as it was supposed to.

"This is Skinwalker calling Home Base, come in, Home Base."

"This is Home Base, you're a go, Skinwalker. What's your report?"

"There's no time for that. I need you to pull up satellite feeds for the last twenty-four hours—give me everything we've got from anything sitting above the city right now."

The bored voice on the other end of the transmission suddenly sounded worried. I'd just gone completely off script.

"That's not something authorized by your mission profile. I'm going to have to get approval from someone higher up before I can do that, over."

The girl who'd been convinced that the Society was the highest good in the world would have simply waited patiently regardless of the danger involved in doing so. The fact that I wasn't willing to do so was a clear sign—to me at least—of just how far I'd traveled since jumping out of that plane.

"No! There isn't time for that. The Citizen-President told me my mission was the most important operation being undertaken by our Society. That means I have authorization to ask for any resources that I think might improve my chances of success.

"I have only minutes to get back to the surface or my cover is blown. Get me the damn satellite feeds right now or you'll be answering to the Citizen-President for having sabotaged my mission."

There were a couple of seconds of shocked silence and then the guy on the other end of the line cleared his throat. "I've got them up now, but if you're wrong it's your head—not mine. What do you need?"

"Approximately forty-four hours ago a group of four individuals were attacked along the southern edge of Brennan's compound. One of the four was abducted by the group and presumably taken back inside the building. I'm betting that they traveled underground for some distance before surfacing, and it is vitally important that you figure out where they went."

I could hear keys clicking as the technician input search parameters. "Okay, I've found the attack. Are you sure you don't have anything else for me to go on?"

"Just that they had to have gone underground, and that they wouldn't be staying down there for long. They'll be headed to one of the neighboring territories to meet back up with their boss."

At least I hoped that was the case. It was always possible that they were from a territory even further away, but that didn't feel like the right fit for the situation. If someone from further away had grabbed Brennan, the odds were that they wouldn't have said anything to Piter or the rest of the warlords who shared a border with us.

"Okay, I've got the computers looking for appearances of the same number of individuals where some of them are injured and being carried by the others, but you're asking for it to search a big area. The computer can do it—and quickly—but it's going to take me some time to run through the false positives and make sure that they aren't the ones you're looking for."

I wanted to swear, but instead I closed my eyes and tried to think. "Tell it to prioritize matches outside of Brennan's compound, but still inside of his territory, and start with the infrared data from just after the sun started to go down. If they've got a tunnel all of the way from their territory into the compound then they probably wouldn't have settled for a simple grab—not when they could have easily used it to move an army inside the compound. That would have let them kill everyone inside here before we...before Brennan could muster any kind of effective response. My bet is that they came up in his territory and had to hoof it over to whatever hole they used to get inside of Brennan's territory."

I was praying that the analyst on the other end of the transmission hadn't heard my slip. I was playing the role of an operative of the Society, someone fully committed to her mission. The person I needed him to believe I was would never identify with Brennan and the others inside of the compound. I didn't know what I was any more—not for sure—but I was no longer the kind of person anyone from the Society would be helping if they really understood what I'd become.

If I had been, I wouldn't be risking everything to save Brennan.

"Okay, I've got the parameters input and have started running through the possible matches. It's still going to take some time though if I have to look at all of them before finding your group..."

With each second that passed I felt like I could sense Jax's men closing in around me. I considered grabbing the transmitter and making a run for it. If I could get out of the compound then there was a good chance that I could reattach the transmitter to the structural steel inside one of the aging buildings and reestablish contact with my analyst. Getting out of the compound could be tricky though. The only way it was even going to be possible was if Jax had really drawn down the normal guard contingent in preparation for his attack on the Muertos.

If the worst came to pass and I got caught on my way out, there would be no reestablishing contact with the Society, which would mean that I'd lose the one resource that had a chance of finding Brennan in time to save the people in his territory.

That wasn't acceptable. I was going to do everything I could to survive the next few hours, but if I got caught, I wanted to be able to tell Jax exactly where Brennan was being held.

Rather than yelling at the analyst, I took a deep breath. "Understood—just hurry. I don't know how much longer I have before someone will find me down here."

Several seconds of painful, dragging silence passed and then he cleared his throat. "I think I've got them. A similar group appeared halfway between Brennan's compound and his southern border. They worked their way two blocks south and then entered another building. The computer is confident that they haven't left the building in the last twelve hours."

My knees went weak, but I managed to keep my voice level. "Okay, assuming that's the grab team, how long will it take you to find where they exit on the other side of the barricade? It's probably safe to assume that they are headed into the territory directly south of this one."

The satisfaction in the guy's voice was unmistakable. "I'll do you one better. I used their trip across the surface from the first tunnel to the second to establish movement rates for them, and then had the computer run a search algorithm in an expanding ring."

"You've got them?"

"Yep, they popped up right on schedule—the same number of people with the same number of injured. This is our group."

I wanted to cheer. If the analyst had been sitting in a room with me I probably would have kissed him.

"Do you have them? Can you tell where they ended up? I need a location where the prisoner is being held."

"I'm advancing the feed right now. The computer has them locked in and is moving things forward at high speed. The algorithms aren't perfect, but once you give the computer a specific enough target to follow it usually does a pretty good job. Worst case I'll have to go back and run it manually...nope, it worked. I can see them walking into a big building at what looks like the center of the territory to your south. From the top it's shaped like a triangle, so it should be easy for you to identify."

"And they don't come out afterwards?"

"Not in that same group—the computer would have caught that. That's not to say that they didn't all come out singly over the next couple of hours, but it's a good bet that the injured individuals at least are still there in that building."

I grabbed onto the pipe to steady my shaking body. "How long would it take you to run it forward and make sure that nobody was carried back out of the building?"

"Maybe twenty minutes—you want to stay on the line while I do that?"

I did, but I knew I didn't have that kind of time to waste. It had been Piter all along, but Jax and Tyrell had dismissed him as a possibility because he'd been so easy to work with up until now. The odds were very good that the triangular building was his headquarters, and if that was the case it was almost guaranteed that Brennan was still there.

I wanted to have the analyst confirm that he hadn't been carried away, but in the end it didn't matter if Brennan was still there or not. I had proof that Piter had been involved and that was all I needed to pick up Brennan's trail if he wasn't still there.

"No, there's not enough time for that. Thank you though—you've been a real champ. I'd like to buy you a drink the next time I'm back home, Analyst…"

"Craft, ma'am. Analyst Craft. I'll take you up on that just so I can hear all about your mission. Twelve-hour shifts are better than wasting my time the way everyone else around here does, but they can still drag on from time to time."

"It's a plan then. Over and out."

I cut the transmission and headed back towards the surface at a fast walk, expecting each time I rounded a corner to be faced with Jax and a dozen other guards with their weapons leveled at me. My pulse was thundering in my ears by the time I made it to the top of the bore, but everything looked surprisingly normal top-side.

I'd expected someone to at least stumble upon the guards I'd left unconscious at the secure entrance, but apparently Jax had everyone working two jobs to fill in the holes left when he raided all nonessential functions to put together his strike force. That was a good sign. I pulled my hat down low over my eyes and forced myself not to break into a full-on run.

A short time later I was approaching the gate on the south end of the compound. The normal detachment was down to just one guy and his attention was focused on the area outside of the gate rather than anything happening on our side of the wall. He gave me only a cursory visual inspection before pulling the bolt on the gate back.

"You got any news?"

I shook my head, barely slowing as I walked past. "Just that they're still stripping all of the guard posts down to the bone. I'd stay and chat, but if I don't get this dispatch delivered I'll be on punishment detail for a month."

"I hear you. Be careful out there—the people on that side of the wall have clued into the fact that something is going on. I'm surprised that you got sent out by yourself. Every time I open up this gate I'm half convinced that someone is going to pop up out of the darkness and try to rush me."

"Yeah, I'll be careful—you too."

I proceeded at a fast walk until the darkness swallowed up the gate and then broke into a run, rifle slapping against my leg. There were plenty of eyes between the compound and the barricade to see what I was doing and wonder what was going on, but none of them were the ones I had to worry about. I kept my speed down to something that a normal human in peak physical condition could have managed, but even so managed to cover the distance to the southern guard post in less than five minutes.

I wasn't wearing one of the balaclavas we'd been sporting on my last visit to the guard post, but that just meant that the lone guard manning the exterior door was less nervous as I approached.

"State your business."

I patted the large pocket along the side of my left leg. "I've got a message to deliver to the basement."

His eyes went wide. After I'd had such an easy time getting out of the compound I'd assumed that Jax and Tyrell hadn't spread the word about my incarceration, but this guard's reaction nearly had me convinced that I'd been wrong.

I thought for a moment that he was going to go for his weapon, but instead he just grabbed me. I was a fraction of a second away from slamming my elbow into his chest with enough force to shatter his ribs, but he got his words out first. They came out in a low hiss.

"We don't talk about the basement out here. I don't care how new you are, if you know about the basement you should know that. That's how rumors start. Now get inside and thank your lucky stars that things are too crazy right now for me to track down your supervising officer so that I can file a complaint."

I stumbled as he pushed me towards the door. I was as shocked as he thought I was—just for different reasons. I'd been lucky—much more so than I'd had any right to expect.

There was only one guard inside instead of the two I remembered from last time, but I still would've had a hard time explaining my presence but for the fact that the first guard had all but escorted me into the building. The guard inside the door gave me a wry smile.

"You look like someone who just had the riot act read to them."

"Yeah, I just mentioned the basement when he asked me why I was here. Nobody gave me the proper countersign to get inside—I figured I just needed to tell him where I was headed."

"Don't worry about it. The odds of anybody out there understanding the significance of what you said are pretty minimal. Just don't let it happen again and I'm sure Yuri will forget about it by the time the week's out. You know where you're headed?"

"Yeah, I think so. Isn't it down the hall to the right?"

The guard smiled. "Yeah, but make sure you've got your orders out where the boys down there can see them. They're even more jumpy than Yuri is."

I nodded my thanks and hurried down the hall, conscious of the fact that someone could arrive at any moment with word of my escape. Part of me hadn't actually expected to make it this far, but now that I had, I was grateful that the last pair of guards were located so far away from the outside door.

It was going to be hard enough to take down two guards who could see me coming. At least this way I shouldn't have to worry about alerting the guard I'd just left behind—unless somebody got a shot off before I managed to neutralize them.

A few seconds later I came round the last corner separating me from the final pair of guards. I made sure I was walking quickly and tried to give myself the air of a junior officer on a new assignment who was worried she wasn't going to get the job done quickly enough.

"Hold up! You can't come running up on us like that. Where are your orders?"

I made a big show of sliding to a stop—made it obvious that I was stopping as soon as he started talking—but doing so in such a way that I actually covered several more feet before coming to a complete stop.

It had gotten me close, but not close enough to do the job without risking one of them getting a shot off and alerting the other guards in the building. There was nothing left to do but try to sell them a lie.

I reached down to my pants pocket as though planning on fishing out the requested orders, and then gasped when my hand came up empty. "They were just there—I swear I just had them."

I let myself stagger to the side as I sped up my breathing. "What am I going to do? Jax himself gave me those orders. He said he needed the insurgents down there to create a diversion. One of the other territories kidnapped Brennan and I just ruined any chance of getting him back because I couldn't keep hold of a simple set of orders."

I'd been hoping that Jax would play the news of Brennan's kidnapping close to his chest, but I'd known it was a long shot. Rather than both of them gasping and dropping the rifles as I'd been hoping, only one of them seemed affected by the news.

The closer of the two guards took a step towards me as though planning on shaking me to get the truth out. "Wait, what are you talking about?"

The further guard didn't take his eyes off of me. "Can it, Stikes. You have no idea whether or not she's telling the truth, and even if she is, it doesn't change our job."

"That's just it, she has to be telling the truth. There's no other reason why they would draw down all of the forces that are usually stationed here. If someone else has Brennan, then all bets are off."

The further guard took a step forward as though planning on trying to calm down his partner. "Pull yourself together—"

I didn't give him a chance to finish his sentence. I'd needed him to be just a foot or two closer to me and now he'd obliged. I sprang forward and slammed my palm into the throat of the first guard as I went past.

He dropped his weapon and reached up to his throat with both hands, but I noticed that only in passing as I lashed out with my foot and blew out the knee of the second guard. The second guard was the tougher of the two of them, but tough didn't even enter into it at that point. The joint was structurally incapable of supporting his weight, but that didn't stop him from trying to get his weapon up where he could fill me full of lead.

I wrapped my hand around the breech of his rifle, simultaneously controlling where the muzzle pointed and pulling it out of battery far enough that even if he did pull the trigger, the weapon still wouldn't discharge. A slight tug on the back of his neck finished off his balance and as he fell forward I slammed my knee into his face.

That was a devastating attack when administered by someone with normal strength; if I hadn't pulled the blow I probably would've killed him. I knew as he recoiled from the impact that he probably wasn't going to still be conscious when he hit the ground, but that didn't stop me from slamming my fist into the side of his neck. I didn't hit him hard enough to break his neck, but even a relatively weak blow to that location would cause his body to temporarily stop pumping blood up to his brain.

As the second guard dropped bonelessly to the ground, I spun back around and put a sleeper hold on the first guard. If he'd been smart he would've gone for his weapon—dangling uselessly from his sling—but instead he clawed desperately at my arm for the ten seconds that it took for his brain to shut down from oxygen deprivation.

Less than twelve seconds after I made my move, both of the guards were on the ground unconscious and I was gathering up their weapons and ammunition. A minute after that, I was slipping through the last vault-like metal door that separated Victoria's freedom fighters from Brennan's southern guard post.

I'd been half afraid when I hatched this plan on the way up out of the bore that I would find the parking garage empty, but my luck held up better than expected. There weren't just one or two insurgents waiting down there when I arrived, there were nearly a dozen of them—and Victoria was among their number.

To say that they were surprised would've been an understatement, and I didn't miss the way that several of them lingered by the rifles they'd been practicing with. Victoria didn't order them away, but she did step forward and give me an appraising glance.

"Unless I'm very much mistaken, you shouldn't be here without Brennan."

I gave her a humorless grin. "You're not at all mistaken, but I have a very good reason why I'm here alone. Slightly less than two days ago, Piter had a team grab Brennan and smuggle him across the border. Given that Brennan is currently being held captive inside of Piter's headquarters, there isn't any way I could've brought him along with me."

A flash of alarm crossed Victoria's face. "If that's true, then why am I hearing about it from you?"

"Because Jax and Tyrell are convinced that Piter didn't do it. They think some gang called the Muertos is responsible. I suspect that they've probably already started their attack on the Muertos, but all that's going to do is weaken Brennan's army so that Piter can swoop in and expand his territory by three or four times what he currently holds."

She shook her head. "Impossible. Piter knows better than that—he still hasn't finished subduing and integrating Jenks' territory. Even if he had, Jax would have to lose nearly half of his people before Piter would have any kind of chance of pulling something like that off. I know next to nothing about the Muertos, but I have a very hard time believing that any one territory is going to be able to inflict those kinds of casualties on a group as deadly as the one Jax will be leading into the assault."

"Sure, Jax and Tyrell will probably roll right over the Muertos, but they will lose people and they won't find Brennan, which means they'll have to go into another territory, and another, and another. Eventually they'll get worn down enough that they'll start taking serious casualties. Once that happens, Piter will be waiting to walk in and take over not just Brennan's territory but also the territory of everyone that we just finished stomping all over. It's the perfect plan—a much better one than kidnapping Brennan and then trying to ransom him back to us."

Victoria was silent for several seconds as she did the math. "So what, you're here hoping you can convince us to follow you into some kind of suicide mission? All based on the off chance that you're right about where Brennan is being kept? Do you have any idea what we sacrificed to be here? If we go up against Piter and lose, it won't be just us who will die. He'll have his goons torture and kill everyone we've ever cared about."

I shook my head. "First of all, I'm not guessing about what went down when they grabbed Brennan. He's here in your territory, in Piter's building. I wouldn't be here talking to you if I wasn't positive of that fact. Second of all, with your help I can all but guarantee that we will be able to decapitate Piter's command group.

"He's trying to make it look like he doesn't have extra people on the border so as not to spook Tyrell and Jax, but all of the buildings along the border have got to be crawling with enforcers right now. He can't be strong everywhere, which means there's probably nothing more than a token set of guards around him. We'll start from inside his outer perimeter and he'll never even see us coming.

"Thirdly, even if we did somehow fail, Piter and his men can't torture and kill everyone you care about tomorrow because they already killed some of those people yesterday or last month or last year. This is a chance to both save Brennan and avenge the people you've already lost. The only question is whether you're going to take it."

I could hear various people shifting around in response to my words. I'd considered lying and telling her that I recognized one of Piter's enforcers in the group that had grabbed Brennan. It had the benefit of being mostly true—after all, I had been there when Brennan was grabbed—but that would've begged the question as to why Jax and Tyrell hadn't believed me and prepped their assault on Piter's territory.

No, telling her the truth—at least as much as I could tell her without revealing that I was a spy—was the better, safer option, but I wasn't thinking about that at the time. I just told her the truth because that was what felt right. I was getting tired of lying to everybody.

I kept my eyes locked on Victoria until she broke the staring contest and turned back to her people. I followed her gaze and saw a group that was obviously torn. Victoria met each of their eyes and then reached over and grabbed one of the guns I'd just taken from the guards upstairs.

"You've all been complaining that we didn't have enough weapons for everybody. We still don't, but once you add what Skye just brought us to the rest of what Brennan has had delivered recently, we're darn close. I don't know if Skye is lying or telling the truth, but she's right about one thing. Without Brennan none of what's happened could've been possible. If there's even a slight chance that he's a prisoner and we can get him out, then I could never live with myself if I didn't at least try.

"Let's go kill Piter."

Chapter 24

I hadn't been sure what to expect with regards to Victoria and her crew. They'd obviously trained with the rifles that Brennan had supplied them, but that did not automatically make them experienced covert agents. I'd figured the best I could hope for, was that they would know the territory well enough to avoid the worst of the regular patrols, and that they would be able to put bullets downrange and on target when the time came.

It turned out that I'd been woefully under-estimating them. Within five minutes Victoria had half of her people armed and ready to go. Every magazine Brennan had provided them with was already loaded, but that still left nearly a thousand rounds of ammo sitting in the familiar metal boxes that Jax's men used to transport munitions.

We all filled our pockets with loose rounds and then three of the guys who hadn't received rifles each picked up an ammo box and we all set out. The old me probably would've taken a spot at the back of the group simply because I'd spent so long believing the highest virtue was not questioning authority. The new me wasn't having any of that.

I took a spot at Victoria's side as we set off through the parking garage, surrounded by pools of illumination from the lanterns that they'd been using as a light source.

"What's the plan?"

Victoria gave me an amused look. "I thought you were the one with the plan."

"Sure. Make my way to Piter's headquarters and then shoot my way inside. It's doable but I'd be stupid not to pay attention if you've got a way to get us inside the building without having to fight enforcers every step of the way."

"Normally I could guarantee being able to get you at least to the building without being spotted, but everything's too much in flux right now. If you're right about Piter having most of his people crammed inside of the buildings along the border, that could mean that things will be easier, but I suspect that what few people he still has out and about will be under orders to move around a lot more than his goons normally do."

I nodded. "Okay, I buy that. What kind of options does that leave us?"

"If I thought we could guarantee that the men armed with rifles would be at their normal spots, then I'd say job number one would be to ambush them so that I can arm the rest of my people, but realistically speaking that's not an option either. Instead I'm going to send out runners to gather the rest of the resistance and the bulk of us will go attack the buildings along the border while you and a small team will go after Brennan during the distraction. Just try not to start shooting people too soon or you'll bring Piter's entire army down on your heads."

"It's a deal."

Things continued to go much more smoothly than I'd been expecting. Once we arrived at the doors up into the ground floor of the building, we all formed a long human chain and passed the lanterns forward so they could be stowed next to the door. Victoria then doused the lights, and we made our slow, careful way through the door.

The other side of the door was so dark that I wouldn't have been able to see my hand in front of my face—even assuming I'd been willing to let go of the hands I was holding onto and break the human chain—but I got the impression that I was being led through a twisted warren of metal and garbage that had been carefully staged to appear impassable from the outside.

The fact that the insurgents knew the path well enough to navigate in the dark was a testament to both their dedication and preparedness. Time and time again, Victoria leaned back to caution me with a whisper about some obstacle or another that I otherwise would have blundered into.

We moved more slowly than I would've liked, but still made remarkable time considering the nature of the obstacles we were trying to navigate around. Just over fifteen minutes after the lanterns went out, we got close enough to the exterior of the building for me to be able to start seeing shapes inside the darkness.

Still communicating via whispers, Victoria made assignments. She split off three of her shooters and two of her other people to accompany me, and then told us to wait until everyone else had been gone for at least fifteen minutes before starting off towards Piter's headquarters.

I followed one of the three shooters in my new team over to a vantage point where we could watch as the rest of Victoria's people trickled out two or three at a time.

"How long do you think this is going to take?"

There was just enough light coming from a small fire burning inside an oil drum out in the middle of the street for me to confirm that my companion was a big redheaded guy I'd noticed back inside the parking garage. He looked like he could've been the brother of the guard I'd knocked unconscious back inside the compound in order to get out of my room.

All I got in response was a grunt. Apparently this guy didn't share the same love of yelling that his twin had expressed. I considered pushing him for an answer, but realized that there was no real benefit to making him dislike me. It was going to take however long it was going to take.

"Can I at least get a name out of you?"

"Jasper."

We passed the next twenty minutes in silence and then he motioned for me to follow him back over to the door where the rest of our team was waiting for us. Five minutes later it was our turn to exit the building. Rather than going out into separate groups, we all left together, guns hanging unobtrusively from our shoulders.

With every block we crossed I half expected for gunfire to break out behind us, but we made it three blocks without running into any enforcers or hearing any evidence that Victoria had started her attack. Jasper was in the lead and stepped around the corner that he'd indicated would give us a straight shot to the triangular building Piter was using for his headquarters, but before I could follow him he reversed course, nearly knocking me off my feet.

"Enforcers, three of them. I don't think they saw me."

I crept forward, trying to get far enough around the corner that I would be able to see what we were up against. "Can we go around them?"

"Sure, but there's no guarantee that's going to be any better. The streets to either side get a lot more foot traffic. That's why I chose this one—less chance of someone seeing the guns and raising some kind of alarm."

He was right, the path he led us on had been remarkably empty of other people, but apparently Piter knew that too—it was probably the reason he'd chosen to station enforcers there.

"So what do we do now?"

"We don't have any choice but to wait until Victoria creates the distraction we need."

I'd been trying not to focus on the clock I could feel ticking away in the back of my mind, but the urgency to find Brennan hadn't ever disappeared. That probably would've been enough all by itself to force me into motion, but I could also feel unseeing eyes watching us, wondering why we'd stopped where we'd stopped.

"It's too risky. You just said it yourself, all it would take is the wrong person walking by close enough to realize that we're armed and we'll have dozens of enforcers pouring out of the woodwork."

I stood back up, but Jasper grabbed my arm before I could move. "I'm not letting you ruin this, Skye. If you open fire on those three it will be just as bad. We'll have swarms of enforcers coming after us and it will ruin things for Victoria and the rest of our people—my people. They'll get massacred."

"So we don't use guns."

Jasper chuckled like he thought I was joking and then frowned when I didn't join in. "Yeah, right. They'd take us apart in seconds. With guns, if we're far enough away then we have a chance of taking out a group several times that size. If we let them close though, all of the advantages shift to the other side. We've been training for two months with our rifles, but they've been training for years with their knives and swords."

I lifted the sling attached to my rifle off over my head and handed it to the guy carrying the ammo case. I debated for a second and then slipped out of my vest as well. If things went poorly Jasper and the others were going to need my spare magazines—besides, the uniform Jax had designed was distinctive enough that I couldn't risk it tipping Piter's men off.

I gave Jasper a humorless smile. "If I don't succeed, then go ahead and wait for Victoria to open the ball. There's still a chance you can make it to Brennan and get him back to the parking garage. Just remember that his ribs are all broken—you'll probably have to carry him out of there."

I slipped away before anybody could stop me and walked casually towards the enforcers. They weren't very good guards—I made it to within five feet of them before anyone bothered to challenge me.

"If you're hoping for some companionship you're going to have to wait for a few hours—we're on duty."

I put a big pout on my face. "Surely it doesn't take all three of you to watch this one little stretch of road."

The closest guard, a massive guy wearing nothing under his leather vest, stepped towards me as though planning on grabbing me. I didn't wait to see whether his intent was hostile. I grabbed his arm and slammed my palm into his elbow, shattering the joint and triggering the start of a pain-filled scream that I interrupted a split second later with an elbow to his throat.

I'd targeted the top of his throat. Unlike when I'd been forced to fight Brennan's guards, I had no qualms with killing any of Piter's men. He went down and I was positive he wouldn't be getting back up.

The next closest guy was thinner and shorter—only barely taller than me—and it shouldn't have been a surprise that he was so fast. I should've known that he would have some offsetting advantage to have earned a place among such a brutal group of men. The adrenaline surging through my system meant that my nanites were once again moving signals up and down my nerves at six times normal speed, but even so the second guard got a knife out and slashed at me before I managed to close the distance between us.

I leaned back and spun slightly to the side in an effort to avoid being cut, but I couldn't risk reversing course—if I didn't keep the pressure on both of the remaining enforcers, that they would realize they should be yelling for help rather than just trying to kill me by themselves. Even as my upper body swayed backwards, my right leg shot forward and hammered my foot into the second guard's ankle.

He nicked my arm, drawing first blood, but I felt the smaller bones in his ankle crunch as they lost the battle against my combat boot and the nanite-infused bones inside it. A split second after his knife flashed past me I grabbed his forearm to control his weapon, stepped in close, and went up on my toes as my elbow came up and slammed into his chin. The force of the blow threw him back into the last enforcer at the same time that it snapped his neck.

The last guard was still unlimbering a big mace from his belt when his partner collided with him. He abandoned his efforts to get his weapon out as the second guard careened off of him, but by then it was too late. I crossed the distance between us in a split second and threw myself into the air, clearing the punch he'd just thrown at me.

It was a kind of attack my instructors would never have approved of, the kind of attack that was only possible for someone who grossly outmatched their opponent, but my nanites made it child's play to wrap my legs around his neck a split second before I slammed into him and threw him over backwards.

I had just enough leverage to break his neck as we hit the ground.

Chapter 25

Jasper and the rest of our team arrived at my side a few seconds after I disentangled myself from the last guard.

"How did you do that? I didn't think something like that was humanly possible."

I shrugged uncomfortably as I slipped my vest back on. "You'd be amazed what's possible with the right training and enough adrenaline flowing through your system. Now let's get moving before somebody shows up and sees all of these bodies."

We made it two more blocks—nearly all the way to Piter's headquarters—before the sound of gunfire tore through the darkness. All six of us dove into the deepest set of shadows we could find and watched as more than two dozen enforcers came running out of the headquarters building and hurried off towards their northern border.

We waited four more minutes to see if there was going to be another wave of Piter's men leaving the building, and each second made me more and more jittery.

"We need to move now, Jasper. There's no telling how long Victoria and the rest can stand up to whomever Piter has hiding in those buildings. If we wait too long there's a chance we'll have to fight our way back out through everyone headed back from that other battle."

Jasper grunted. "Yeah, but if we move too soon then all the guards left in the building are going to be on high alert still. Besides, once we shoot the guards outside the building we're going to have enforcers popping up all over."

I gritted my teeth and then moved further to the left, leaving the deepest part of the shadows, so I could get a better look at what we were up against. Whoever was running Piter's security detail had left two men behind to guard what Jasper had indicated was the only exterior door into the building.

I'd already proved several times that under the right circumstances I was more than capable of taking down two enforcers with my bare hands, but these didn't look like the right circumstances. They were too far apart for one thing, and they both looked much more on-the-ball than the last group I'd taken out. Not only that, both of these guys were equipped with rifles—the fruit of Piter's trades with Brennan.

The lighting was pretty bad or we never would've been able to hide this close to them.

There was a chance that I could sneak up on one of them and neutralize him before he got a shot off, but that wouldn't do anything to stop the second guy from raising an alarm. I could see one plan that seemed like it might work, but it wasn't playing to my strengths. Even worse, if I failed not only might I die, I would be depending on Jasper and the rest to stop the second guard.

I scooted back over next to Jasper. "Who's the best shot out of the people we have here?"

"Me. Why do you ask?"

"I'm going to work my way closer to the guy on the right. I'm pretty sure I can take him before he even knows I'm there, but I may not be able to take down the second guy. Go ahead and put your sights on him. When I make my move you'll know, and if it looks like I'm not going to be able to take him out quickly enough, put a single shot into him. There's still a chance one shot will bring down the wrong kind of attention, but we're a heck of a lot more likely to be able to blend in with the commotion coming from the north with just a single shot."

I moved off before Jasper could respond, but I honestly couldn't have said if my abruptness was to stop him from raising objections or if it was to stop me from talking myself out of what I was about to do. Going up against people with swords and knives was bad enough, but facing down men armed with high-velocity rifles was a step beyond even that.

My nanites meant that I could conceivably dodge most melee attacks, but nobody was capable of dodging a bullet. I was just going to have to hope that I was fast and quiet enough to survive what was coming. It sure would've been nice to be wearing body armor.

I crept forward, moving slowly and trying to stay low enough that the flickering light from the oil-drum fires wouldn't outline me. The closer I got to my target the more likely it was that I was going to be able to take him and his partner out quickly enough to avoid alerting the people inside the building, but with each inch I moved forward, the odds of being seen went up drastically.

When I was still twenty feet away, I reached down into my boot and slipped out the knife I'd taken off of the guard outside my room. It made crawling that much more difficult, but the blade was blackened and I was going to need it if somebody noticed me before I was ready to initiate my attack.

I adjusted my course slightly, trying to keep what was left of a rusted oil drum between me and the closer guard. The adrenaline flowing through my system was making it hard to keep from shaking, but I managed to get to the oil drum without making any noise.

I was within ten feet of my target now and couldn't realistically count on getting any closer without being seen. I took a deep, quiet breath, reversed my knife so the blade stuck out in front of me, and then exploded out around the barrel that had been concealing me.

I covered more than four feet with my first step, moving at a speed that would've been the envy of any participant in the Anniversary Games back home. Neither of the guards realized what was happening until my left foot hit the ground and launched me forward five more feet. By then it was too late for the first guard.

My blade took him in the chest as my left hand swept his barrel off to the side. It was a killing blow, one that was so close to instantly fatal that it hardly mattered whether he'd lost consciousness or not by the time I ripped the blade free of his body.

I pivoted to the left, spinning on the ball of my left foot as the knife came back by my ear in preparation for a throw that I wasn't convinced I could make. As my wrist snapped forward and the knife went spinning away from me, a trio of shots rang out in rapid succession and I cursed.

The knife sank home in the second guard's throat with a sickening thunk and then I stumbled as the pain hit me. I'd thought that Jasper had shot the second guard before I could throw my knife, but I'd been wrong. There hadn't been three shots because he'd forgotten to change the selector over on his rifle, there'd been three shots because the guard had just shot me.

I looked down fully expecting the blood I found coursing down my arm, but knowing that

I had to confirm I hadn't been hit anywhere else. I hadn't, which meant I could keep fighting—at least for as long as it took me to bleed out.

Jasper arrived at my side a second later, my rifle in his left hand. "You're hit!"

"Yeah, but we don't have time to do anything about that—any second enforcers are going to come pouring out of the building."

I grabbed my rifle out of his hand as I was speaking and then turned and charged towards the doors. Hopefully his people would be smart enough to grab the guards' weapons as they went by. I hit the doors at a run, throwing them open with my injured shoulder, and stepped into a killing field.

Anyone else would've died within the first second of entering the building. Unlike some of the other gang leaders, Piter hadn't traded any of the weapons he'd gotten from Brennan to other territories. He'd been stockpiling them, and based on the hail of bullets headed towards me, he hadn't sent any of his people with rifles out to watch the border.

Only two things saved me. The first was that I'd come into the building at a dead run—and I was much faster than any normal human. The second was that Piter's people had been so low on ammunition that they'd never been able to practice with their weapons like they should have.

The entryway into the building was a three-story atrium that had seen better days, but the second-floor balcony on the west side was still functional and the better part of a dozen people were lined up there waiting for me as I entered the building. A whisper of sound brought my head around just in time to see the gunners and my training stood me in good stead. Rather than stopping and trying to return fire, I dug down deep for every ounce of speed I possessed and streaked across the broken marble floor as the wall behind me exploded in a deluge of gunfire.

The door I was headed towards seemed impossibly far away. I was moving at more than thirty-five miles per hour, which meant, it wasn't going to take me more than a second or two to make it to shelter, but I wasn't sure I was going to have that much time.

The trail of destruction along the wall to my right followed me with unnatural speed as the gunners tried to track my movement. With each step I could feel them catching up to me, and with each step I became more and more sure I wasn't going to make it to cover. I was two steps away from the doorway and positive that my next step was going to be my last when a second source of gunfire cut loose behind me.

I thought I was dead. It only made sense that Piter would've positioned a second group of men where they would have a clear shot at anyone who'd managed to cross the kill zone, but for once the most likely explanation wasn't the correct one.

THE SOCIETY

Jasper and the others hadn't been quick enough to make it inside the building before the shooting had started, but they'd been smart enough to fall back to where they would have a clear line of sight to the gunners targeting me.

They opened fire on the enforcers through the windows, and my last step forward into safety was accompanied by the sound of shattering glass.

No place inside of the city—other than Brennan's compound—was very well-lit, but Piter's men had moved what light sources they had down to the first floor so they would have better visibility in the kill zone. That meant that Jasper and the others were mostly aiming by the light of their targets' muzzle flash, but their efforts were good enough to cause the enforcers to take cover, and that was all I needed to disappear into the doorway I'd been aiming for.

I brought my rifle up to my shoulder as I slowed down and assumed the bent-kneed gait I'd been taught in training. It was slower than the sprint I'd just been using, but had the advantage of providing a stable firing platform, which the most important thing at that moment.

I could still feel blood trickling down my arm, but I had to make it up to the second floor and eliminate Piter's gunmen if Jasper and the others were going to have any chance of survival. My nanites were just going to have to do the best they could.

Ears straining for any clue of what was up ahead of me, I came round a corner and someone grabbed a hold of my gun, yanking me forward. I had only a second to react. Judging by the force with which I was pulled forward, I was up against someone who was much bigger than me, so rather than pulling backwards to maintain my position, I threw myself forward.

I used the enforcer's hand on the barrel of my gun as a pivot and slammed the butt of the weapon into the side of his head. That got me out of the way of the knife he tried to jam into my gut, but it didn't do anything to stop the sword his partner was wielding.

The slender length of steel took me in the abdomen—down low, on the left side—but my opponent was nothing more than a thug with delusions of grandeur. He'd let his excitement to land a blow on me pull him off balance, and I took ruthless advantage of that.

I went with the inertia from my blow to the head of the first enforcer and continued around in a circle, wincing as the sword tore free of my stomach. The enforcer hadn't even had time to realize how badly he'd erred before my right foot swept his leg out from underneath him. I grabbed his right arm—mostly to keep him from cutting me by accident as he flailed for balance—and then used it to change the direction of his fall and slammed him headfirst into the floor.

The sound of gunfire had changed in the few seconds it had taken me to deal with my latest two opponents. Brennan had been very careful about the number of rounds he'd allowed to leave the compound, which meant that Piter's men had probably burned through a significant percentage of their reserves in their attempt to kill me, but they had Jasper and the others outnumbered by more than two to one.

The reduced volume of fire coming from above was a good indication that the enforcers had realized exactly that, but I didn't like the sound of the shots coming from my level either. It no longer sounded like they were all coming from rifles pointed into the building. It sounded like some of the insurgents had been forced to start dealing with threats from other directions.

I bit back a curse as I cleared another doorway that was thankfully free of hostiles and headed up the stairs. This was exactly the reason it had been so important to make it inside the building before we started shooting at people. Jasper and the others were being surrounded, which meant it was only a matter of time before they were all dead. If I was right that Piter had kept all of his guns in the hands of people inside the building, then the insurgents at least didn't have to worry about gunfire coming from multiple directions, but they were still in trouble.

The ambush when Piter's people had grabbed Brennan was plenty of proof that some of his men were expert archers and the insurgents were going to be just as dead from an arrow through the throat as from a bullet through the chest. I had to give them somewhere to go, had to make it safe for them to retreat into the building.

I kicked the second-floor door open and then stuck my head out for just long enough to assess the situation. I ducked back behind cover a split second before someone filled the space I'd just been occupying full of bullets. I waited for half a heartbeat and then threw myself forward before the door could finish rebounding off of the wall next to it.

My timing had been perfect. The gunner had just let go of the trigger to avoid burning through the rest of his ammunition when I appeared as if by magic four feet past the door, rifle at the ready and already acquiring my first target. I stroked the trigger and was rewarded with a three-round burst that took my target on the left side of his chest.

It was the first time I'd ever fired a rifle in a real combat situation, and I was surprised at the godlike detachment I felt as I lined up my second target and put three more rounds downrange.

Somehow when I'd agreed to the Citizen-President's mission I hadn't actually expected to have to kill anyone. I'd trained for the possibility, mastering as many different forms of combat as possible in the window I'd been allowed, but it had still taken me by shock when

I'd been forced to kill Bash and the other enforcer on my first night inside the city. That had been a frantic, scary experience. I'd killed because I'd had no other choice, and I'd done so knowing full well that my nanites couldn't fully offset the advantage in the size and weight of my two opponents.

Each fight since then had been the same way. Blurs of motion in which I'd matched my limited training and nanites up against men who were older and more experienced than me, some of whom had been training for decades.

This, though, this was different. My nanites seemed to have realized that the fight had shifted. Rather than speeding up the neurons running between my brain and my limbs, they'd kicked my brain into high gear. It was like there was a fiber-optic cable running from my eyes to my brain and then down to my trigger finger.

I was still bleeding—losing twice as much blood as before—but the fight had changed into something I felt like I couldn't lose. I moved like a machine, with metronome-like precision as I identified targets and executed them. I could still die, I wasn't any more able to dodge a bullet than I had been five minutes before, but I was up against men who were woefully unprepared to face me on these terms.

The enforcers who'd come within fractions of a second of killing me only moments before had been reduced to silhouettes that crumbled with every stroke of the trigger. I calmly moved across the balcony and killed every single gunner in less than ten seconds before being forced to take cover from fire coming up from Jasper's position.

"It's me. The balcony is clear. You're free to fall back into the building."

The abruptness with which incoming fire dropped off was all the confirmation I needed that Jasper's team had heard me, but I waited for a couple of seconds to make sure before standing back up to take in the situation outside. It appeared as though the two dozen enforcers who'd been dispatched to help deal with Victoria's assault had returned, and they were making life difficult for the insurgents.

I identified an archer who seemed to be giving Jasper a particularly tough time, and drew a bead on him. It was difficult given the poor lighting we were dealing with. That was actually the only reason that Jasper and others hadn't managed to cut the enforcers down within moments of their arrival. The flickering light from the few fires burning in the area provided plenty of shadows, and this was exactly the kind of fight the enforcers were used to from the turf wars they'd spent their entire lives fighting.

They had spread out and were slowly working their way in close enough to be able to use the weapons at their disposal. Jasper and the others were slowing their advance with semi-targeted bursts into any shadow that seemed to be moving, but they were up against the same problem that had been plaguing Piter's gunmen. They had a lot more ammunition at their disposal, but it wasn't endless and already two of the insurgents had been forced to stop firing so they could load fresh rounds into empty magazines.

Not for the first time, I wished that my nanites were capable of improving my night vision, but there was nothing to be done about that particular problem. I studied my aim, breathed out half of the air in my lungs, and squeezed my trigger again. There was a yell of pain, and then the archer stumbled out into plain sight and one of the insurgents finished him off.

I was tempted to stay there and help cover my team's retreat, but all that would do was burn up what little ammunition I had left against targets that were little more than ghosts. No, I needed to work my way deeper inside the building.

I reached down and ripped a swath of fabric off of the shirt of one of the men I'd just killed. I begrudged the time it took me to tie the material around my stomach, but it couldn't be helped. Blood loss would kill me if left unchecked for long enough, but that wasn't the only danger I was up against.

Nanites were capable of infiltrating any part of my body, but they primarily used my circulatory system to get around. Every drop of blood that I lost contained nanites that I desperately needed if I was going to be able to free Brennan.

Under ideal situations, direct pressure on a wound was enough to stem the blood loss, which also meant that the nanites had a much easier time accelerating the healing process. The pressure meant that the nanites could gather at the sides of the cut and form a kind of molecular net that would keep the blood inside me at the same time that it helped pull the edges of the wound together so that I could heal cleanly and quickly.

The nanites had no doubt done their best to stem the blood loss, but without something to counteract the internal pressure forcing them out of the body, their efforts had been severely hampered. I couldn't afford that—at least not until I had Brennan safely back to the compound.

I grabbed another strip of fabric and used my teeth to tie it around my arm, and then set off as I heard Jasper and the others enter the building.

"It's clear up here—you can probably scavenge some more ammunition off of the bodies—but be careful. There's no guarantee that someone won't come in behind me and ruin your day."

"You're not going to wait for us?"

"I can't afford to, Jasper. If we get bogged down they'll surround us and cut us to pieces. I've got to keep moving, got to keep them off balance."

Jasper didn't sound particularly excited at the idea, but he didn't try to stop me. "The word on the street is that Piter runs everything out of the fourth floor. That's your best bet as to where he's holding Brennan."

"I hope you're right. There aren't enough of us to lock down the exit and conduct a room by room search of this place at the same time."

"Yeah, we probably should've thought of that before we let Victoria send such a small group."

I nodded—fully aware he probably couldn't see the gesture in the darkness—and headed back towards the stairwell.

The trip up the next two sets of stairs was a balance between stealth and speed. There was no way of knowing how many people were on the third floor, but it was a good bet that at least some of them would actively resist me if given the chance. That meant I was going to have to bypass the third floor and just hope I could move quickly enough once I got to the fourth floor that I wouldn't have to worry about someone attacking me from behind. It wasn't a very good plan, but hopefully Jasper and the others wouldn't be too far behind me.

I reached the fourth floor and wasn't surprised to find the window blacked out. This time I chose to go in fully committed. I backed up several steps and then charged forward, leading with the shoulder that had already seen so much abuse in the last fifteen minutes.

If Piter had been smart he probably would've just blockaded himself inside the fourth floor until his people could regain control of the streets. Then again, I wasn't all that surprised that he'd chosen not to bar the door. Warlords and gang leaders ruled primarily through causing fear among the general populace, and a different kind of fear among their enforcers. Once someone like Piter started showing signs of fear, his days were unavoidably numbered.

Piter couldn't afford that—especially not after the losses he'd already suffered. I hit the door leading out of the stairwell with every ounce of force my hundred-and-twenty-five-pound body could muster, and it barely slowed me down at all.

I caught only flashes of my surroundings as I stumbled into the room. It was massive, taking up nearly the entire floor. They'd obviously knocked out walls to create a more intimidating space. There were a surprising number of candles scattered about the space, creating a soft flickering light that made it easy to see the primitive luxury of a city despot.

There were girls scattered around the periphery of the room—all young, all wearing too few clothes for how cold it was. The center of the room was dominated by a large metal throne which was currently surrounded by an even dozen bodyguards. Twenty feet away from the throne, Brennan was chained to one of the structural steel beams that rose vertically to the ceiling.

THE SOCIETY

My heart skipped a beat when I realized that I'd found Brennan, but there wasn't time to dwell on his presence because Piter had stationed one of his men less than five feet from the doorway and a rusty, jagged ax was headed towards my head.

I got my rifle up just in time to deflect the blow. I even managed to avoid losing any fingers, but it was a close thing. I was strong—stronger than I had any right to be—but there were limits to what even cutting-edge nanites were able to do.

I'd been moving at something like twenty-five miles per hour when I ran into the ax, and it had carried a respectable amount of kinetic energy all by itself. Despite my best efforts, the enforcer's blow drove my rifle back into my chest and knocked me down.

For once I was grateful that Brennan hadn't yet mastered the art of manufacturing rifles that were more plastic than metal, like we had back home. A rifle like that probably would've been sheared through by the blow from the ax that had just taken me down, but the heavy compound-manufactured rifle I was carrying turned the blow without sustaining any critical damage.

I hit the ground hard enough to knock the wind out of me, but as I slid backwards towards the door to the stairwell, I whipped my rifle around and put a three-round burst into the chest of the enforcer who'd just tried to decapitate me. Acting on instinct, I slapped the ground with my left hand, throwing myself to the right as the two guards with rifles opened up on the space I'd been occupying a second before.

I needed to be moving, needed to make myself a harder target, but there was simply no good way to do that—not starting from a sitting position. I rolled through one complete revolution and then used my right elbow to stop my momentum with a suddenness that I was hoping would make the two gunners overshoot me.

The pain was intense. I'd just broken one or more of the bones in my arm, but my trigger finger still worked and I returned fire with a smoothness beyond anything I'd ever demonstrated in training.

It was surreal to see the near-constant strobe of my enemies' muzzle flashes blooming like orange flower petals. I knew a child could probably take out the stationary target I presented at this range, but I forced the fear surging up inside of me back into the little box where it had been living all night.

My first burst took the guard on the left through the throat and he dropped like a puppet whose strings had been cut. A hot awl of fire sliced my left cheek a split second before the wall behind me exploded, and then my crosshairs settled over the figure of the second guard and I stroked my trigger again, blowing a hole in his chest where his heart had been only moments before.

I rolled to my feet, gun at the ready despite the pain in my right arm. I felt like a porcelain doll who'd had a hammer taken to her and then been put back together with chewing gum, but I refused to quit—not now, not when I was so close.

A few of the enforcers closest to the two I'd just killed looked like they wanted to make a play for the two priceless rifles. I couldn't allow that.

"Anyone who moves is dead. This can all be over—just remove Brennan's gag and free him. There's no reason for me to gun all of you down."

Piter shook his head, top hat swaying with the motion. "I'm not stupid. If I let Brennan walk out of here I—and all of my men—will be dead before the week is out. Brennan can't let this kind of provocation go any more than I could if I was in his shoes. All we need to do is rush you. You won't be able to kill all of us, and once you're dead it's only a matter of time before my men reestablish control of my territory."

"It may have escaped your notice, but there's a running firefight all along your north border. The only way you were going to survive this was if Jax and Tyrell continued to think that you'd had nothing to do with Brennan's abduction. I'll admit that you are way down on their list of suspects, but even they won't be able to ignore the kind of commotion taking place just across the barricade from them. Even if by some miracle you kill me, there's another team headed up the stairs as we speak. That doesn't matter though, because Jax and Tyrell will be attacking your territory within an hour or two of sunrise.

"You're going to lose your territory no matter what you do at this point, but I'm willing to offer you a head start. Even Brennan's reach has its limit. If you started now you could probably bribe your way across two or three territories and put yourself safely beyond retribution.

"It's a good offer, Piter, you should take it. I guarantee you that the team behind me isn't going to let you off that easily."

Piter shook his head, not even bothering to rise from his throne. "You severely overestimate both your skill with that gun and the number of bullets you have remaining in that magazine. You could be the fastest person on the earth and still not manage to put a new magazine into your weapon before we get to you."

I tried to do some quick math in my head. I didn't remember doing a tactical reload back on the balcony, but I was pretty sure I'd done so out of simple force of habit. Brennan's rifles had twenty-five-round magazines, but it was common knowledge among the guards that you were asking for a jam if you put more than twenty-two rounds in them.

A tactical reload meant that I would have replaced my magazine before I'd shot it dry, which meant that there would have still been a live round in the chamber when I slammed a new magazine home. That meant that I'd entered the fourth floor with twenty-three rounds. Killing the three men I'd killed so far had taken nine shots.

Piter was right, I didn't have enough ammo left to take them all down—not unless I switched over to single shot, and if I did that I wouldn't be able to gun them down quickly enough. It was ironic. I probably was the single fastest person in the entire world, but that wasn't going to be enough to save me—not with a broken right arm.

I put on the bravest front I could. "Maybe you're right. Maybe I can't kill all of you, but I will kill most of you. You're not worth dying for, Piter, and everyone in this room knows it. More importantly, I'll definitely take you with me when I go down."

I did my best to read the mood of the gathered strongmen as I talked, but there were still too many cultural differences between them and me. Brennan's compound had been alien enough to push my acting ability to its outer limits, but this was a whole different world. Brennan was trying to recreate civilization; Piter couldn't have cared less about any of that.

A long burst of gunfire from beneath us broke the stalemate, and I brought my rifle back up to my shoulder in the smoothest motion I was still capable of. Beth had been right, I moved like greased lightning, but Piter had obviously been waiting for me to make my move. He grabbed the arm of one of his bodyguards, pulling on it as he threw himself out of his throne.

I tightened my finger on the trigger and the bodyguard jerked as my bullets tore into him. Piter never would have been fast enough to avoid my fire by himself, but he'd pulled his guard into the path of my bullets and saved himself in the process.

"The guy who kills her gets a territory of their own!"

It was like someone had run a live current through the enforcers. They charged forward, completely heedless of the danger, and I cut them down with three-round bursts as quickly as I could.

They should have spread out, but in fairness there was only so much they could do given that they were all headed toward the same point. Every burst of fire I sent into the crowd took down at least one person. Brennan's rifles were heavy old beasts. They were murder to pack around all day, but their sheer weight meant that they could fire a heavier load than we'd used back home.

More often than not, my bullets tore through their original target and collided with someone behind them, but I was going through my ammunition too quickly. I started to fall back and then remembered that the door to the stairwell had swung shut behind me. There was nowhere to go.

I pulled the trigger again and this time the gun didn't respond with the three-round burst I'd asked of it. The slide locked back partway through the firing cycle—my magazine was empty. I hit the magazine release as I darted to the right, trying to buy myself time to reload, but I knew it was a futile effort.

Without the support of my left hand, my right arm nearly wasn't up to the task of keeping ahold of my gun. It dropped towards the ground with alarming speed, but I just gritted my teeth as I went for my last spare magazine.

The enforcers had been trimmed down to numbers that would have been nearly manageable under other circumstances. The closest one wound up with his club, aiming to crush my skull in, but I kicked him in the stomach, crying out from a combination of pain and the effort of trying to keep my weak arm from dropping my rifle.

I was at less than top form, but I still managed to generate enough force with my kick to pick him up off of the ground and fling him backwards into his friends. He still would have crushed my head if I hadn't leaned backwards from the waist as I drove my foot into his midsection.

The magazine had caught on my vest, but it came free to the sound of ripping fabric as I spun to the side in an effort to avoid a knife to the ribs. I was nearly successful, but added another wound to my rapidly failing body as the knife creased me.

I slammed the magazine—full of bullets and therefore heavy enough to serve as a decent improvised club—into that opponent's temple and then screamed once again as I tried to bring my rifle up to where I could force the magazine home.

It was no good, the arm had taken too much damage. It was physically capable of lifting the rifle, but my will was insufficient to force it to operate around the pain.

A slender, remarkably quick enforcer stepped over his fallen companions. He was eager to be the one to take me down, and as his sword darted towards me I knew that I was out of time. I tried to dodge to the side, hoping that would be enough to avoid the cruel point of his weapon, but all of my speed still wasn't enough to let me get completely out of the way.

The sword took me through the back on my right side. I was pretty sure that it had just taken out my right kidney. I was going to die within the next couple of minutes without medical assistance. I hadn't managed to dodge the attack, but that was okay, I'd accomplished something else with my spin.

The top of my rifle slammed into the wall next to me a fraction of a second before the magazine clicked into place inside the receiver. The wall provided the resistance I'd needed, did what I couldn't bring myself to do.

I released the bolt, driving a new round into the chamber with a flick of my thumb, and then fired off a three-round burst, aiming blindly behind me at the swordsman who had just impaled me. I shouldn't have been able to hear any-thing—not after so much sustained gunfire—but the sound of his body hitting the ground was undeniable. Even more welcome was the fact that the tension on the sword disappeared as he let go of it—a fraction of a second before he would have ripped it free and sealed my fate.

I turned, rolling along the wall through half of a revolution, and then gunned down the last four enforcers in quick succession. I would have already fallen if not for the support the wall offered, but even with that extra help, it was all I could do to get far enough around to take in the rest of the room.

The women had scattered in an effort to get out of the line of fire, but I wasn't concerned about them. Most of them were victims, but saving them wouldn't change the bigger picture. Saving Brennan very well might. If I could get him out, there was a very real chance that he could transform the city into something else, into a place where girls even younger than me didn't have to sell themselves into prostitution.

I found Brennan after just a second or two of searching, but that just confused me. I must have lost even more blood than I'd realized. My vision was starting to go a little blurry, but it almost looked like Brennan was standing now, no longer tied to the steel beam.

Piter was standing behind him, knife to his throat, but even that wasn't the most surprising thing. Brennan's shirt was open, and there were dozens of signs of the abuse he'd suffered at Piter's hands over the last twenty-four hours, but there were no bandages, no steel brace with rods running into his ribs, nothing to indicate that just a few days before he'd been at death's doorstep.

"Put your gun down. You're obviously just seconds from falling over, and I still hold all of the cards. As long as I hold Brennan, you can't do anything to me."

Piter's voice distracted me from Brennan's inexplicable recovery. I wanted my questions answered, but I forced myself to focus on the most important things, the things that had brought me this far.

"I'm not going to let you walk out of here with Brennan as a hostage, Piter. I know how that scenario plays out. Nothing we could give you would ever convince you to give him up."

"My freedom—"

"No. There's no way for me to guarantee that you'll release him once you cross over the border to your nearest ally. You can let him go and I'll still give you a head start, or I kill you. There is no third option."

"Don't lie to me, whore. I saw how you looked at him. You love Brennan, you're not going to risk killing him. Maybe you've been lying to yourself all this time, but you can't lie to me. If you want to guarantee Brennan's safety then put the barrel of your gun in your mouth and pull the trigger. With you out of the way, I won't have any reason to hurt Brennan—he's more valuable to me alive than dead."

"Don't do it, Skye!"

The sound of Brennan's voice gave me a lifeline to cling to. Piter had pulled the gag away from Brennan's mouth, probably expecting him to beg me to kill myself to save him. Piter stuck the point of his knife a quarter of an inch into Brennan's neck.

"Not another word out of you, Brennan. As for you, *Skye*, don't listen to him. He's nothing more than an idealist. You and I know better than that. You're already dead. Frankly I'm surprised that you're still able to stand. Every heartbeat pushes more of what little blood you have left out of your body. All you would be doing is hurrying along the inevitable."

"Maybe, but I don't have to stop you, Piter. All I have to do is delay you long enough for the rest of my team to get here."

I hoped it was true. The gunfire from below us had started to die out, but there was no way to be sure if that was because Jasper and the others had managed to cut down their opposition or if they'd run out of ammunition.

"You're mistaken, Skye, time is most definitely on my side. You're going to die, but if you make me wait for one second longer, I'll cut off his hands when I finally get to safety. Kill yourself and save him—isn't that a small sacrifice for love?"

The sights on the top of my rifle seemed to be moving around independently of my will. I was much too weak to keep the rifle steady enough to guarantee a shot. Even if I'd been stronger, taking a shot at Piter would have still been risky. After slamming the top of my rifle against the wall like I'd just done, it was virtually guaranteed that the sights were no longer lined up. I'd managed to mow down those last few enforcers, but that had been at extremely close range.

Two futures stretched out before me, and it took me only a second to choose one. I held my breath as the barrel of my rifle moved, and then I stroked the trigger and put all three rounds into Piter's head—the only target I had with so much of his body hidden behind Brennan.

"I guess I'm not willing to sacrifice myself for someone else after all."

It was an impossible shot, but I managed it and then fell to my knees, rifle dropping from hands too weak to hold it. My reality went fuzzy for a time. I lost at least several seconds, maybe as much as a minute, but the next thing I knew Brennan was kneeling next to me.

"I've got to get this sword out of you, Skye."

It felt like the words were coming to me from the top of a deep hole. It was hard to summon up the energy required to respond, but somehow I managed.

"Can't—it will just speed up the bleeding. Piter was right, I'm a dead woman. It's just a matter of time now."

Brennan reached over and picked up my rifle. I thought for a second that he was going to deliver a mercy blow and put me out of my misery, but he simply pointed it at a set of windows and fired off a long burst of bullets that drained the clip dry.

"Don't, Brennan. You're going to need—"

I wanted to finish the sentence, wanted to tell him that he was probably going to need that ammunition to fight his way down to Jasper and the others, but my strength was gone. I watched numbly as Brennan ran over to two of the first enforcers I'd shot after leaving the stairwell—the two who'd been carrying the last of Piter's rifles.

Brennan ripped one of the magazines out of the rifles on the floor and jammed it into my rifle before turning and emptying the entire magazine out into the night. The magazine from the second rifle was likewise discharged, and then Brennan was running back toward me.

"This is going to hurt, Skye, but we don't have any other options."

Before I could ask him what he meant, he pulled the sword out of my back and jammed the super-heated barrel of my rifle into the wound. The pain as my wounds were cauterized was nearly enough to force me unconscious, but he slapped me.

"Don't close your eyes! You've got to stay awake."

I tried to tell him that he was asking too much, that there wasn't any point in continuing to fight, but the words wouldn't come out.

A second later he picked me up and slung me over his shoulder. "Stay with me, Skye. I saw a couple of spare magazines on the two guys you shot. Let me get them and then we'll get out of here."

I lost some more time. I'd wanted to surrender to the blackness, but Brennan had asked me not to—apparently that was enough to make me keep fighting. There was no way of telling if I failed and that was why time got fuzzy, or if my mind had just been pushed too far, but all I got over the next hour or so were flashes, images and bits of sound.

We were going down a set of stairs, surrounded by Jasper and two other guys. We were passing an endless parade of fires burning in decaying oil drums. Brennan turned around and for a brief moment I saw the barricade in all of its jury-rigged glory. There was yelling—signs and countersigns—and then someone was laying down covering fire from above.

My nanites must have finally been getting on top of the damage by that point, because I started sticking around for more of the journey after that. I saw Victoria and the first few of her people come through the barricade as Brennan carried me deeper into his territory.

I knew that he wanted to stay and help with the fighting, wanted to stay at the barricade providing cover fire until all of Victoria's surviving people made it to safety, but he didn't—because getting me medical help was even more important to him than all of that.

By the time that we made it to the compound I was recovered enough to speak, but there was too much commotion as Brennan ordered half of the remaining guards off of the wall to join the fighting on the southern border.

He delayed for just long enough to make sure that his orders were being followed and then continued on toward the headquarters building—carrying me across his shoulder, completely unconcerned about the fact that he didn't have any bodyguards, anyone to help stop an attack if some disgruntled employee like Jerome saw him.

"Brennan, this isn't safe."

"Nothing is safe, Skye. I've been telling myself that for years, but I didn't really believe it until Piter's men grabbed me—not down in my gut. Maybe you're right, maybe I should have brought a couple of guards along, but then I would have been taking away three of us who should have stayed at the barricade and helped out Victoria's people. I couldn't justify pulling others off too—not just to protect me."

"Then why didn't you stay there too?"

"Because the only thing worse than betraying the people who depend on me is the thought of watching you die. I'm getting you to Tyrell if it kills me. After everything you've done for me it's the least I can do."

I tried to struggle, but I was just too weak to make him put me down. "No, Brennan. You have it all wrong. You were the one who saved me."

"You need to stop moving around, Skye. Once you're better I'll give you anything you want—anything that's within my power to give—but until then you're going to hold still until Tyrell gives you a clean bill of health. It would kill me if anything happened to you."

I would have kept arguing, but somehow we'd arrived at the secure entrance to the headquarters building and Brennan was setting me down on a stretcher just outside the door. I looked up into the night sky and saw something that made my blood run cold.

There were lights high above the city, lights that shouldn't have been there. They weren't contained fires positioned at the top of one of the skyscrapers, they were electric lights mounted to one of the Society mobile command centers.

That could only mean one thing.

Everyone in the city was going to die.

Chapter 26

Despite my best efforts, I briefly lost consciousness as we headed down the stairs. When I came back to, I was on a hard metal table in my room, but I wasn't alone. Brennan was there with Tyrell, and the pair of them were deep in conversation.

"I'm pretty sure that she's going to recover—it looks like you got the bleeding stopped in time—but I don't know if it's going to make any difference, Brennan. Now that the ants have moved one of their mobile command centers overhead it's entirely possible that none of us will make it out of here alive."

Tyrell sounded remarkably calm for someone discussing the likelihood of his death. It didn't make any sense—there was a thread there that I was missing—but Brennan responded before I could home in on it.

"Yes, I know. I saw it too, several hundred tons of superweapon floating so high above us that nothing we have could possibly bring it down. It's ironic—two hundred years ago that thing would have been nothing more than a giant deathtrap, but now it's untouchable, a giant blimp that floats over to the next target the Betrayer wants destroyed and then drops tungsten rods from so high up that they hit with the destructive power of a nuclear weapon. All of the damage, none of the radioactive fallout.

"You're sure that Katya isn't going to be able to get us out this time?"

"I'm afraid so. I haven't heard from her since the transmission telling us to expect the arrival of a covert operative. I suspect that she's either been captured or been forced to go to ground."

"Does Jax know?"

"Not the specifics, but enough to realize just how much trouble we have headed our direction. He's got a bone to pick with you, by the way."

"I know—he's right, too. I took too many risks and it nearly cost us ten years of work. I guess I was just so focused on the ants that I forgot about the smaller threats."

My eyes were still closed—if I was going to figure out what they were talking about, I needed to keep them from realizing that I was awake—but it sounded like one of them leaned in closer to the other and whispered something too faint for me to make out.

Desperate to hear what they were saying, I held my breath, hoping that would make a difference, but that still wasn't enough to turn the whispers into something intelligible. After several seconds I gave up and sucked in the air that my body was so insistently demanding.

Breathing deeply sent a stabbing pain through my side where I'd been stabbed. Apparently the nanites were having a hard time dealing with all of the cauterized flesh.

I gasped from the pain and Brennan was at my side a second later. "Skye, are you okay?"

It was time to play up my injuries. A normal person probably wouldn't be conscious for another day or two at least. I needed to throw the two of them off my scent—make them think that I was going to spend the next two days unconscious so that I would have a chance to get out and do the things that I knew needed to be done.

I nodded sleepily. "Yeah, I just breathed funny and it hurt."

"I'd tell you to stop breathing, but I'm worried that you would take me seriously. Tyrell is going to give you something for the pain—do you need anything else?"

I started to shake my head tiredly, and then stopped and opened my eyes, blinking like it was all I could do to keep them from closing again. "You said I could have anything I want?"

"Yes. Anything."

I winced as Tyrell injected me with something that my body didn't actually need. I was already well on the way to being back to one hundred percent, which meant that absent the special chemical marker used back in the Society, my nanites were going to assume the painkillers were an unwanted foreign substance and break down the morphine before it could affect me much. All Tyrell was doing was wasting good painkillers, but I couldn't tell him that.

Instead I focused on what Brennan had just said. "Does that include your generator? If I asked you to stop working on it and destroy all of your notes would you do that?"

Brennan frowned. I expected him to refuse, or to at least ask why I wanted him to abandon his life's work, but he didn't do either of those things.

"I stand by my word, Skye. Once you've recovered and I'm sure that you've had a chance to really think about what it is you want, we can talk again. If your answer is unchanged, I'll destroy that generator and count it a small price to pay for you having saved me not just once, but twice."

I suspected that he thought I was still too drugged up to realize what it was I was asking, but it was a start. I felt guilty about deceiving him like that, but it was the only way I knew of to save his life. I let more sleepiness into my voice, distorting my words nearly to the point of being unintelligible.

"Thanks, Brennan."

"No, Skye, thank you. I'm going to be here when you wake up—I'm not going anywhere."

Tyrell cleared his throat. "There really are a number of things that you should be seeing to right now, Brennan. I know it's hard, but..."

I smiled faintly, eyes closed. "It's okay. I'll be here when you get back."

Brennan stood, but I didn't realize what he was planning until his lips brushed my forehead. It was like he'd just run an electrical current through me. We'd held hands before now, but that had strictly been to misdirect people into thinking that I wasn't a real guard. This was something else entirely, and it took me so much by surprise that I nearly sat up and ruined the illusion I'd been trying to create.

"Duty calls, but I won't be gone long. I'll see you in a few minutes, Skye."

I listened as the two of them walked to the door and let themselves out. Lying there, eyes closed and motionless, for the next fifteen minutes was one of the harder things I'd ever forced myself to do, but I couldn't afford to have them come back in and find me up walking around.

Once I was confident that they weren't returning, I sat up and looked around my room. Things looked much like I remembered with a couple of new additions. A rifle was once again sitting prominently on the shelf designated for it and I had a full set of new magazines and several boxes of ammunition. It was a pretty compelling sign that Brennan, Tyrell, and Jax trusted me again.

That wasn't unexpected given that my rescue mission had been successful. In truth I was much more surprised to find a new dark, wide-brimmed hat to replace the one I'd lost while fighting my way into the heart of Piter's territory.

There was a note from Lexis pinned to it.

Every time I think that I've nearly balanced the ledger between us, you go off and do something crazy that puts all of us further in your debt.

I quickly dressed in my guard uniform, being careful to do up all the straps on my vest so that my uniform was closer to regulation than the way that Lexis had envisioned it. I considered the hat for several seconds before pulling the note off of it and setting it on my head. The hat was very similar to the one I'd lost, but there were subtle differences in the way it fit that all of the guards had been trained to recognize. Hats like this one were part of the uniform for a special subset of Jax's people. The regular bodyguards didn't wear them, but the special forces group that had no doubt been right at the tip of the spear last night in the assault on the Muertos did, so I put the hat on in the hopes that it would help make people think I was someone other than myself.

It was a long shot, but once again, I didn't have any other choice. I'd spent days worried about how I was going to reconcile my duty to the Society against my growing loyalty to Brennan, and I wasn't going to just sit passively in my room when I finally had a chance to make everything right. I would just have to hope that we were even more thinly stretched now than we'd been before I'd led the attack on Piter's territory.

I'd been listening carefully as Brennan and Tyrell left in an attempt to determine whether or not Brennan had posted guards outside of my room. Given the commitments Brennan had on his limited pool of trained personnel, it didn't make a lot of sense for him to station anyone outside my door, but I wasn't positive that I was going to be able to leave until I opened the door and saw with relief that the hall was empty.

I made it all of the way up to the door outside without running into anybody else, which was a marvelous stroke of luck, but that was nothing compared to the surprise awaiting me at the top of the stairs. Rather than the two guards I was accustomed to seeing, today there was only a single uniformed figure awaiting me, and he looked like he couldn't have been a day over sixteen.

Rather than avoiding eye contact as I'd originally planned, I met his gaze squarely and gave him a crisp salute as I walked past. He didn't even seem to register my face—the simple fact that I was in uniform, the uniform of the special forces group no less, was enough to convince him that I had every right to be going in and out of the secure areas of the building.

The journey to the bore and then on down to the location where I'd left my transmitter was equally uneventful and only minutes after leaving my room I was pressing the transmit button.

"This is Skinwalker to Home Base, come in, Home Base."

"This is Home Base; I've been receiving disturbing reports recently, Skinwalker."

My heart dropped in my chest—I recognized that voice. The low-level analyst I'd been expecting had been replaced by the Citizen-President himself.

"I'm very sorry, sir. I would like to explain, but I'm not sure that would be a good idea on an unsecured channel. The important thing is that I've completed my mission. I've become Brennan's confidant and he's promised to stop development on his generator. You can call off whatever strike you've been planning, there's no longer any need."

The Citizen-President sighed. "I'm afraid, that's not going to be possible, child. The situation is changing. It's no longer going to be enough for us to simply ensure the destruction of the device. Within the next few hours I'm going to authorize a strike by our military forces. Our brave men and women will be going into the city to capture and extract the device."

"That's never going to work, sir. I know that the...grubbers...can't possibly match our technological superiority, but their numbers are nothing short of incredible. Even if every single spare military unit was mobilized to come into the city I don't believe we could hold a perimeter around the compound for long enough to secure the device. Not against every warlord and gang leader in the entire city."

"You're absolutely correct, which is why we'll begin the attack with an extensive, prolonged series of high-altitude strikes designed to lay waste to everything outside of the compound where you're currently located. That will ensure that we won't have to face any opposition from the rest of the city. Our ground forces should then prove more than sufficient to mop up inside of the compound and secure the device."

My mind was whirling. The news that the Citizen-President was authorizing strikes meant that Brennan was in extreme danger, but that couldn't be the only reason I was having such a hard time processing what I was hearing. I'd known from the moment I'd seen the mobile command centers that everyone inside of the city was in danger, so being informed that everyone was still in danger shouldn't have come as such a shock.

Then it hit me. "Sir, the destruction of the city and all its inhabitants goes directly against the precepts. I understand your concern about the device, but life inside of this compound is changing in incredible ways—in good ways. We've been hoping for more than a century that the grubbers would redevelop civilization on their own, but this is the first time that we've seen it actually start to happen. We need to find a way to protect our Society without destroying the seeds of civilization that are starting to grow here."

"I understand your hesitancy, Skinwalker—to be honest I have similar feelings—but that doesn't change the fact that this is what must happen. There are things you don't know yet, important things. Once you're back here safely behind the barrier, I will bring you up to speed, but that's simply not possible right now. Given all of that, I have to ask. Are you prepared to do your duty to our great Society? I know you said that you were one of Brennan's confidantes, but I need to know that you're not going to let that relationship affect your judgment."

"Yes, sir. I am prepared to do the right thing. I would ask, however, that you give me two days in which to make arrangements down here. I believe that I can lure the vast bulk of the guards into one place so that they can be destroyed with a single high-altitude strike."

The silence as my proposal was considered was torturous. With each second that passed I could feel my nerves winding tighter and tighter, but eventually he cleared his throat. "I can't give you two days, but I can give you twenty-four hours. That only works, however, if you get back to us twenty hours from now with the coordinates of where those guards are going to be located."

"Yes, sir. Consider it done."

"I'm putting a lot of trust in you, Skye. Don't let me down."

"No, sir. I won't."

I turned off the transmitter and stumbled back up towards the surface. Nothing made sense to me anymore. I'd always understood the necessity of keeping the cities from uniting against us. It was a distasteful job, but one which was unavoidable, which was why we used firebombing to destroy the ringleaders while leaving as many people and as much of the infrastructure as unharmed as possible.

The use of the mobile command centers was supposed to require the approval of every single franchised citizen. They'd been built and deployed more than forty years ago under the agreement that they would never come within less than a hundred miles of any grubber city without a Society-wide vote, but the Citizen-President hadn't said anything about a vote.

My world was turning upside down, but I was sure of only one thing. If Brennan had been in the Citizen-President's shoes, possessed of complete technological superiority and the ability to destroy an entire city from tens of thousands of feet up, he wouldn't have chosen to exercise it without at least trying to talk to the people he was about to kill.

I had to talk to him—had to warn him about what was going to happen. I knew it was going to ruin any chance of something happening between the two of us, but I also knew that I couldn't live with myself if I didn't come clean and tell Brennan everything.

I popped the top buckle on my vest open and pulled off my hat as I approached the secure entrance to the headquarters building. Every moment counted, and it didn't matter how young the guard at the door was, he wasn't going to tell just anyone who asked where they could find Brennan. I needed to look like myself.

"Has Brennan left the building since you came on duty?"

"I'm not sure that I should be sharing that information, ma'am. I mean, that's classif—"

"Do you know who I am?"

"I…ah, no, ma'am."

"My name is Skye, and I'm on Brennan's personal guard detachment. I wouldn't be asking about him if it wasn't important."

"I thought you were injured in the fighting."

"Do I look injured?"

"Well, no, but the scuttlebutt said—"

"I don't have time for this, soldier. You have exactly five seconds to tell me how long you've been on duty and whether you've seen Brennan leave the building or I will see you busted down to cleaning latrines for the next six months."

"Two hours, ma'am! I have not seen him leave, ma'am!"

I nodded and brushed past him, sticking my head in operations on my way down the stairs for just long enough to verify he wasn't there. I checked the cafeteria, and then headed directly to his bedroom, but he wasn't there either. If it would've been anything less important I probably would've given up at that point. I felt like I'd checked everywhere, and then I realized where he had to be.

The drawdown of the guards who otherwise would have been posted inside the building meant that I made it all the way to the door just in front of the stairs that led down to Brennan's workshop before I encountered anyone, but that wasn't as surprising as the fact that it was Tyrell who I practically ran into as I entered the small guard room.

"Skye, what are you doing here? How are you even up and walking?"

"Tyrell, I'm sorry I can't explain right now, but it will all make sense once I've had a chance to tell Brennan what's going on. Is he down there? I have to see him."

"He's down there, but I'm not letting you past without more explanation than that."

I'd never been this desperate about anything before. My drive to rescue Brennan from Piter had come close, but even that need hadn't been as powerful as this. I'd grabbed my rifle on the way out of my room because a guard without a weapon attracted far more attention than one with. Tyrell was unarmed, which meant I had him even more outclassed than normal, but it never even crossed my mind to shoot him.

My desperation meant that there was plenty of adrenaline flowing through my system. I streaked forward intending on disabling Tyrell without doing any permanent damage to him, but he sidestepped me and slammed his fist into my side just above my short ribs in one smooth motion.

The crack of breaking ribs was shocking, but it had nothing on the sheer surprise of seeing Tyrell move that quickly or the impossibility of any normal human breaking my nanite-reinforced ribs so easily with nothing more than their bare hands. Still reacting out of reflex and training, I spun around and tried to land a blow to Tyrell's neck, but he checked my attack with a punch that left my arm numb and useless and then swept my feet out from underneath me.

I hit the ground hard—harder than I had in years—but tried to roll to my feet nevertheless. Only Tyrell had somehow ended up on top of me, fist cocked back for what I knew would be a killing blow if I moved so much as an eyelash.

"I'm not going to let you kill him, Skye. I don't care how much he trusts you, this ends here."

I should've told him that I had no intention of killing Brennan, that hurting Brennan was the last thing on my mind, but I was too busy trying to reconcile all of the impossibilities I'd just been faced with.

Tyrell didn't have Jax's massive size and reach. In fact, he was only marginally taller than I was, which meant that any confrontation between us should've come down to nothing more than speed and experience. I'd been injected with cutting-edge nanites the likes of which this world had never seen before, which meant that the speed advantage should've been solidly on my side, but that hadn't been the case. Tyrell had practically flickered from one place to another so fast that I almost hadn't been able to even follow his movements, let alone counter his attacks.

I looked up at him and asked the one question I had to know before I died. "Who are you?"

"Unlike you, Skye, I've never lied to anyone inside the compound. My name really is Tyrell, but you would probably know me better as the Destroyer."

Acknowledgements

Writing The Society involved venturing out into new ground. I've done a little bit of sci-fi writing, but by and large, my editors and advance readers haven't been exposed to that side of my writing. I was a little worried that some of them wouldn't make it through to the end of The Society, because it was so different from my other works. When you add in the fact that this was the first book where significant parts of it were dictated rather than typed, there was a lot more work at every level from editor through advance reader and Launch Team, but they all pulled through like champions. My editors, RJ Locksley and Amy Jirsa-Smith were as amazing as always and I'm very grateful for their help.

An equally heartfelt thanks needs expressed to my advance readers. Thank you, Mom, Dad, Matthew, Shalese, Lachele, Mimi, Mark, Kim, Janelle, Jenine, Mei and Heather.

I would also like to say thanks to Merissa at http://archaeolibrarianologist.blogspot.com/ for her ongoing efforts to get the word out about my books, all of the members of my Launch Team, and all of you readers who take the time to tell your friends and family about my books.

Finally, as always, the biggest thanks goes to my wife, Katie. A lot of things haven't gone according to plan this year, but we're still trucking along, releasing novels, and most of the thanks for that goes to Katie. Not only has she been my trusted first reader, she also did the breathtaking cover for The Society, and I'm grateful for that, and everything else she does. Thank you Katie!

About the Author

Dean Murray is a prolific author with dozens of titles across multiple pen names and more than half a million copies of his work currently in circulation.

Dean started reading seriously in the second grade due to a competition and has spent most of the subsequent three decades lost in other people's worlds.

Things worsened, or improved depending on your point of view, when he first started experimenting with writing while finishing up his accounting degree. These days Dean has a wonderful wife and two lovely daughters to keep him rather more grounded, but the idea of bringing others along with him as he meets interesting new people in universes nobody else has ever seen tends to drag him back to his computer on a fairly regular basis.

Keep up to speed on Dean's latest projects at deanwrites.com.

Stone Heart

Dani's new home isn't just another stopover in a long chain of places she'll never see again, it's the home of both Caine and Jerek, two guys like nobody she's ever met before. One represents the best friend she's been hungering for, and the other represents something much more.

It should be the perfect recipe for a fairytale, but Caine and Jerek live in a dark, shadowy world and one of them is hiding secrets that will change everything, secrets that relate directly to Dani.

Reborn

True love never dies.

A new arrival at Selene's high school is about to turn her entire world upside down. She's never met anyone so attractive—or so mysterious—before this, but Jace's unyielding insistence that they've known each other for decades can't be denied—not given how familiar he feels to her.

In the hidden world of gods and fairies what you don't know can get you killed faster than anything else and only those you love have any chance of saving you.

Broken

Adri Paige's arrival in Sanctuary thrusts her into a dangerous, shadowy world most people don't believe exists, and places her in the middle of a war between darkly handsome Alec Graves and charismatic Brandon Worthingfield that threatens to consume the entire town.

On the surface, both Alec and Brandon are nothing more than average high-school guys, but as Adri is pulled ever more deeply into their conflict she realizes that one of them wants to kill her. Adri needs to decide who to trust before her time runs out once and for all.

The Greater Darkenss

Dean writing as Eldon Murphy

Something powerful is stirring in the darkness. Something so ancient that even creatures who've been alive for hundreds of years have long since discounted this new threat as nothing more than myth.

Normal humans will be caught in the crossfire, but then that's always the way of things. Geoffrey has no memory of his past life or any idea how to survive in the violent, dangerous world in which he's trapped. Despite his best efforts, he's about to find himself in the middle of a conflict that threatens to sweep away everything, and everyone he's been fighting so hard to protect.